A Runaway Heiress, a Powerful Rancher—
Their Secrets Could Bring Heartbreak or Bind
Them Forever. . . .

SELINA—She was innocent, yet lies and desperation had brought her to Morgan Kincaid's door. She had to win his trust, but if he knew the truth, would she lose his love forever?

MORGAN—A bitter marriage and a brutal accident had left indelible scars. In spite of himself, he wanted Selina, but as the fierce Montana winter closed in, a wall of icy fear and uncertainty hardened his obstinate heart.

CELIA—Morgan's child. Angry, rebellious, she, too, had a secret that threatened to destroy the tender bond between father and daughter.

CLAY PRESCOTT—Charming, seductive, he'd loved Morgan's first wife and he was only too willing to befriend Selina, to comfort her, to betray Morgan—again.

ALBERTA BODINE—Her first fateful whim had thrown Selina and Morgan together. Her second could send Selina to the gallows.

D0456424

QUANTITY SALES

Most Dell Books are available at special quantity discounts when purchased in bulk by corporations, organizations, and special-interest groups. Custom imprinting or excerpting can also be done to fit special needs. For details write: Dell Publishing Co., Inc., 666 Fifth Avenue, New York, NY 10103. Attn.: Special Sales Dept.

INDIVIDUAL SALES

Are there any Dell Books you want but cannot find in your local stores? If so, you can order them directly from us. You can get any Dell book in print. Simply include the book's title, author, and ISBN number, if you have it, along with a check or money order (no cash can be accepted) for the full retail price plus $1.50 to cover shipping and handling. Mail to: Dell Readers Service, P.O. Box 5057, Des Plaines, IL 60017.

SNOWFIRE

by

Jessica Douglass

A DELL BOOK

To Kerry,
for caring

Published by
Dell Publishing Co.
a division of
The Bantam Doubleday Dell Group, Inc.
1 Dag Hammarskjold Plaza
New York, New York 10017

Dell ® TM 681510, Dell Publishing Co., Inc.

ISBN: 0-440-20075-X

Printed in the United States of America

April 1988

10 9 8 7 6 5 4 3 2 1

KRI

Chapter 1

Selina shivered, fighting down a surge of panic. It was not the coolness of the April night that raised the gooseflesh on her arms, but rather the chilling terror she sought to leave behind. Like a hawkswept bird she darted from shadow to shadow, avoiding the circles of light from the flickering gas lamps standing guard over the streets. Turning, she dared a glance over her shoulder, her gaze skittering up California Street to the monied elegance of Nob Hill. She'd run a quarter mile from Gideon's mansion, but she knew even if she were a thousand miles away she would not feel safe. She doubted she would ever feel safe again.

Dark circles rimmed her deep brown eyes, and the normally delicate planes of her face were pinched and drawn. Stray locks of her chestnut hair had tugged free of her severe chignon. Gideon would not be pleased. She shuddered. Gideon was dead.

She twisted the wedding band on her left hand, wincing as the movement sent a slicing pain through the raw welts on her palms. Gideon was dead; Marelda would find her. Marelda would exact her revenge.

Selina hurried on, scurrying past the garish signs that beckoned all around her, seeking to lure the wary and the unwary alike to brothels, saloons, and opium dens. She shut her mind to the bawdy laughter and leering propositions. So close to the hill, yet so infinitely removed, life here flourished in darkness.

With a gasp Selina flattened herself against the cold brick of a saloon alcove. A police paddy wagon thundered out of the night, three pair of straining horses pounding up the hill. Above the cacophony of hooves, wheel rims, and cracking whips she heard the barked commands of two uniformed officers as they ordered a cable car to a halt barely twenty-five feet from where she stood. As the conductor threw his brake, the policemen leaped aboard the tram to move swiftly from passenger to passenger.

"She's not here, Sergeant!" the patrolman declared.

"Sure'n she's got to be," the sergeant called

back. "The call come in barely five minutes ago. How else could she have got away?"

"She could walk."

"A lady? Amongst this godforsaken lot? They would've ate her alive."

"She'd be better off if they have. She'll get no lady's privileges now, not after what she done."

"Hush now. No sense alarmin' these good folks. We'll find . . ."

Selina jerked away from a hard poke in the ribs. She whirled to find herself face-to-face with a brassy-haired woman lurching out of the saloon.

"This corner's taken, missy," the woman hissed, reeking of cheap perfume and even cheaper liquor.

"Please," Selina stammered, "I'll be going in just a minute. I . . . my shoelace came undone."

The woman's bloodshot eyes raked Selina from head to foot. "Lord," she sniffed, wavering slightly when she made as if to plant her hands on her ample hips and missed, "I don't know what I'm worryin' about. Ain't many men'd want a tumble with a dowdy piece like you. Still, you may have more to ya than the eye can see." With unexpected violence she lunged at Selina, shoving her into the glare of the street lamp. "Like I tol' ya, this corner's taken."

Straightening, her heart hammering, Selina managed to keep her back to the street. She closed her eyes, nearly sick with relief to hear the jangle of harnesses and creak of leather that told her the police wagon was continuing up the hill. But there would be more police wagons; Marelda would see to that.

Selina bit back tears and took a long, steadying breath, drawing in the wet, welcome scent of San Francisco Bay. The water, shimmering serenely less than a mile away, teased her, enticed her. If only she could make it to the Ferry Building! But it was too dangerous. The police could be waiting for her there.

Once more on the run, Selina risked another terrified look back toward Gideon's three-story Victorian mansion atop the hill. Lanterns blazed like serpent's eyes from the windows of the upper floor. Marelda would have roused the entire household by now, exhorting the servants to join the hunt. At this moment they could be fanning out along the streets and alleys, searching.

She had to find a place to hide, a place to think. Selina forced her increasingly unstable legs to support her for two more blocks, remembering St. Mary's Church, a strategically placed thorn in the side of the bay front's ongoing chaos. She'd never actually been inside the church, but she'd often heard the servants speak of it. Collapsing against its heavy oak doors, she sobbed her prayer-filled thanks on finding them unlocked.

Small votive candles provided the only illumination in the church's cavernous interior. Along the walls, stained-glass windows, muted by darkness, were strangely comforting. Selina ducked into an oak pew, but immediately felt too exposed. Stumbling to her feet, she crept back to a confessional. Easing open the penitent's door, she sank to the floor in one corner of the small cubicle, hugging her knees to her chest.

She hunched there, trembling. Swirling images from an hour—a lifetime—ago crowded into her mind, weaving around her, tightening their blade-sharp threads . . .

Selina was standing in the master bedroom of her husband's mansion, staring at his lifeless body, the ancient Chinese dagger protruding grotesquely from his chest. The ruby eyes set in the carved-dragon hilt seemed to follow her, accuse her, as she backed across the lush Aubusson carpet in the center of the massive bedroom. She pressed a hand to her mouth, trying desperately not to be sick. Yet when she tried to feel something, anything, for this man who had been her husband for five years, the only emotion that swept over her was overwhelming relief.

She had to think what to do. If she were found with his body, she would be blamed. She started toward the door, then stopped. Who in this house could she turn to? Worse—how far would she get with no money?

Biting the inside of her lip, she turned to the twenty-dollar gold piece lying on the night table beside the canopied bed. Her insides lurched as she thought of why Gideon had placed it there. But that didn't matter now. Nothing mattered but that somehow she free herself from this nightmare that had begun when she was sixteen years old.

Scooping up the coin, she stuffed it into the pocket of her threadbare cotton dress. Perhaps there would be time for her to . . .

Her gaze flew toward the sound of the creaking door.

"Gideon, dear, I thought you might like a bit of tea before you retire. I've . . ." A silver tray and its contents crashed to the floor, dark tea seeping through the exquisite tapestry. Selina watched the wizened features of her mother-in-law freeze for just an instant, then blaze to life.

"My son!" Marelda Hardesty shrieked, her wrinkled face contorting in disbelief. She dropped beside Gideon's body, cradling his head in her arms. "Gideon, my dearest, what has she done to you? *What has she done?*"

Selina took a step back.

Marelda raised her eyes to Selina, her face white with fury. "Witch! Murderess! You've killed him!" She looked once more at the body of her son, her gnarled hands clutching at the lapel of Gideon's blue silk waistcoat. "My dearest, speak to me! Speak to Mother, please."

"I didn't kill him, Marelda," Selina ventured. "You know that. You must have seen—"

Marelda's face contorted with hate. "No one will believe you. No one!"

In that split second Selina knew every other choice was lost to her. To live, she had to run.

Selina bolted for the open window, evading Marelda's bony grasp by inches. As she grappled her way down the latticework outside, the spear-tipped wrought iron tore at her dress and gashed her palms.

"I'll see you hang!" Marelda screamed after her. "I'll see you dead!"

The words echoed and re-echoed in Selina's mind as she raced down the hill. She stumbled once, chancing a look back. Marelda still stood in the lighted window, her black crepe dress billowing behind her, making her appear every bit a winged specter from hell. Marelda would be the devil's own partner to make good her threat.

Selina pressed her hands to her temples and cowered inside the tiny confessional. She was so tired . . . She closed her eyes. Marelda couldn't find her here. . . .

Selina awoke to the feel of a hand on her shoulder. In a rush her terror returned and she struggled to her feet, lashing out blindly at the black-robed presence that sought to pin her hands to her sides.

A gentle voice penetrated her haze of terror.

"It's all right, miss. You've nothing to fear here. Please, are you ill?"

Selina found herself staring into kind gray eyes. A priest.

His hand moved to grip her elbow as she began to waver unsteadily. He guided her up the center aisle of the church, pausing to genuflect in front of the altar, then led her through a series of small rooms and corridors to an adjacent building.

In the rectory the priest directed her toward a cane-back chair by a circular mahogany table. The aroma of frying eggs and bacon drifted in from the kitchen, unsettling Selina's already queasy stomach.

"Eat first, then we'll talk," the priest said.

It struck Selina then that it had been a very long time since anyone had been kind to her. Her eyes burned, but she would not let the tears fall. "I can't stay," she whispered.

A plump, matronly woman bustled into the room, carrying a plate laden with food. Selina didn't miss her initial shocked expression, but it was quickly replaced by a too-bright smile.

Selina shifted nervously.

"As you can see, Mrs. Rafferty," the priest said, "we'll be having a guest for breakfast."

Mrs. Rafferty placed what had obviously been the priest's breakfast in front of Selina.

"Thank you, but I . . . I'm not hungry," Selina protested.

"Nonsense, dear," the woman said, her eyes darting uneasily to the newspaper just inches from Selina's left hand. "A hearty meal takes the edge off the bleakest day."

Nothing could take the edge off this day, Selina thought, but said nothing.

"You mind Mrs. Rafferty," the priest said. "Eat. We'll talk later. Whatever it is, you're safe."

"Father Thompson likes to take in strays," Mrs. Rafferty said.

"Now, Maggie, let the child eat in peace." He shooed the woman out of the room, then left after her, saying, "Where's that boy of yours? I've got chores to be done. It's not like him. Danny's usually chafin' at the bit . . ."

The sound of Father Thompson's voice trailed off into the rectory. Selina picked up a fork, but managed only to push the food around on her plate.

What was she going to do? She couldn't stay here. A church's sanctuary would mean nothing to a woman like Marelda. Yet, perhaps the intensity of the search would wane if she remained for a day or two.

Her fingers strayed to the newspaper and an eerie sensation stole over her. The paper was an EXTRA edition of the *Examiner.* Trembling, she unfolded it, then stared at the blazing front page headline.

HARDESTY HEIRESS SOUGHT FOR MURDER.

The paper shook in her hands as she read on.

Prominent mining entrepreneur Gideon Hardesty was brutally stabbed to death last night in his magnificent Nob Hill mansion. San Francisco police chief Robert Prine issued a statement shortly after midnight naming the only suspect in the slaying as Hardesty's widow, twenty-one-year-old Selina Michaels Hardesty.

Marelda Hardesty, the victim's mother, was inconsolable. "Gideon loved her so; he doted on her like a precious treasure . . ."

Selina closed her eyes, a scalding anger coursing through her. *Precious.* She had meant less to Gideon than one of his trinkets. When she could breathe steadily again, she read further.

"I want her hanged," Mrs. Hardesty said. "I'm posting a reward . . ."

Jumping to her feet, Selina peered into the corridor, relieved to find it empty. She dared stay here no longer. Mrs. Rafferty obviously had recognized her. Even now she could be alerting the police.

Rushing out a side door, she ignored Father Thompson as he called, "You're safe here, child!"

She was safe nowhere, and if she hadn't been certain before, she was the instant she stepped into the mid-morning sun. Newsboys were hawking copies of the *Examiner* on every corner.

Keeping her eyes downcast, her pace deliberate, Selina headed toward the bay. She paused only long enough to grope for the coin in her pocket, fearful when she did not at once find it. Her heart started beating again only after her hand closed over the cool metal. How far could twenty dollars take her?

She halted abruptly, recalling the trust fund that had been set up for her in accordance with her parents' wills. She'd seldom thought of it these past five years because Gideon had not allowed her access to it. Now that he was dead . . . No, she was being foolish. Marelda would most certainly have the bank watched. Someday she would think of a plan to retrieve her money, but for now she had but one coin.

"Get along with ye, miss," a strange voice prodded.

She looked up, startled to realize that she had been standing in the same spot for several minutes.

"Go on, now, get away! I don't need no beggars hangin' around my pastry shop."

She moved off, staring down at her tattered dress, the angry scratches on her palms. Her hair, too, must be a sight.

"Find the murderess! Get the reward!" A young boy zigzagging along the sidewalk shoved a leaflet into her hand. He was forcing the flyer on every man, woman, and child on the street. She stared at the white paper with its bold black lettering and the painfully accurate line drawing of her face. Her hand shook.

FIVE-THOUSAND-DOLLAR REWARD . . . FOR

THE APPREHENSION OF SELINA MICHAELS HAR-
DESTY, WANTED FOR THE MURDER OF HER HUS-
BAND GIDEON HARDESTY ON THE NIGHT OF
APRIL 30, 1886. THE MURDERESS IS FIVE FEET
THREE INCHES TALL, OF SLIGHT BUILD WITH
REDDISH BROWN HAIR AND BROWN EYES. SEND
INFORMATION TO PINKERTON AGENCY . . . OR
TO MARELDA HARDESTY, NOB HILL. More details
followed, including a description of what she had
been wearing when last seen.

Five thousand dollars. Selina's throat constricted. In this part of the city there were men
who would kill for five cents. Her pace quickened.
At every turn she now felt she was being watched.

Anxiety riding her hard, Selina ducked into a
secondhand clothing and sundries store not far
from the Ferry Building. It was a calculated risk,
but she had to change her appearance. Spending
two precious dollars, she quickly emerged with a
package under her arm.

Reaching the wharf, Selina skirted dozens of
cable cars and bustling passengers and made her
way inconspicuously to a fare booth. Just as she
rounded a last vacant tram, a hand snaked out and
seized her violently.

"Let me go!" she cried, struggling to free herself
from the viselike grip of a scraggly-looking little
man with pock-marked cheeks.

"Not likely, miss." The man leered, displaying a
toothless grin. "I ain't never had my hands on five

thousand dollars before." He waved a flyer in her face. "It's you, ain't it? You're the one they're all lookin' for." His grip tightened on her elbow.

Selina swung her package at him out of sheer terror. Freedom was just yards away. All she had to do was get to a ferry.

Easily fielding her blow, the man threw her package to the ground. "They're going to hang you, missy. That's the tale all over the city. I never seen a woman hanged. Oughtta be some sight."

He twisted her arm behind her back and, keeping it at a vicious angle, propelled her up the street away from the wharf. They both knew she didn't dare call for help.

"What's you got there, Larkin?" A bullish-looking man stepped out of an alley and into their path.

"Get out of the way, Zeke," Larkin demanded, though Selina thought she detected a trace of fear in his squeaky voice.

"That the murderess?" The big man's jowls twitched eagerly.

"Yeah, and she's all mine."

Zeke made a grab for her. "Not anymore."

Larkin growled, "I found her first! You got no right."

Zeke smashed a beefy fist into Larkin's face. "Now I got a right."

But Larkin, still hanging on to Selina, pounded back at Zeke like a maddened terrier. Selina winced, fearing at any second one of their punishing blows would land on her. The sound of flesh on flesh sickened her, reminding her . . .

She wrenched free as the two men escalated their attack, and ran. Scooping up her package, she sped for the landing. Slamming down her fare, she raced for a ferry just as it was pulling away from the pier. From its deck she watched Zeke and Larkin storm onto the wharf, still battling. A policeman—probably stationed there, Selina suddenly realized, to watch for her—stopped them both.

"Thank God for greed," she murmured. To her bitter disappointment the two men abruptly improved their behavior, and the policeman let them go. As the ferry pulled away she saw them heading for the ticket booth. The next boat would not be leaving for at least ten minutes.

Across the bay in Oakland, she made good use of her head start and walked briskly to the railroad station, keeping her head down. Checking behind her to make certain no one was watching—how quickly the habit was becoming ingrained—Selina then hurried inside the ladies' lavatory. She crossed to a steel basin and opened her package, extracting a large bottle of ebony-colored liquid. Setting the package out of the way, she leaned over the sink and quickly worked the coal rinse into her chestnut locks.

When she emerged from the lavatory Selina was

wearing a simply styled calico dress, with a dun rebozo wrapped around her damp, newly darkened tresses.

Around her, hundreds of voices caught up in hundreds of conversations created a dull roar that outstripped all but the piercing whistle of steam engines blasting relief from full-bellied boilers. On a spidery maze of dual tracks trains chugged and puffed, gorging and disgorging passengers bound for dreams unknown. Here among the throngs of travelers, porters, and workers Selina felt a welcome rush of anonymity at last.

"Board!" Conductors called out again and again. "Stockton, Red Bluff, and points north. Los Angeles, Tucson . . ."

Hurrying now, fearing Zeke and Larkin might easily guess she would come here, Selina waded through the sea of human traffic, making her way toward a Central Pacific ticket agent.

"Where to, miss?" the bespectacled clerk asked from his booth.

She'd given no thought to where. Just away. "North," she blurted. "I mean . . . my uncle lives in . . . in," she recalled a name, "Red Bluff." Her deceit embarrassed her. She had no uncle, had no one. Shoving a coin at the man, she took her ticket and turned to go.

"Don't you want your change, miss?"

"Mrs. . . ." She stopped, staring at her wedding ring. Never again would she name herself

Mrs. Hardesty, but she'd given no thought to a new identity. "Mrs. Smith. Yes, please. I'm sorry."

She gathered up her change and, checking quickly over her shoulder, walked brusquely toward the train. It was scheduled to leave in fifteen minutes.

As Selina walked, she twisted the symbol of her five-year bondage to Gideon Hardesty. Tugging it free of her slender finger, she clenched the small gold band in her fist. A tide of bitterness ripped through her. With a grim smile, she dropped it to the floor and kept walking.

"Board, miss?" inquired a portly uniformed conductor as she hurried up to the twenty-five-car train.

"Yes, sir," she said, handing him her ticket. She stood there, nervously smoothing her skirts as she waited for him to return it. The man was studying her appearance, and the longer he looked, the more curious he seemed. Was something already amiss? Thankfully, he said nothing and merely handed back her ticket.

Once aboard she hurried to check her appearance in the mirror of the train's lavatory. The irony of her new preoccupation with her appearance did not escape her. Gideon had spent five years indoctrinating her on the virtue of plainness, condemning any hint of what he pronounced "feminine frippery," even forbidding her the tiny pleasure of scented bath soaps. She'd told herself it didn't matter. But oh, how long it had been since she'd even had so much as a ribbon in her hair.

With a resigned sigh she took advantage of a small needle-and-thread case in a cupboard near the wash basin, repairing two tiny rents in the skirt of her secondhand dress. Ribbons weren't important right now. Staying alive was. Feeling a shade more confident, she made her way back to a Pullman car.

Welcome relief mingled with exhaustion as Selina sank into a plushly upholstered seat. Not caring if she ever moved again in her life, she turned a tired but triumphant gaze out onto the bustling platform. She had done it. She was free! Marelda would never find . . .

She straightened, an odd movement in the terminal capturing her attention. A bear-sized man was lumbering from ticket agent to ticket agent. Horror pulsed through her.

Zeke.

Chapter 2

Trembling, Selina pressed her forehead against the window of the Pullman car, searching the crowded terminal for any sign of Larkin. But Zeke was alone.

The thought came from nowhere. It was a long ferry ride across the bay. She knew, *knew,* no one would ever be seeing Larkin again.

Selina's skin grew cold as she watched the brutish Zeke question conductors, porters, anyone who would listen, shoving a copy of Marelda's flyer in their faces.

For a moment a crowd of boarding passengers blocked her view—children, parents, a man lugging a huge sample case, a tall, buxom woman in an outrageously provocative red silk dress . . . When they were safely on board and her view clear, Selina's breath caught. Zeke was talking to the bespectacled Central agent, who was nodding his head.

Selina panicked. She had to get off the train. She started to rise, but sank back. Where would she go? No, the train was her best chance. She would just have to be calm. The train would start moving any minute.

She shrank back from the window, but her fear once again compelled her to check on Zeke.

He was coming toward the train.

She tensed, praying the train would depart.

The train whistle screamed, and as the conductor shouted "Board!" Zeke picked up his pace, elbowing down the platform.

The conductor waved his lantern, signaling the engineer, just as Zeke reached him.

The train lurched into motion.

Selina held her breath, willing the train to pick up speed, her gaze riveted on her pursuer. As the thickset Zeke huffed alongside, the conductor pointed at a gold watch he'd extracted from his vest pocket. When Zeke tried to shove the flyer at him, the conductor pushed the paper away. For an instant, Selina was certain Zeke would drag the conductor from the train and board in his place, but Zeke stopped cold.

The platform had ended.

As the train moved out, Zeke's eyes met hers through the glass. He crumpled the flyer in his fist.

"You'll see me again, little lady!" he roared, the threat piercing the closed window. "You'll see me again!"

A horrified shudder coursed through Selina, but she forced herself to be calm. No one else aboard knew who she was—and no one seemed to pay Zeke any mind.

"Dang drunk," the conductor pronounced as he passed Selina. "Railroad's got to do something to keep riffraff like that out of the station."

"Amen," Selina sighed. But there would be no keeping the "riffraff" out of her life. Marelda's flyers could be all over the state in a week. How much longer before they were all over the country as well?

She slumped back, feeling suddenly more alone than she had when her parents died five years ago. A sad smile touched her lips along with a familiar irony that the deaths of the two people she loved most had led to her hellish marriage to Gideon.

Selina had been a late surprise in the lives of Jeremy and Colinda Michaels. They had pampered her from birth. Selina's father, a history professor with a naturalist bent, had instilled in her a sense of awe and wonder for the wilderness and all of its creatures. Cherished nature trips had stretched to months of living off the land during which they had studied the habits of condors, wolves, elk, bears—"Anything your father can get his eyes on," her mother would say, laughing.

Her mother. An accomplished pianist, Colinda provided the sense of humor and zest for living that made Selina's childhood soar with happiness.

But in the end her parents had sheltered her too much. The hard realities of the world had seldom intruded on Selina's life, leaving her unequipped to cope with the crushing devastation brought on by their deaths. They had taught her to survive in the wilderness, but not in a day-to-day life without them. She had been lost, completely vulnerable. And Gideon had been ready.

She recalled how innocuously Gideon Hardesty had come into their lives. Selina's father had accepted an archaeology professorship at Blakeley, a private San Francisco college funded by the Hardesty empire. The position had seemed the answer to her father's dreams that long-ago autumn in 1871—a chance to teach the subject he loved and to relish extended summer holidays with his family.

Soon after arriving at Blakeley, six-year-old Selina and her parents had been invited to dinner at Hardesty House. When the moment came for her father to introduce Selina to the handsome golden-haired Gideon Hardesty, she had promptly stuck out her tiny hand. With a low bow and a grave smile, Gideon had accepted it.

"Such a charming man," her mother had beamed. "Such an utterly charming man."

As charming as a cobra, Selina thought bitterly, seeking to change the direction of her thoughts.

She laid her head back, allowing the clacking of wheels on iron rails, the gentle rocking motion of the car itself, and the tranquillity of the passing greenery to soothe her aching spirit. She took the time finally to study the scrupulously maintained appointments of the railcar. Plush upholstery and hand-carved woodwork enhanced the soft blue velvet drapes. Inlaid woods, marquetry, and ornate lighting fixtures all bespoke the elegance train travelers had once held in awe, and now expected as their due.

She smiled at the printed placard near the door. *Please take off your boots before retiring.*

"Hi, honey, this seat taken?"

Selina gasped. It was the woman in the red silk dress.

"I . . . I'm not looking for company," Selina said as tactfully as she could manage.

"Yeah, I noticed you looked kind of down at the mouth. Figured maybe you were lonely or homesick or somethin'. I'm alone myself—and I do hate to be alone." She plopped herself down in the seat facing Selina. "Ah, that takes a load off the bunions. And, see, now neither one of us is alone." She stuck out her hand. "My name's Bertie. Bertie Bodine. Short for Alberta." She made a face. "What's yours?"

Feeling awkward, Selina accepted the handshake. "Sel . . . Sally . . . Sally Smith."

"Well, Sally, how far are you going?"

"My . . . my uncle's in Red Bluff."

"Red Bluff. Never been there. Been everywhere else, though."

"Everywhere?" At once Selina chided herself. Why was she encouraging this conversation? The woman was a monument to garishness. People couldn't help but notice her—and that would call attention to Selina.

Bertie plunged on, "Been in mining camps in Nevada. Cattle towns in Kansas. Wherever men and money meet, I like to step in and introduce myself."

Selina found herself smiling. Just listening to Bertie was proving a balm to her bleak mood. The woman sat there, spinning tale after tale, each one wilder than the last.

". . . Them claim jumpers never stood a chance." Bertie grinned, finishing up one particularly outrageous yarn. "Showed 'em a little leg"— she lifted her skirt to her knees—"and my man got the drop on 'em."

Selina felt her cheeks heat.

"Of course," she said conspiratorially, "That ain't the kind of stuff I been tellin' Mr. Morgan Kincaid, you can bet your boots on that."

"Who?" Selina could not recall having heard the name in Bertie's outlandish discourse.

"Morgan Kincaid, my soon-to-be husband." Bertie struck a pose. "What do you think, can I fool some Montana dirt farmer into marrying me? Maybe I'll even get a few dollars out of him over a year or two. Got no real roots anywhere, Lord knows."

"You're engaged?"

Bertie withdrew two letters from her beaded reticule. "From my fian-see."

"That's nice," Selina allowed, not particularly relishing a shift in subject to marriage.

"Hope he ain't too ugly, if you know what I mean."

Selina frowned, bewildered. "You don't know what your fiancé looks like?"

"Nope. Never met him. I got hooked up with the Ladies in Waiting Mail Order Bride Service in Frisco. This Mr. Kincaid wrote, gave a list of what he wanted, and I fit the bill." She chortled. "Well, sort of . . ."

Selina's natural curiosity was piqued. "You're marrying a man you've never met? Whom you know only through . . ." She looked at Bertie's hand. ". . . two letters?"

"Yep. Why not? Already had me three other husbands I *did* meet! They didn't work out neither —'cept Horace. He died. But he had a smile on his face, if you get my drift."

Selina didn't want to get Bertie's drift, but she was forced to admit the woman had a point. She had known Gideon nearly all of her life—but the façade he'd presented to the outside world had done nothing to prepare her for the reality of marriage to the man. "Does this Morgan Kincaid know about the other three . . . I mean . . ."

"Hey, what he don't know don't bother me none. Right? I figure he's got to be ugly as a tree stump anyway, if he's got to resort to gettin' a woman through the mail." Bertie shoved the letters at Selina.

Selina balked. "Oh, no, I couldn't."

"Go ahead. You look like you could use a little entertainin'. Readin' somebody else's mail always perks me right up. See what you think."

"No, really."

"A real cold bastard, I'll wager. But since he sent me ticket money and all, I figured he must have some cash, even if Montana is in the middle of nowhere."

Selina held the letters in her lap, but she couldn't bring herself to open either one of them. Finally she handed them back to the woman. "I can't, Mrs. Bodine . . ."

"Call me Bertie. We're gonna be on this movin' box car more than a while. Twenty-two miles an hour is nice, but it's still three days from here to the Judith Mountains and Kincaid's ranch. He calls it Wolf Trail. Can you imagine? I must have had rocks in my head to agree to this whole thing."

In spite of herself, Selina was enjoying Bertie's company, but a warning voice reminded her not to get too close to anyone who might later be questioned by the law. Reluctantly she shifted her gaze to the passing terrain, hoping Bertie would take the gentle hint. Of course she didn't.

"Maybe gettin' hitched again ain't such a great idea, huh, Sally?"

"Then why did you agree to it?"

" 'Cause they give me fifty dollars at the Mail Order Service." Bertie paused reflectively. " 'Course I had to have one of the other gals help me with what to say. I ain't been to school too much, and this Mr. Kincaid wanted practically a schoolmarm for his kid. Told him I was a governess once . . ."

"He has a child? Then his wife is . . ."

"Plumb dead, I hope."

Selina leaned back in the seat. "I beg your pardon?"

"I mean, I don't hold with no man havin' two wives like some of them Mormons over by Salt Lake, you know."

Selina rolled her eyes. Maybe Bertie shouldn't go to Montana to marry this poor unfortunate widower. The shock might be too great for both of them.

"Listen to this part," Bertie said, opening one of the letters.

Selina held up a hand in protest, but Bertie barreled on.

"My dear Mrs. Bodine," she began, looking up at once. "Did you ever? 'My dear Mrs. Bodine'!"

She chuckled and looked again at the crisp blue stationery. "After reviewing your qualifications sent to me by Ladies in Waiting, it would seem you may be the woman to suit my purpose."

"Whatever will you do when you get there and he discovers you're not what you represented yourself to be?"

"Oh, honey, I'll be a hundred miles from anywhere. What's he going to do? Throw me back on the train? I'll have to stay over a little while." She patted her ample bosom, shoving the letter back into its envelope. "Believe me, honey, if he's breathing, he won't be askin' me to leave when I get through with him."

Selina gasped, certain her eyes were wide as China plates.

"Well, what else keeps a man in line?"

"You mean you would . . . willingly . . . be . . . in—" she stumbled over the word. Oh, good heavens, how could she even be talking about such things with a complete stranger?

"Intimate?" Bertie mocked, then sobered, sensing Selina's discomfiture. "I'm sorry, dearie. Are you of a . . . shall we say, *untouched* condition?"

Selina stared at her hands. She made no response.

"Sex is the best way to keep a man toeing the line. And if he's well made, well, who am I to say it won't be a marriage made in heaven?" As she said the last, Bertie leaned over in her seat and winked at the medicine drummer some four rows back. The man smiled back broadly.

Selina was grateful for the respite. She was trying with everything in her to keep her revulsion from showing on her face.

Tears stung her eyes as she thought of Gideon's subtle and not so subtle humiliations over five years . . . She had no use for sex. The very idea nauseated her.

"He's sure a good-lookin' one, ain't he?" Bertie grinned, poking Selina in the knee.

She followed Bertie's gaze. The drummer was now primping shamelessly, smoothing back his hair, grinning, leering, twirling the ends of his handlebar mustache.

Instantly Selina returned her attention to her hands.

"You really should learn to cheer up, honey," Bertie chided, her voice oddly gentle. "You're a purty little thing under those godawful clothes. You can't hide it from me. I got an eye for such. I used to hire the girls at a saloon in Tucson. Try wearin' a little makeup. Put a little color in your cheeks." She opened her reticule, pulling out a tiny vial. "Here." She placed the perfume into Selina's hand. "That'll make you feel better. Buy yourself a sunshine-yellow dress, and get rid of that crud you got hidin' the red in your hair. And why on earth you got it stuffed under that ugly scarf . . ."

Bertie made to reach for it, but Selina jerked back.

"Skittish little thing," Bertie said. "I suppose your mama and papa brought you up real strict, warned ya to stay clear of such as me, eh?"

"I . . . uh, haven't been well for a long time. I haven't been out much."

"I see." Bertie's brown eyes brimmed with sympathy. "Well, you'll get some color back in your cheeks in Red Bluff. Probably a wide-open little town. Maybe your uncle can line you up with a cowboy."

Selina choked. "I'm not looking for . . ."

"Don't give me that, honey. There's something else I can tell about a woman. You got what it takes to please a man in the bedroom. But you just ain't been usin' it, have ya?"

"Please, Bertie . . ."

"Take it easy. I'm wantin' our drummer boy for myself, not for you." She dropped her hankie, making an exaggerated display of retrieving it. Leaning over, she also managed to make an exaggerated display of her cleavage. Lifting the hankie, she blew a kiss at the drummer, then tucked the hankie seductively between her breasts.

The drummer rose and strode over. "I sincerely hoped to reach the hankie before you did, ma'am." He tipped his derby hat.

"Well, why not reach it now?"

Selina's eyes all but leaped from her head as the

man tugged the lace free of Bertie's bosom, then
held the delicate fabric to his mouth.

Bertie laughed and followed the drummer to his
seat. Try as she might Selina couldn't bring herself
to take her eyes off them. She found herself growing envious of Bertie. The woman lived her life as
she pleased, not giving a whit about society's approval. It had been so very long since Selina had
felt spontaneous or impulsive about anything.
Would she ever feel free again?

Her gaze fell on the two letters Bertie had left
lying on the seat. She reached over and picked
them up. Drawing a deep breath, she marched
over to Bertie.

"Excuse me, Mrs. Bodine, you left these. Your
fiancé, remember?" She was unable to keep the
censure out of her voice.

"I changed my mind, honey," Bertie said,
laughing. "I found me a new beau."

The train slowed, then stopped. Selina gripped
the seat to keep her feet.

"Looks like as good a place as any," Bertie said,
peering out the window. She and the medicine
drummer rose, arm in arm.

Selina held out the letters. "Wait! What
about . . ."

Bertie started toward the door, then looked
back, her bawdy laughter filling the car. "I've got
an idea, honey. *You* take him!"

Exasperated, Selina made her way back to her seat.

Fingering the letters, she felt a twinge of sympathy for the man. His fiancée would never arrive. She would likely never even write to explain her change of heart.

How could Bertie be so thoughtless? Mr. Kincaid was probably some painfully shy older man desperate for a bride.

Throw the letters away, her mind prompted. She had enough trouble of her own without burdening herself with the problems of a man she'd never met. But though long minutes passed, she did not loosen her grip on the two envelopes. With a resigned sigh, she extracted the letter with the earlier postmark, shaking off the feeling that she was somehow trespassing.

Morgan Kincaid. She noted the strong signature, the short, almost abrupt sentences, the terse up-and-down penmanship. The words were just as terse. Not exactly a man to warm a woman's heart. But then, there was no such creature.

Still, in the words she sensed an underlying pride and a genuine concern for his young daughter.

My dear Mrs. Bodine. Selina studied the salutation that had so tickled Bertie, deciding it was not meant as an endearment, but merely written out of a sense of politeness.

After reviewing your qualifications sent to me by

Ladies in Waiting, it would seem you may be the woman to suit my purpose. Since the death of my wife three years ago, my daughter, Celia, now ten, seems more and more in need of a feminine influence in her life. I cannot promise you an easy time of it. Montana can be harsh, the winters cruel. I make no promises. We will have a trial meeting, and if both parties are agreeable we will go ahead with the wedding. Of course, the intimate details of the marriage will be discussed only after we've seen each other.

Selina scowled. Of all the arrogant—! He wouldn't even discuss having an intimate relationship with Bertie until after he'd seen her.

Selina jammed the stationery back into the envelope and tossed both letters onto the seat. She was not going to involve herself. Why tell the poor fool he'd been jilted? Served him right for selecting a wife the same way he ordered feed.

But the letters drew her back again and again, until for no reason she could fathom, she stuffed them into the pocket of her dress just as the porter came by to help her pull down her berth for the night.

Sleep proved elusive. Selina's painful memories crowded out any hope of a restful night. She remembered the knife, Gideon's scream, the gurgling sound deep in his throat. She closed her eyes. She was so frightened, so very frightened.

Bertie appeared out of the darkness, floating, ephemeral, holding out the letters. *You take him.*

Then she saw him: the Montana rancher stalking the width and breadth of the rail station, pacing impatiently as he awaited his mail-order bride. He was tall and dark, though his features were indistinct. Bertie flounced off the train. The man padded toward her. Like a wolf. Then it wasn't Bertie. It was Selina who stood there. The wolf padded closer.

Abruptly, the image vanished and Gideon rose up like a specter, cackling. "No man will have you! I've taken care of that. You're mine. Even dead. You're mine. Come, my sweet Selina. Come."

He was holding something in his hand, coming toward her. Threatening. No, never again! No man would ever degrade her again.

Marelda circled above them, shrouded in black, screeching. "You'll hang, witch! You'll hang. You can't hide from me. There's nowhere you can hide."

Selina twisted, whimpering. The dream softened. Mountains. Awesome snowcapped mountains loomed in front of her. Summer in the Sierra Nevadas. Fishing, hiking. Her last summer with her parents.

A knock sounded on the door of her parents' home. She opened it. Gideon, looking so very sad. "I'm sorry, Selina. Your parents have been killed. A carriage accident on the way to the campus.

Please, come to the house. I insist. You'll stay with mother and me. I'll take care of you now. It's what your parents would want."

Kind, so kind. And she was so alone.

Take care of you.

The wedding. The wedding night. Gideon.

She awoke strangling on a scream, cut short. Gratefully, no porter came to investigate. Trembling, she lay back in her berth, and watched while the darkness outside turned gray with dawn.

To avoid arousing suspicion, the next day Selina disembarked at Red Bluff, but only long enough to purchase another ticket, this time on a Northern Pacific train, knowing it would take her out of California. Where didn't matter, though she found herself rattling on to the clerk about some sort of extended holiday. Why was she telling him anything? Why didn't she just keep her mouth shut?

To escape the notice of any observant passengers she went to the station washroom and sifted the coal rinse through her hair once again. The dark bottle was nearly empty. She told herself it was just as well. She disliked the gritty texture it gave her hair. Selina laughed at the absurdity of it, wishing the texture of her hair were the only problem in her life at the moment. With a heavy sigh she boarded the next train.

In the face of all the uncertainties that lay ahead, she had managed one concrete conclusion.

A place to hide wasn't enough anymore. She had to find a place to live, to be free to mend her hurts.

As the day passed, she pretended to doze, praying she would attract no more company. She looked up only when she noticed the silence. The train had stopped. Perhaps it would again take on water from one of the frequent towers along the track. But why was a passenger coming on board?

Her heart leaped. The passenger was wearing a badge.

He walked along the aisle, stopping at each seat, speaking to each traveler. Selina adjusted her scarf, praying the darkened tresses peeking out above her forehead looked more natural to the lawman than they had to Bertie.

The man reached her seat. A square-jawed man of about fifty, he tipped his hat politely. "Morning, Mrs. . . . ?"

"Good morning, Marshal."

"Sheriff. Sheriff Avery Cain."

"What . . . uh, what can I do for you, Sheriff?"

"Looking for a lady named Selina Hardesty. She's wanted for murder."

"Really?" Selina gasped, knowing she had to bluff her way through this or she was lost. "How dreadful."

"Yes, ma'am. You don't quite match the description, but— Might you be carrying some proof about who you are?"

"Proof? You think I . . . ?"

"Just talking to everyone."

"Of course. Well, I don't know what constitutes proof." She tried to smile, but failed.

"Somethin' with your name on it."

"Name?" She didn't remember consciously making the decision, but some core-deep instinct to survive gave her the words. "I . . . I'm traveling to meet my . . . fiancé." She fumbled in her pocket for the letters, holding them out to the lawman. "See? They're addressed to me from . . ." Lord, what was the rancher's name? "Morgan . . . Morgan Kincaid."

"And your name, ma'am?" the man persisted.

"My name?" Selina swallowed. "Why, I'm Bertie . . . Alberta Bodine."

Chapter 3

Morgan Kincaid slammed a hand against the side of an empty stall, the normally welcome scent of new hay and horses doing little this morning to ease his mounting agitation. Damn! Why had he asked Alberta Bodine to marry him? A woman, sight unseen, would be arriving at Wolf Trail in two days, and she was going to be his wife.

He paced angrily, kicking straw out of his way with his boots. He was a fool. A man couldn't mail-order a wife, much less a mother for Celia.

As he paced he deliberately nurtured his anger, needing it to keep other, more loathsome emotions at bay. He blamed no one but himself for his untenable situation. A temporary lapse in judgment and he'd somehow all but bought and paid for a wife. Surely there was a way out, a way to salvage his self-respect without hurting the innocent victim of his stupidity—the widow Bodine.

He raked a hand through his night-black hair, unconsciously pausing to touch the leather patch that shielded his ruined left eye. His fingers strayed no further. He wouldn't have to worry about reneging on his offer. One look at him and Alberta Bodine would renege for him.

"You're doin' it again, ain't ya, boss?"

Morgan glanced toward the long-haired, dark-skinned man ambling out of the early dawn sunlight to join him in the shadowed interior of the barn. Chino Black Hawk, half Comanche, half Texan, and all cowboy, walked with a bow-legged gait that attested to more time spent on horseback than on foot in his twenty-nine years.

"I don't recall asking your opinion," Morgan said, in no mood for his foreman's uncanny ability to read him as easily as he would the trail of a stray steer.

"You never ask anybody's opinion." Chino grinned. "That's why you're wrong so damned often—at least when it comes to women."

Morgan's already black mood grew darker still. "Isn't it about time you headed out?"

"The train delivers her to the water stop at noon tomorrow," Chino allowed, with a voice that suggested they'd already had this conversation once too often. "I think I'll make it." He tugged thoughtfully on one end of his full mustache. "You know, it's plumb amazing how you timed this lady's comin' so near to spring roundup. Gives you a chance to marry up with her, then desert her for five weeks. Real convenient, if you ask me."

"I didn't ask you, and she's here for Celia, not me."

Chino said nothing, but the look in his dark eyes made Morgan shift uncomfortably. He feigned work on a harness he'd told one of the hands to repair. "Just remember, I want her to come into the house alone."

Chino stooped to pick up a piece of straw, running it absently through his calloused fingers. "You should be makin' this trip yourself, you know."

"I've got a ranch to run."

Chino snorted. "Hell, we both know why you ain't goin'."

"Don't say it, Chino."

"Morgan, no woman on this earth could ever make as much of that scar of yours as you do."

Morgan's jaw clenched. "That's enough!"

Chino heaved an exasperated sigh. "That temper of yours ain't long enough to measure. But you mark my words, if this lady is worth her salt, it won't be Ceecy gettin' the better part of the bargain."

Morgan stared at the harness, a fierce tide of bitterness surging through him as he pictured the maimed ridge of flesh that snaked from above his blind left eye down to his jaw, where it trailed out and up in three jagged streaks across his cheek.

Chino called it a warrior's face. His own opinion was not nearly so noble.

"You saved my life once, Morgan," Chino said quietly. "Now it's time you saved your own."

Morgan didn't look up as Chino led two bay geldings out of the barn. "You gotta stop judgin' all women by Lenore. She meant to hurt you—and you let her."

Morgan swore, but Chino seemed not to notice, setting himself to the task of hitching up the bays. Damn his half-breed hide! Rubbing a hand over the back of his neck, Morgan assured himself he was not making comparisons between his late wife and what he assumed to be some frump of an aging widow. Alberta Bodine hadn't found it necessary to be specific about her age in the three letters she'd written him, but she *was* a widow. He considered it unlikely she would be younger than his own thirty-eight years. She could even be older. A frumpy, dowdy, aging, plump little widow . . .

He stiffened. Damn, oh, damn, why was he dwelling on the woman's appearance? It made no difference. This was nothing more than a business arrangement, made for Celia's sake.

He straightened, his good eye narrowing. He had not seen Celia this morning. She had been up and out of the house before dawn. Already knowing what he was going to find, he stomped back to the rear stall. It was empty. With his mouth set in a grim line, Morgan headed out of the barn.

His gaze shifted from the one-story log house to the sprawling series of corrals and outbuildings that made up the home base of Wolf Trail Ranch. Ignoring the awesome sight of the Judith Mountains three miles to the north, he gazed at the small blond figure perched atop the uppermost rail of the far corral. He strode toward Celia, thinking how daily she was growing to look more and more like her mother, in spite of the fact that her clothes more closely resembled his own.

Celia was shaking out a lariat, tossing it toward a prancing pinto stallion.

"I told you not to mess with that horse, girl," he said, striving to keep his tone even. "He's not full broke."

Celia turned to glower at her father. "I can manage any horse on this ranch."

"Just do as I say for once. And remember, I want you cleaned up and wearing a dress the day Chino comes back with Mrs. Bodine."

The girl leaped to the ground, swatting the dust from her trousers. "I ain't bein' nice to no stupid old lady, and you can't make me. I don't need her. You think you can make her be my ma. Well, she can't. My mother's dead!" She bolted away from him and raced toward the meadow.

He thought about going after her, but decided against it. It would only make a bad situation worse. Besides, he'd heard the sound of a horseman approaching. Squinting, Morgan looked east

into the sun to see Clay Prescott riding in on a
blaze-faced sorrel. "Perfect," he hissed under his
breath. "Just perfect."

Morgan made no move to welcome Prescott,
standing his ground as the sun-bronzed mus-
tachioed rancher dismounted and strode over to
him, hand outstretched. "Mornin', Morg."

Morgan accepted the handshake, though he
continued his icy appraisal of his closest neighbor.
"What the hell brings you here, Prescott?"

"What kind of a greeting is that from one partner to another?" Prescott chided, his attempt at
levity not quite ringing true.

"Going fifty-fifty on one bull hardly constitutes
a partnership."

"A prize Oregon shorthorn," Prescott corrected. "What the hell do you call that beast—
King something or other—"

"King Patrick," Morgan supplied, wishing the
man gone. Prescott's knowledge of breeding stock
was cursory at best, and Morgan was skeptical
about the man's sudden interest. Prescott was
overseer of the Lazy C, headquartered some thirty
miles east. As long as the man kept the Lazy C
turning a profit, its absentee owners, a wealthy
conglomerate of Europeans, were satisfied. And
that Prescott did turn a profit year after year Morgan credited to the fact that he at least had enough
sense to hire wranglers who knew as much about
cattle as Prescott did about making money. "Pat-

rick's calves are scattered all over the south range. You'll be seeing them in three weeks at roundup. So why don't you tell me what really brings you to Wolf Trail?"

"You wound me," Clay said, doffing his broad-brimmed gray Stetson long enough to smooth back his sweat-dampened yellow hair. "I can't wait to see those baby beeves. A couple of your boys told one of my hands they were the best they'd ever seen."

Chino strode over to stand near Morgan, ignoring Prescott's outstretched hand. "You could have had Stubby or Pete show you those calves right then, Mr. Prescott," he said, naming two of Wolf Trail's year-round wranglers.

Prescott's smile never left his face, though it was no longer in his eyes. "Well," he said slowly, "I guess I will admit to being a trifle curious about that other little matter. It isn't every day a man orders up a wife by mail." It was a deliberate attempt to goad Morgan.

Chino took a step toward Prescott, but Morgan held up a restraining hand. "Don't waste your time." To Prescott he said, "Chino will be meeting the train. Alone."

Prescott's eyes took on a knowing look. "Don't want her to leap back on the train, huh?"

"You son of a—" Chino lunged toward Prescott. Morgan stepped between them, putting a hand on Chino's chest to stop him. "Leave it be. I mean it." Prescott hadn't moved.

Chino scowled darkly. "You don't have to take that from him!"

"He's not worth it. Besides, he's leaving." Morgan looked pointedly at Prescott.

The blond rancher shrugged, letting the subject drop for the moment. "I ride with Chino, or I follow him. It makes no difference to me, but I intend to see those calves. Half of them belong to the Lazy C. Is it my fault the calves are in the same direction as the train?"

Morgan wished again that he could have avoided involving the Lazy C with King Patrick. When the bull had been offered for sale, Morgan hadn't had enough capital on his own, having spread himself thin buying stock last fall. But he hadn't hesitated to approach Prescott. In spite of their antagonistic relationship, each man knew a potential bonanza when he saw one. That they hated each other seemed almost a bonus. Neither would let the other get away with anything. Still, Prescott seemed more determined than usual to draw blood today.

Morgan's guard stayed up as Prescott headed over to Chino, now tying off the reins of the buckboard team. "Has Morg seen a picture of this woman?"

"Damn you!" Morgan spat. Moving quickly, he gripped Prescott's shirtfront. "Wasn't it enough your flirting with Lenore? You intend to move in on this one, too?"

Prescott made no attempt to free himself. "You know there was never anything serious between your wife and me. We were friends, that's all."

Morgan released Clay with a snort of disgust. "Why don't you just head back to the Lazy C? We'll be seeing enough of each other at roundup."

"It's a free country. I'll ride where I like."

Chino was about to climb aboard the wagon when he seemed to reconsider. "I think I'd best bring an extra blanket," he said. "There's one in the barn. The lady might not take to a chilly night on the plains."

"You don't think Morgan can keep her bed warm for her?"

Morgan backhanded Prescott across the face, sending him sprawling butt first into the dirt. He stood over him, splay-legged, his chest heaving with what it cost him not to beat the man senseless. "Get on your horse. Get off my land. Now."

Without looking back, Morgan stomped over to the corral, incensed that he'd let Prescott get to him. For four years he'd believed himself immune to jibes like Clay's. But now, faced with meeting a strange woman . . . He imagined first the horror in her eyes. Then the pity.

He should have warned her, but he hadn't been able to find the words. How do you tell a woman you're a freak? God, how Lenore had come to loathe the sight of him, how much he loathed it himself. The Bodine woman would be no different.

Maybe she'd missed the train. Maybe she'd changed her mind. Maybe— He whirled toward the sound of splintering wood. The sharp cry that followed sent him sprinting toward the barn. Prescott followed on his heels. They found Chino lying on his back at the base of the ladder that led to the hayloft, one of its middle rungs hanging jaggedly. "Meant to fix that blasted thing," he said, struggling to rise.

"What hurts?" Morgan asked, hunkering down beside his friend.

"Leg." Chino grabbed his left knee. "Twisted it bad."

"Is it broken?" Gently Morgan tested the leg for motion.

"I don't think so. But it feels like I'm gonna be on my back for a while."

The full implication of Chino's injury struck Morgan like a fist.

Clay hadn't missed it either. "I'd be glad to fetch the merry widow," he said.

"No!" Morgan snapped. "You won't fetch anyone. But you can make yourself useful and help me get Chino to the bunkhouse."

Together they carried the stricken foreman to the squarish clapboard building some fifty yards beyond the main house. "Easy," Morgan said, settling Chino onto one of the lower bunks. "Keep that leg still."

Chino lay back on the straw-stuffed mattress. "I'll be all right. Just need to keep my weight off it for a while."

"You can leave now, Prescott," Morgan said, straightening.

"You sure you don't want me to meet that train for you? I'd consider it a real privilege."

"I'll just bet you would." Morgan jerked his head toward the door. "Get out. Now."

Smirking, Prescott tipped his hat and left. Irritating Morgan Kincaid seemed to afford him almost as much pleasure as a ledger book filled with black ink.

"I don't know how you keep from killing him," Chino growled.

"Times like this I don't either." Morgan shook his head. "To hell with him. Let's get your boots off."

Chino winced as Morgan tugged off first his right boot, then the left.

Morgan's brow furrowed. "Just which leg did you twist?"

"The right. Hurts like hell."

"Yeah, I'll bet. Especially since you were favoring your left when I came into the barn."

"Musta twisted 'em both."

Morgan looked grim. "I know why you're doing this."

"Doing what?" Chino drawled, his dark eyes innocent as a babe's.

"You're a real bastard, you know that?"

"Uh-huh."

Morgan blew out an exasperated breath. "You'll keep an eye on Celia for me while I'm gone?"

"You know I will." Chino grinned, then grimaced for all he was worth as he rubbed both legs. "See you in a couple days, boss. Have a real nice trip."

Morgan headed out of the bunkhouse and strode across the ranchyard toward the waiting buckboard. He supposed he'd known all along that it was his responsibility to meet the train. He just hadn't wanted to admit it.

He climbed onto the wagon seat, refusing to entertain the jumble of possible scenarios of what might happen when Alberta Bodine saw him for the first time. If he thought about it too long, he'd never leave the ranchyard.

Ignoring Prescott, who guided his sorrel alongside the buckboard, Morgan gigged the bays into a trot. Unconsciously his left hand reached to adjust his eyepatch. He caught himself, curling his fingers into his palm. Tomorrow he would meet his mail-order bride.

Chapter 4

Morgan paid little attention to the passing terrain and even less to Clay Prescott, who, despite Morgan's irritation, made it his business to come along. Expansive grasslands gave way to clumps of sagebrush and back again, but his thoughts, despite his best efforts, focused sharply on Alberta Bodine. He'd read her letters several times before making his decision to acquire a mother for Celia. He reminded himself now of the solid, practical reasons for bringing a woman to Wolf Trail.

The woman's qualifications as governess were unimpeachable. She'd spent two years in the employ of a man she'd termed "an influential bay area widower." *The children, bless their hearts, were lost to me when my employer's relatives took charge of them after his tragic death. Subsequent temporary positions have proved unsatisfactory. I am anxious*

*for a permanent arrangement, thus my association
with Ladies in Waiting.*

She was a widow. She would know how to run a
household. *Norman, bless his soul, was a beneficent
provider until he was taken by the cholera. Friends
say I am a steady sort, not quick to anger, and a
fair cook. I would be grateful if we could come to
some sort of agreement, Mr. Kincaid.*

He'd admired her forthrightness and her obvious education. Though she had not been specific,
her flair with language suggested schooling beyond
what was typical for girls. Celia could read and
write, but he wanted so much more for her. His
own attempts to tutor her these past two years had
left him bewildered and frustrated, as though she
deliberately refused to learn just to defy him. He
hoped Alberta Bodine could break through the
child's stubbornness.

"Are those some of the King's offspring?"

Morgan grimaced. He'd almost forgotten his un-
wanted traveling companion. Prescott already had
asked the same question a dozen times since they'd
left the ranch six hours ago. "Patrick's are all farther south. We'll probably catch sight of some late
this afternoon." He paused, then added, "I trust
that will appease your sudden interest in cattle
breeding so you can head back to the Lazy C."

"Afraid I'll follow you to the train? Catch a
glimpse of the new bride? I guess you wouldn't
want her making comparisons . . ."

Morgan fingered the reins, his jaw tightening. Why did Prescott seem to forever bait him? In his life Morgan had never been a man to back away from an argument. Debate, a duel of words, had been a large part of what attracted him to the study of law after the war. But he could not debate the reality of the scar that marred his face.

He shook his head, forcing away the self-pity he loathed. He thought instead of that long-ago decision to become a lawyer. It all seemed so distant, as though it were part of someone else's lifetime, not his own.

Morgan had been only twelve when the war broke out. By its end, he'd lost everything. Willowsong, the Virginia plantation that had been in Kincaid hands for six generations, lay in ruins; his mother and younger sister reduced to living at the charitable whim of friends. His father and brother . . . His mind veered sharply from the memory.

Instead he recalled the night he'd listened to his mother sobbing herself to sleep in the servants' quarters of a Richmond banker. Morgan had vowed to restore the Kincaid name, the Kincaid pride. He struck a deal with the banker, promising to return the man's money twice over if he would finance Morgan through Harvard. Through school Morgan worked every spare hour at any odd job he could find to pay for a private residence for his mother and sister.

He managed to finish in the top one percent of

his class, accepting a position with a noted Richmond law firm. With a negotiated advance and a hefty bonus, he paid back the banker and even made arrangements to buy back Willowsong. The purchase agreement was in his pocket at graduation. He was going to surprise his mother that evening at a celebratory dinner. She died of a heart attack on her way to the ceremony.

He stayed in Virginia another year, then took his sister, Marcette, and moved to Houston. The girl had become unmanageable, flirting with socially prominent men twice her age whose marital status was of little or no consequence to her. In new surroundings he'd hoped . . .

Morgan shut out the dark memories, holding the spirited bays to a trot for another hour before pulling up to prepare a midday meal. Building a quick fire, he started a pot of coffee, then readied a skillet full of beans and bacon, gesturing unenthusiastically to Prescott.

"Been a long time since you and I shared a campfire, Morg," Clay said, sipping gingerly at a cup of the scalding brew. "Since before Lenore . . ." He looked at the ground. "I'm sorry. There I go again. I can act like a real jackass sometimes. I don't know what gets into me."

Morgan poured himself a cup of coffee. "Forget it." He wanted the subject dropped.

"Can't." Clay straightened. "I really mean it. I'm sorry."

Morgan said nothing, ladling a plateful of beans from the pan. Nothing was ever going to let him trust Clay Prescott, not even an apology.

Clay seemed determined to keep up the chatter. "I can't believe you asked this Bodine woman here on the basis of a couple of letters."

Morgan glared at him. He had no intention of discussing his personal life with Clay Prescott. The ranch hands on both spreads had found the impending arrival of Alberta Bodine irresistible range gossip for weeks. Prescott's prying, though, skated well past the bounds of normal curiosity.

"Well, I hope this woman helps," Prescott said. "Ceecy's a good kid." He threw the dregs of his coffee on the campfire.

Morgan finished and broke camp, his thoughts troubled as they resumed their trip. He and Clay had never made any pretense of being friends. Clay had been appointed overseer of the Lazy C not long after Morgan set up Wolf Trail, and he'd taken an instant and obvious liking to Lenore. At first she'd been merely flattered. But after Morgan's accident Lenore had grown more and more remote, and Morgan had become more and more suspicious. Her long solitary rides led ultimately to overnight sojourns. For a woman who detested sleeping on the ground . . .

He followed her once to a line shack fifteen miles from the main house. He waited, out of sight. Clay rode up a half hour later. Morgan re-

turned to Wolf Trail and never said a word to either one of them. He never followed her again.

And yet like any neighbors they were there for
each other in times of trouble. They exchanged information, lent each other equipment, tolerated
each other's ways. When the Lazy C banded with
other ranches to rid the range of rustlers a few
years back, Morgan had not joined in, but neither
had he interfered. Justice had been swift, if not
entirely legal, for more than a dozen outlaws. And
the number of stolen cattle had dropped signifi-
cantly since.

"Whoa!" Morgan yanked back on the reins.
"Prescott, take a look at that." He pointed south,
about a mile ahead. Streaks of black circled and
dipped against the cloudless blue sky.

Buzzards.

"Probably a deer," Prescott said, unconcerned.

"I don't think so. They're right above that patch
of buffaloberry bushes. Some of Patrick's calves
were grazing there a couple of days ago." He
snapped the reins, sending the bays into a quick
canter.

When he heard the piteous bawling of a calf in
trouble, Morgan leapt from the wagon and
sprinted toward the far side of the tangle of chest-
high shrubs.

Then he saw it.

"Damn."

The calf lay on its side, thrashing weakly some

thirty feet into the thorn-flecked bushes. The body of its mother lay sprawled on the plain twenty yards away, her carcass bloated and torn.

He studied the ground. Wolves had made the kill, and the buzzards now were busily taking their share. As he approached the carcass, hundreds of horseflies rose above it as a single mass, buzzing furiously. When he moved off, the flies dropped again to feed.

A dead wolf lay just outside the circle of bushes, its belly sliced open by the cow's horns.

Prescott dismounted and strode over. Morgan stood in front of the thorny shrubs, assessing how best to approach the calf. It had likely bolted into the brambles in terror, gotten itself tangled up, and now was unable to free itself. "With a whole cow to feed on, those wolves didn't bother with the calf. But they could be coming back tonight."

"Too bad we don't have any strychnine with us. We could salt the carcass."

"I don't use poison. I don't like it. Poison doesn't discriminate. It kills whatever eats the meat." Morgan returned to the wagon, retrieved his gloves and a pair of wire cutters, then made his way carefully through the shrubbery. Bright green leaves shielded dull brown flowers that in two months time would turn into juicy red buffaloberries.

"So the world loses a few buzzards, maybe a

bobcat," said Prescott from the sidelines. "So what?"

"So I happen to believe that even the wolves have their place in the scheme of things. I don't like it when they eat my livestock, but I won't use poison. Ever. I've seen ranchers use so much of it, they foul their own water and kill their own cattle."

"I doubt I'll ever understand you, Kincaid."

"I doubt I'll ever ask you to try, Prescott."

Gingerly Morgan freed the two-month-old calf. The animal was so weak from hunger and exhaustion it no longer struggled.

"Looks pretty pitiful," Clay said. "You'd best shoot him."

"No. I think I can keep him alive. I'll take him back to the ranch. I've got a cow that'll wet-nurse him." He lifted the calf, carrying him to the shade of the wagon. "He's one of Patrick's. I don't want to lose him."

"Aren't you forgetting something? Or should I say some*one*?"

Morgan lifted his hat, brushing a hand through his dark hair. For the first time in two months he had actually forgotten the widow Bodine. For five minutes. He considered his options, knowing already he had none. Prescott could never take proper care of the calf.

"It looks like you're going to get first look after

all, Prescott." He didn't succeed at keeping the edge out of his voice.

"It'll be my pleasure . . . to deliver your intended to Wolf Trail."

"Just get one thing clear."

"I'm listening."

"Keep your mouth shut . . ." He adjusted the eyepatch. ". . . about me."

"Whatever you say. I still think it would be better to warn her. Maybe that way she could even pretend it doesn't bother her."

Morgan stood there trying to decide if Prescott was indifferent, malicious, or both in his constant needling. He finally decided it didn't much matter.

They set up an early camp upwind of the carcass. Morgan tended the calf, easing some water down its throat as best he could. Though the men heard wolves howling in the timber some four miles distant, the pack made no appearance near the camp. At dawn Morgan gently settled the calf over the saddle of Clay's sorrel.

"Train arrives at the water tower at noon."

Clay climbed onto the wagon.

"Remember what I said, Prescott."

Morgan watched the buckboard until it was out of sight. Maybe he *should* have put the calf out of its misery. The calf licked his hand. He smiled, patting the coarse brown head. "You win, little fella. We'll find you a new mama real soon."

He rode slowly, not reaching Wolf Trail until

late afternoon. Before he'd had a chance to dismount Chino was out of the bunkhouse and rushing toward him.

"What happened?" the foreman demanded.

Morgan explained.

Chino swore. "I should've followed you."

"You seem remarkably fit," Morgan drawled, enjoying a modest revenge, "for a man who seemed so close to having two broken legs yesterday morning."

Chino stared sheepishly at the ground. "What can I say, boss? It was a miracle."

"Never mind," Morgan said. "Just help me with this calf."

Chino carried the nearly limp brown-and-white bundle, matching Morgan stride for stride as the two men headed for the barn. "I can't believe you sent Prescott to meet Mrs. Bodine."

"What choice did I have?" He cast a glance around the yard, then changed the subject. "Where's Celia?"

"Out riding her mare."

"Well, let's see what we can do about presenting this fella to his new mama, shall we?" He swung open the door of the middle stall. "Whoa, Lady," he soothed, patting the placid beast on her huge rump. "Got a surprise for you." In minutes the milk cow had accepted the orphan and the calf was nuzzling greedily at her udder.

Satisfied, Morgan left them alone. Outside, he

glanced skyward, almost unwillingly checking the position of the sun.

Chino seemed to read his mind. "Clay should have picked her up at the water stop by now."

"Uh-huh."

"They'll spend the night on the trail."

"Uh-huh."

"You're scared to death, aren't you?"

Morgan stiffened. "If anyone else had said that to me . . ." Then he shook his head. "Terrified."

He spent the rest of the day working himself to a state of near exhaustion, refusing to entertain any of the contradicting emotions seething inside him. He was no easier on himself the next day, spending his time attacking the most physically demanding chores on the ranch—chopping wood, mending fence, anything to keep his mind occupied.

Toward dusk he brought himself up short, telling himself he should relax, clean up. Alberta Bodine could arrive at any time. Again he checked the south horizon for any sign of the buckboard. Using the blue bandanna around his neck, he wiped off the day's sweat and grime and headed toward the house. He paused only long enough to call to Celia.

She peered out at him from her favorite retreat, a treehouse in the towering cottonwood along Ford Creek that meandered three hundred yards behind the house.

"Remember, young lady, I want you presentable when Mrs. Bodine arrives."

His daughter gave him a reluctant nod.

Morgan did not press her. In his present mood he would only further cripple their deteriorating relationship. With a resigned sigh, he ducked into the house.

The wooden structure boasted a full complement of glass windows and was far more elaborate than most homes in Montana, a concession he had willingly made to Lenore, knowing how much she had detested leaving Houston. Each room offered its own mute testimony to how far he had gone to make her life on the ranch as comfortable as possible.

Hands on lean hips, Morgan stood just inside the door, trying to envision Alberta Bodine's reaction to what Lenore had pronounced "little better than a tipi." The main room, the largest in the house, was dominated by a fieldstone fireplace in its center. On its opposite side the fireplace served to heat the kitchen. On the floor in front of the hearth lay a rug sewn from the finest bearskins. Unwillingly, he recalled how he had once tried to seduce Lenore on that rug. Abruptly, his gaze shifted to admire the Shoshone shield and spear on the wall above the mantel.

The most incongruous thing in the room had to be the Baldwin grand piano, which took up much of the area to the left of the fireplace. Lenore had demanded the thing be brought out, though she played only rarely and badly. Morgan had been well aware that her motives were anything but musical. She had wanted to upstage the neighbors. Discovering that the vast majority of her neighbors were of the four-legged variety had become one more reason for her to hate her new home.

Morgan crossed the main room, heading down the south hall to the back of the house. At least here one of Lenore's demands had actually become a pleasant convenience for himself and Celia. He stepped into the indoor bathing room off the kitchen, relishing the idea of soaking his aching muscles. He made good use of the zinc bathtub with its running water, pumped directly into the house from pipes laid to a nearby underground well. Alberta Bodine could hardly accuse him of being uncivilized about a lady's more delicate comforts.

After toweling his lean, hard body dry he settled the towel around his hips and headed to his bedroom. The sun was gone. Clay's trip was taking too long. The delay only exacerbated Morgan's mounting unease.

He stood at his dressing table, staring into the oak-framed mirror. Life on the range had long ago taught him the expedience of shaving by feel. He wondered sometimes if he used the mirror deliberately to taunt himself with his own image. He studied his reflection. Critical, assessing, he tried to see his face for the first time, see it through a woman's eyes. But he could not.

Shaking off this latest bout of self-pity, he mixed his shaving lather and scraped the day's stubble. His face, except for the scar, was deeply tanned.

Four years.

He closed his good eye, remembering the blood that had been everywhere. Lenore's screaming. Celia standing to one side, ashen faced.

After he had healed he made the mistake of going to Lenore's bed. She'd been sitting up, filing her nails, her lush sun-colored hair tumbling across her satin-covered pillows. When he entered the room, she turned her head away in revulsion. "I couldn't bear for you to touch me now."

"You couldn't much bear it before." God, how he had hated the defensive sound of his voice. Lenore had moved her things into the guest bedroom that night. Morgan never slept with her again.

He knew his imminent meeting with Alberta Bodine had rekindled his memories, but that didn't make bearing them any easier. He padded over to the small wardrobe, wanting only to pull on a clean pair of dungarees and a shirt. But something prodded him to select a well-cut dark gray frock coat and trousers, a pale blue silk shirt, and a string tie. He ran a thumb over the fine fabric of the jacket, recalling the last time he'd worn it: the day he'd resigned his position as a full partner in the prestigious Houston law firm founded by Lenore's father.

Forcing his thoughts to the present, he finished dressing and ran a brush through his dark hair, giving his reflection a last sardonic smile.

Returning to the living room, he crossed to his desk and pulled out the three letters Alberta Bodine had written him. He reread them by the dim light of an oil lamp. The woman still came through as intelligent and steady. He only hoped she would be the catalyst he needed to mend his broken relationship with Celia.

He frowned, realizing his daughter had not yet come in from her treehouse. He'd done a pathetic job of being a father to her these past three years, if her increasingly rebellious behavior was any indication. He didn't know how to reach her anymore. He'd tried strict discipline, tried being lax, tried everything he could think of, but it was as though she didn't want anything to do with him. It hadn't been so for the first six years of her life. He had relished being a father, relished the obvious adoration in his child's hazel eyes. But something had gone seriously wrong. Whatever it was, even if it cost him a measure of his pride, he intended to try his damnedest to fix it.

Losing her mother had been hard on Celia. Still, Morgan had at least shielded her from the more bitter truth, that Lenore had been deserting not only him but Celia as well the night she died.

Shoving the letters back into the desk drawer, he crossed to the piano, poking at the keys. The thing was hopelessly out of tune. He ought to break it up for firewood. Its presence was a constant reminder of Lenore's pretentiousness. But someday perhaps Celia would want to learn.

At the fireplace he lifted a bottle filled with an amber liquid, poured himself a drink, and belted it down. The time was too close now. He could no longer quell thoughts he wanted no part of, thoughts that sent a long-suppressed heat through his blood.

God, what had possessed him to mail that last letter to the Bodine woman two weeks ago? He'd told her, as delicately as he could manage, that there would be times when as a man he would expect . . . No. He would tell her tonight that he'd changed his mind, that he'd had too much to drink when he wrote the letter. This was a business arrangement. He would slake his physical needs elsewhere if it came to that. Still, he prayed Alberta Bodine was the ugliest woman on earth.

It would be all right then if she didn't desire him. Because he wouldn't desire her.

He let out a disgusted breath. He stood there, balancing his lust against her appearance, when his deepest terror was that she would do exactly the same to him. Yet he couldn't seem to help it; couldn't stop it.

He pictured her then for one fleeting instant—
her body ripe, lovely. And in her eyes he saw a
sickened horror when she looked at him.

He poured himself another drink.

Chapter 5

Selina had to get used to the name. Alberta Bodine. She said it to herself over and over as she paced in the knee-high grass beneath the huge wooden water tower. The train had been stopped for more than half an hour, but the hissing of hot boilers taking on water continued to disrupt the stillness of the vast meadow.

"I hope you're not too worried, Mrs. Bodine," the conductor said, wading through the grass to join her. "This is the exact spot Mister Kincaid sent word he'd meet you. The wire said noon, and it's just a little past that now."

"I'm not worried, Mr. Barnes," Selina replied, thinking, *I'm just scared to death.*

The conductor extracted a gold watch from his vest pocket, checked the time, looked at the train, then checked the time again. He gave Selina a nervous smile.

Selina said nothing. She knew what he was

thinking. The boilers were filled now, and he had a schedule to keep. Yet she was reluctant to make his departure easier by assuring him she would be all right here alone. What if Kincaid didn't show up?

The conductor cleared his throat. Evidently Selina's anxiety did not take precedence over the Northern Pacific's arriving in Miles City on time. "I'm afraid the train is going to have to leave now, ma'am."

"I understand, Mr. Barnes."

"I'm sure he'll be along any minute."

"Of course."

She watched as Barnes climbed aboard.

At first she misunderstood his murmured "thank God," ascribing it to her not becoming hysterical about being stranded. Then she lifted her eyes to follow the conductor's gaze northward. About three miles distant she spied a thin plume of dust. A wagon. Her heart pounded.

"That'll be Mr. Kincaid," the conductor said. "Never met the man myself, but hear tell he's one big rancher in these parts. You could have done a lot worse, Mrs. Bodine."

She closed her eyes, an unwelcome shudder shattering her fragile composure. She already had done a lot worse.

Mr. Barnes slipped his watch back into his vest pocket and waved at the engineer to start the train.

"Good luck to you, ma'am," he called above the

departing shriek of the train's whistle. He sounded as if he thought she would need it.

For long minutes after the departure of the train Selina concentrated on the advancing dust cloud, even as her mind unaccountably leapfrogged to a dozen different images of Morgan Kincaid. She pictured him in every guise from Blackbeard to Jane Eyre's Mr. Rochester. She shook her head. She was being a fool. Morgan Kincaid was likely some modestly educated middle-aged widower of average looks and average intelligence, no more, no less. She would be his wife, for now, because she had no choice. But she would somehow convince the man that her only duties on his ranch should involve his daughter.

Taking in long, deep breaths of crisp, spring air, Selina tried in vain to calm her thudding heart. Impulsively she reached into her pocket, extracting the tiny vial of rose-scented perfume Bertie had given her. Quickly—before she had time to change her mind—she daubed a little behind each ear, then forced her attention to the landscape.

She managed a tiny smile. In every direction she saw mountains, some huge, castellated, and snow-peaked, others less lofty but no less beautiful. Billowy hills carpeted with grass greening in the May sun unfurled all around her, the color so pervasive it was as though she were immersed in an emerald lake.

A magnificent land.

Morgan Kincaid's land. She felt a sudden kinship with a man who would choose to live in a place so wild and free. Land ideal for cattle, with its ubiquitous buffalo grass and pungent sage. A land on which to build dreams. And, she suspected, a land on which to end dreams as well. For all the splendor of this valley, she sensed it held the capacity to be harsh and unforgiving.

The closer the wagon drew, the more she found herself questioning her sanity at attempting her monumental deception. Maybe she should have stayed on the train? No, she'd been through all that. Thanks to the loquacious Sheriff Cain everyone aboard had learned she was a mail-order bride. Kincaid's isolated ranch would be a serendipitous haven for now. Perhaps the rancher would even be sympathetic. Maybe she could tell him the truth.

She trailed a hand along one of the tower's wooden support posts. Tell him she was fleeing a murder charge? Suppose he alerted the law? Yet if she explained that she was innocent, that Gideon had been a beast . . .

Selina trembled. How could she tell any man the truth about Gideon?

Her heartbeat quickened as the buckboard drew nearer. She could just make out the figure of a man in a gray broad-brimmed hat guiding the two-horse team. When he neared and raised a hand in greeting, she discerned a flash of even white teeth.

"Whoa!" the man called, jumping down from

the buckboard before the horses had stopped completely. He strode toward her, doffing his hat to reveal straw-colored hair. His grin was easy under his thick mustache, and his gray-green eyes sparked with a genuine warmth. She found herself liking him at once.

"Mrs. Bodine?" he said, reaching out his right hand.

She accepted the warm handshake. "Mr. Kincaid."

"No, ma'am."

She withdrew the hand. "I beg your pardon?"

"My name's Clay Prescott. Morgan couldn't make the trip. I manage the Lazy C about thirty miles east of Morgan's Wolf Trail."

"I see," replied Selina, though she didn't see at all. "Is Mr. Kincaid ill?" My goodness, how old and infirm was the man?

"No, he's not sick. Just got a little side-tracked. He's a busy man."

Too busy to meet his future bride? She couldn't decide which emotion she felt more keenly—alarm or irritation. Was Clay Prescott a scout to find out if she was presentable enough? Would he send up smoke signals for yes or no on the way back? And why was she so concerned about Kincaid's disgraceful manners?

She pushed away the thoughts as Prescott helped her climb onto the buckboard. She was all too aware of how his hands lingered on her waist, but she didn't want to put the man in his place. She couldn't afford to offend him.

He seemed to be looking for something now, his gaze quizzical. "Beggin' your pardon, ma'am, but where's your luggage?"

Selina's mind raced. "I . . . I don't have any."

His eyes widened. "Nothing?"

She dared not claim she was robbed, since Mr. Kincaid might launch an investigation on her behalf. "I . . . I lost track of it in Oakland. It was misplaced. Onto another train. They assured me they would have it sent on when they located it."

"Well, don't you worry that pretty little head of yours, Mrs. Bo— May I call you . . . Alberta?"

She flinched, wishing there were some way to have him call her Selina, but said only "Bertie."

"Bertie?" He looked dubious. "We'll have to come up with a better monicker than that."

As they drove Clay proved himself quite amiable, talking incessantly, mostly about himself.

Finally, toward dusk Selina felt secure enough in his company to ask a few questions of her own. "Mr. Prescott . . ."

"Clay. We're very informal out here."

"All right, then, Clay. Could you tell me what Mr. Kincaid is like?"

"You wrote to him, didn't you?" He chuckled. "You agreed to marry him. And *now* you're asking what he's like?"

"There's only so much you can glean from letters."

"So what do you *think* he's like?"

She studied Clay Prescott covertly, deciding he was a man used to charming his way with women. But despite her growing ease with him, she found herself curiously unwilling to share her assumptions about Morgan Kincaid—that he was arrogant, terse, dour, and . . . thoroughly mystifying. She told herself she didn't want to chance Clay carrying tales back to Kincaid, but there was a deeper reason for her reticence. At least some part of her reluctance stemmed from the defensiveness she had perceived in Kincaid's letters. She decided to reverse the subject. "What did he tell you about me?"

"He told me he needed a woman."

She blushed heatedly.

"I mean for his daughter," he said too quickly, and she knew his innuendo had been deliberate. "She's a little hellion, let me tell you. You'll have your hands full bringin' that little gal to heel. In fact, I doubt a little strip of a thing like you is going to stand a chance."

"I've failed before I've begun?"

"Of course not. But Morgan can't handle her, and he's her father."

"Sometimes an outsider can see things more clearly."

He looked so thoughtful that for a moment she

feared she had made some mistake, but he appeared to shrug it off and continued lightly, "I heard you were a governess once."

"Yes," Selina said, remembering what Bertie had rattled off, "for two children, after my . . . my husband died. That was quite some time ago."

"You hardly look old enough for anything to have been 'quite some time ago,' Bertie."

"I . . . I was married at . . . at fourteen. An arranged marriage to a . . . much older man." She swallowed the bile as the story brushed too close to the truth. "When he died I had to do something. He left me penniless."

"Sounds like you're a survivor, Bertie. Maybe you *will* work out with Celia. Morgan's another story. No woman can . . ." He clamped his jaw shut, then looked to the east. "See that knoll? That's where . . ."

He droned on, Selina only half listening. She had noticed the deliberate shift. What wasn't he saying about Morgan Kincaid? She waited for a break in Clay's monologue, then plunged in. She needed to know as many details as possible about the man before she met him face-to-face. "How long has Mr. Kincaid been ranching here?"

"About five years now, I think. He and Lenore . . ." He stopped abruptly.

"Lenore was his wife?" Selina prompted.

Prescott nodded, but did not continue.

"It's none of my business, but how did she

. . . ?" Her voice trailed off as she detected a barely perceptible stiffening in Clay.

"An accident," he said. "She fell off her horse."

"How tragic. Was she very old? Oh, please, never mind." She corrected herself quickly. "I'm sorry. I shouldn't be pestering you with these questions. I just want to make a good first impression, that's all."

"Well, let me tell you, Bertie," he said, his eyes softening, "you've made one mighty fine first impression on me."

Again she felt her face heat. The man was being painfully obvious. And he was Morgan Kincaid's friend? She clasped her hands in front of her, relieved when he returned the subject to himself.

Night hadn't yet fallen when he pulled up the horses, announcing it was time to make camp. With no ranch house in sight she supposed she should have seen this coming. Still, she didn't hide her disappointment. "Couldn't we keep going?" she asked.

"Morgan doesn't expect us until tomorrow. No sense traveling in the dark."

"Oh." She hoped he didn't notice her sudden nervousness. Taking a deep breath, she told herself she was being foolish. There was nothing to be frightened of here.

Clay set about bedding down the horses, then built a campfire and cooked dinner.

"Pretty simple fare," he said. "Bacon and beans."

"It smells wonderful. I haven't eaten since breakfast."

"You should have said something," he scolded gently. "We could've stopped earlier."

"No, this is fine. Really." She smiled. "I doubt I'll even be able to eat all of this." She surprised herself, though, finishing off one plateful and helping herself to another. In truth "breakfast" had consisted of a slice of bread she'd sneaked from a dining car. She hadn't dared spend any more of her meager funds on food. If Kincaid's ranch didn't work out, she would have to use what money she had left for one last train ticket—anywhere.

"You don't have to keep that scarf on, you know," Prescott said, lighting a cheroot and sitting back against the spokes of the rear wagon wheel.

Selina's hand fluttered upward. She had washed out much of the darkening rinse on the train last night, but her hair was still far from presentable. "You embarrass me, Mr. Prescott. Without my luggage, my personal things, I haven't been able to maintain my hair properly at all. My first order of business at Mr. Kincaid's will be a lengthy soak in a tub."

She flushed at the unmistakably lusty glimmer that came into the man's eyes.

"I think you'll find Morgan's bathing room just

the place for that lengthy soak, Bertie. And if you ever need anyone to scrub your back . . ."

"Mr. Prescott!" she cried, outraged.

"I meant no offense," he demurred. "Honestly."

He gave her such an obviously affected guileless grin that she almost laughed. The man was so secure in his own conceit that he couldn't imagine she was anything but captivated by his charm.

She yawned broadly. "I hope you'll forgive me, Clay, but I'm really very tired. I'm not used to so much traveling."

"Of course. And here I keep chattering."

Prescott prepared a bed of blankets for her beside the buckboard, then spread out his own a few yards distant.

Selina lay down, uncomfortably aware of him so near. Fear rose again. All at once she felt terribly alone. What defense would she have against Prescott, Kincaid, any man?

No more than she'd had against Gideon.

She could run. She'd tried it twice. Each time Gideon had found her, and each time he had locked her in her room, the second time for five months, allowing no one to utter so much as a word to her. Even so, she had been planning a third attempt the night Gideon died.

Here in such wide, open country, she knew she could live off the land. Yet she didn't want to run, not if she didn't have to. An isolated ranch house was preferable to constantly checking over her shoulder. Surely the Morgan Kincaid she'd perceived in Bertie's letters would not have sent a man to meet her who could do her harm. Convinced of that, she closed her eyes and slept.

The next day Prescott was even more amicable, keeping up a steady stream of chatter about his successes as a ranch manager. She listened avidly until his tales of success began to include lurid tales of Montana justice.

"Hanged three rustlers that day," he said, finishing up a story about a murdered ranch hand and several hundred stolen cattle.

"Please, Clay," she interrupted, unable to bear any reference to hanging. "I'd really rather you changed the subject."

"I'm sorry, Bertie. Sometimes I don't think before I talk. A lady doesn't need to hear about a lynching, after all."

"No," she murmured. "A lady doesn't."

Thankfully, he returned to his favorite topic—himself, regaling her with adolescent exploits on the high seas. "Sometimes I think I should go back to the ocean—that I'll never be completely at home on land."

She suspected that comment was the first bit of gut-level insight into the real Clay Prescott she'd heard since he'd picked her up at the water tower. And it was all too brief, as he seemed to catch himself, returning the subject to his managing the Lazy C.

Dusk had long since fallen when they reached
Wolf Trail. She was certain Clay had kept the pace
slow so that he might continue rattling on to her.
Though the night chill now seeped into her bones,
she made no mention of her discomfort. She could
well imagine the man settling his arm around her
shoulder under the pretense of warming her.

Even in the darkness she was struck by the earnest quality of Wolf Trail. She sensed the pride
here. Comparing the ranch house to Gideon's
forty-room mansion, she found the ranch house
infinitely more to her preference. Strangely, she
felt safe here. And at home. It was eerie how the
feeling overwhelmed her at that instant. But she
quickly ascribed it to her need for security and let
it go at that.

". . . I'd better leave you alone now," Clay was
saying.

"Yes, that'll be fine." She felt a renewed surge of
anxiety. To cover her feelings she asked with false
lightness, "Does Mr. Kincaid have many men
working for him?"

"About half a dozen, more during roundup."
He gripped her hand as he helped her from the
wagon seat, then did not release it, instead bringing her hand to his lips. "If you need anything, you
holler, all right? I'll be bunking over tonight."

Selina tugged her hand free, absently rubbing
away the feel of his mouth. "You're expecting me
to have some difficulty, aren't you?"

He seemed about to say something, but changed his mind and tromped off toward what Selina presumed was the bunkhouse.

Selina's heart pounded as she approached the door to the main house. On the other side was Morgan Kincaid.

Taking a deep breath, she raised her hand and knocked softly. When no one answered, she opened the door.

In the dimly lit interior of the house, shadows flickered eerily along the walls, cast by the dancing light of flames crackling in the hearth. Beside the fireplace stood a tall silhouetted figure. Selina's heart hammered in her chest. He was certainly being boorish, just standing there like that. Surely he was aware of her. She frowned, catching the faint scent of whiskey mingled with woodsmoke.

His arm was on the mantel, his right profile lit by the blaze. She smiled tentatively, but he seemed not to be looking in her direction at all. He had pleasant features, handsome even. Dark where Clay was light. The plane of his jaw was well carved, and in a fanciful moment she decided it hinted at a stubborn streak. As she watched, the corner of his mouth quirked, as if he were amused by something, though she sensed, oddly, bitterness rather than humor. It was then she noted the thin black strip angling across his forehead away from her line of sight. What . . . ?

He turned slowly. In the darkness she could not

discern the color of the uncovered eye that now openly assessed her, nor could she decide which emotion he was trying harder to conceal. Defiance? Fear?

She stared at him, at the wicked scar that marred his perfectly sculpted features. And she knew, *knew* he'd staged their initial meeting deliberately for full effect. What was he expecting her to do? Faint?

Her lips thinning, she advanced toward him, her temper set free for the first time in five years.

Chapter 6

"I am cold, dusty, tired, and certain parts of my anatomy ache abominably, Mr. Kincaid," Selina railed. "Sending someone else to bring me here was bad enough, but for you to pull *this* despicable stunt is inexcusable. Now I can turn right around and leave, or you can assure me that this is as childish as you get!"

She watched his good eye widen in astonishment, then narrow with anger, seeing clearly now its color as blue, painfully blue. Even more clearly she saw that he was not at all accustomed to anyone using such a tone with him. And in truth she wondered why she had been foolish enough to do so now. Perhaps it was because she knew she could turn and run for Clay.

Suddenly contrite, she backed away several paces. Things already were going badly, and he hadn't yet uttered a word. How would this tall, imposing stranger react? Gideon would have . . .

"Are you finished?" he asked.

She nodded. "I'm sorry. I should never have—"

He raised a hand, and involuntarily she flinched, but he did not move toward her. "I'm Morgan Kincaid," he said unnecessarily, and she was certain she detected a nervous note in that baritone voice. Could he have been as wary of this meeting as she?

She straightened, studying the way he fidgeted with a peacepipe on the mantel. He was obviously ill at ease. Had he changed his mind about the marriage? No, surely not. Then what could put such an intimidating man so on edge? The words from Bertie's letter leaped across her mind. . . . *the intimate details of the marriage will be discussed only after we've seen each other.* Her eyes widened. He had written those words not out of arrogance, but fear—fear that his prospective bride would reject *him.*

Selina felt an odd stirring in her heart. There was something about his defiant stance that touched her. He had expected her to be horrified, even cruel. His theatrics had been a defense, a diversion to make sure she didn't see his hurt.

She hugged her arms tight against her, searching in vain for some inane comment to make, lest he see how disconcerted she was by the conflicting emotions that assailed her. Needing the distraction, her gaze swept the room, and for the first time she noted the piano. She gasped. A Baldwin.

Impulsively she crossed over to it, caressing its fine mahogany surface. It was magnificent. She ached to sit and play. The piano had always given her comfort. At times her music was all that kept her sane during those long years with Gideon. But she resisted the urge, not certain how Kincaid would react.

He crossed to the horsehair divan and sat down, fingering a glass of whiskey in his left hand but not drinking it. "I think we'd better talk, Mrs. Bodine."

Reluctantly, she stepped away from the piano, seating herself on the opposite end of the divan. She linked her hands in front of her.

"I'm sorry." His voice was so soft she thought at first his apology might have been just wishful thinking on her part. As he sat there, he kept the left side of his face averted at an exaggerated angle. No matter how she shifted she saw only his right profile. The habit seemed ingrained, protective, and again she felt the stirring of an emotion she couldn't name.

"In your letters," she began, because he did not, "you said you needed a mother for your daughter Cecelia."

"Celia," he corrected, any defensiveness vanishing with that single irritated word.

She worried about her mistake, but he seemed to dismiss it to carelessness.

"You can't be her mother, but I think a female

influence would be beneficial. There aren't too many women in Montana."

The smoothness of his speech and the trace of a decidedly unwestern accent piqued her curiosity. She upgraded her estimation that he was only modestly educated. But for now she had no intention of inquiring about the man's personal background. Better to keep the subject on what she perceived as his paramount concern—his daughter. "I'm sure I could be of help to Celia, if I knew more . . ."

The door banged open and a bundle of unrestrained energy burst into the room.

Selina's eyes widened at the sight of the girl. Filthy jeans, a filthy shirt, and an even filthier face gave no clue at all as to the child's gender. Only the blond braids hinted that this was Morgan Kincaid's daughter. She couldn't have been any dirtier if she had deliberately rolled around on the ground.

"I told you to bathe and wear a dress," Kincaid said, his tone more exasperated than angry.

The girl planted her hands on her narrow hips. "And I told *you* I don't want a new mother. It's *your* fault my real mother is dead. If you hadn't . . ."

"Celia!" He rose to his feet, furious.

"What did you do, Pa?" the girl went on defiantly. "Make sure she was plain?" Celia wrinkled her nose at Selina.

Selina laughed spontaneously. Of all the things for the child to say. Gideon had spent five years accusing her of being too feminine. "Thank you, Celia. Truly."

"You *like* being plain?" the girl challenged. "My father doesn't like being ugly!" Turning on her heel, she bolted from the room.

Very slowly Selina drew in a breath and let it out. She had most certainly walked into the dragon's lair. She could feel the frustration and embarrassment coming from Morgan Kincaid in waves. She longed to tell him she didn't think him ugly at all. Her father had often regaled her with tales of Blackbeard, Jean Laffite, and other brigands of the high seas. With his dark good looks, his eyepatch, and his scar, Morgan seemed the perfect pirate. But she dared not tell him anything so personal.

"Damn. I'm sorry." He stiffened, obviously upset about his swearing, and just as obviously tired of saying he was sorry. His broad shoulders sagged. "I'll have one of my men take you back to the water stop tomorrow."

Her stomach knotted. "Why?"

"Surely you must want to leave after that little scene."

"She seems very troubled, but not intentionally cruel."

"Thank you for that."

"Does she miss her mother terribly?"

"I will not discuss my personal life. . . ."

"Then how am I to help her?"

He paced the length and breadth of the wide room, though he was careful to avoid the bearskin rug on the hearth. "This arrangement was a mistake from the first. But it was my mistake. You can be sure I'll pay you for your trouble."

Selina controlled her rising panic. She had nowhere to go but into the teeth of the widening search for her. She couldn't let Kincaid send her away. Not yet. She stood up, facing him.

"Mr. Kincaid, you asked me to come here, to risk life and limb to journey to a place where I know no one. You owe me more than money. More than five minutes of your time. You owe me the chance to make good on our bargain. I need a home, and you need a caretaker for your daughter." Her mind raced. "Perhaps a time limit. Three months—the summer. If there's no progress, then I'll go."

He crossed to the fireplace, inhaling the pungent woodsmoke, needing suddenly to get away from the heady fragrance of Alberta Bodine's rose-scented perfume. Covertly he watched her twist her hands in front of her. The woman was frightened, but trying her best to put up a good front. To be honest, he had put her through a hell of a lot already. She had a right to demand something in return. He couldn't very well send her away because she wasn't what he'd expected.

She was much too young, barely past twenty.

Her face was dusty and her clothes drab, but the curves evident under her simple dress made him wonder just how plain the girl really was. Her complexion was flawless. Her lips . . . He slapped a palm down on the mantel, whipping his head around as she all but leaped toward the door. He grimaced. She was as skittish as a newborn fawn.

"Mrs. Bodine," he began, choosing his words with care, "you can't stay here for an entire summer without . . . going through with the marriage. It wouldn't be proper. I have no other woman here to act as chaperone."

Selina almost laughed, partly with relief and partly from amusement. This man was most certainly an enigma. Chaperone? He was concerned about propriety here in the middle of nowhere? Concealing her thoughts, she replied calmly, "Then we'll marry as agreed. If you deem my progress with Celia inadequate by the end of the summer, we'll divorce."

"You would accept such a social stigma?"

"I've endured far worse, Mister Kincaid." She wished the words back at once as his gaze grew searching.

"I don't know," he said slowly.

"I realize your first thought is for your daughter. In fact, I can appreciate her feelings. I lost my parents in a carriage accident some time ago." She cringed at her foolishness. She dared not be so specific again, at least not until she had found Bertie's letters. For all she knew, Bertie had told him her parents were alive and well and running a brothel in Sweden. She cleared her throat and continued, "I believe I could be of help. And you do want her brought up to date on her lessons."

He ran a hand absently over his jaw. "The circuit preacher won't be by for two or three weeks."

"I'm sure a house this size has more than one bedroom."

He straightened. "That it does, Mrs. Bodine. That it does."

She wondered at the undercurrent in his voice, but continued: "I may stay in the spare one, then?"

"Permanently?"

She steadied herself. They were skirting a subject that had to be explored before she dared agree to anything. "You . . . you said we would discuss intimate matters face-to-face."

"I explained all that in my last letter."

She swallowed. Last letter? Had there been more than the two? What else might she not . . . ?

"I'm a man. There are times when I'll make use of your body in bed." His tone was harsh, belligerent.

If he had struck her, he would have done her less harm. She backed away, her eyes wild. *Use* of her body? Dear God, was Morgan Kincaid merely Gideon in another guise?

At length she managed to whisper, "Your daughter is most important to you, Mr. Kincaid?"

"Of course."

"Does it seem wise, then, to frighten the woman you wish to make her new caretaker?"

He sent her a shriveling glare, then stormed out of the room.

She staggered to the divan, her knees giving way as she reached it. Her whole body trembled. Maybe she should ask Clay Prescott to take her back to the train. She didn't need to live another nightmare.

Hand on her chest, she tried with everything in her to stop shaking. She needed to control her terror, to think clearly. Somehow she had to understand Morgan Kincaid. She sensed an abiding bitterness in the man, more than just rage over the scar on his face. He was an angry and unpredictable man. How unpredictable was evident by the way he had stalked from the room just now. What on earth had provoked him?

She closed her eyes. Did he need a reason? Gideon had required none.

She stood, shifting closer to the fire. But the heat of the flames did nothing to warm the chill in her soul.

Morgan stood alone in his bedroom, staring into the mirror. *Does it seem wise, then, to frighten the woman you wish to make her new caretaker?*

Frighten.

With the notion of sharing his bed.

With an oath, he drove his fist into the looking glass.

Chapter 7

Standing before the fire, Selina wondered what she was supposed to do next. The hallway down which Kincaid had disappeared loomed like some dark tunnel. Did he expect her to . . .

She jumped, startled, twisting toward the sound of a loud thud followed at once by the sound of shattering glass. Allowing herself no time to think, she bolted down the corridor, shoving open the door to Kincaid's room.

He stood near the room's center, clutching his left fist in his right hand. Selina's gaze immediately took in the shattered mirror. His string of muttered curses halted abruptly as she hurried over to him.

"Get out!" he snarled.

Selina flinched, but held her ground. "You're bleeding," she said.

"I noticed," he snapped, adding too quickly,

"The damned mirror started to fall. I . . ." He stopped, then crossed to the wash basin, where he picked up a towel and swiped it across his scraped knuckles.

"Let me do that," Selina said. She prayed her sudden wild nervousness wasn't evident to him. She deliberately kept her eyes averted as she took the towel and dipped it into the fresh water in the basin. "Do you have any whiskey?"

He nodded toward the nightstand beside the bed. "Thirsty?" he murmured, as she crossed over to it.

How could a man lace one word with so much sarcasm? She ignored it, deciding it was his way of channeling her attention to his mood, rather than his actions. He'd slammed his fist into the mirror. The only unanswered question was why he would be so foolish.

Opening the small door of the nightstand, she extracted a half-full bottle of Cyrus Noble. Yanking out the cork, she dampened the cloth with the liquor.

"This will sting a bit," she said, holding the whiskey-soaked cloth to his raw knuckles.

He sucked in his breath but did not jerk the hand free. "A bit?"

She retrieved a red bandanna from his wardrobe and wrapped it around the injured hand. Try as she might to remain detached, she found herself studying those long fingers, the calloused palms, the sun-darkened flesh. Powerful hands used to hard work. Disconcerted by such unsettling awareness, she tied off the bandage with a quick, agitated motion. "You should keep it covered for tonight."

He flexed his fingers, seeming to assess the damage. She sensed he was assessing her as well. "I don't recall nursing being a part of the talents you listed in your letters, Mrs. Bodine."

"I'd hardly call bandaging a cut 'nursing,' Mr. Kincaid." She tried and failed to meet his gaze, then winced inwardly as he stiffened and turned away. It pained her to have him thinking that she avoided eye contact with him out of any unease with his disfigurement. Yet how could she tell him that it wasn't what she saw that terrified her, but what he might see?

"I'm really very tired, Mr. Kincaid. If you could show me to my room?"

He wasted no time leading her down the hallway and across the house to a corridor of rooms along its south side. "Celia's room," he said, pointing to the one on the right. He did not bother to check to see if the girl had yet returned. "The bathing room is at the far end of the hall, just off the kitchen." He stepped up to the center room. "This one will be yours. For now."

He opened the door, leading the way into the darkened interior. "I'll light a lamp for you."

As he did so, Selina turned toward the sound of the front door opening. Celia stormed in, looking even more disheveled than before. She stomped across the front room, pausing only long enough to give them both a defiant glare, then slammed into her bedroom.

Selina wondered if the girl had escalated her hostile behavior as a result of her arrival. She had no time to dwell on it as Kincaid struck a match and lit a bedside lantern. She stood stunned as the flame's glow illumined the room's opulent appointments.

French provincial predominated. Selina admired the delicate styling of the four-poster bed and its matching tallboy, then noticed the three-tiered standing shelves abutting the near wall, each shelf literally crammed with decorative glassware at the expense of the individuality of any particular piece.

She recognized the Steigel detailings on a wine decanter. Waterford crystal sat logjammed among Staffordshire, while a cherub-embellished Venetian bowl lay dumped unceremoniously inside a larger bowl blown from French colored glass. The only continuity in the collection was in the equally distributed layers of dust coating every exposed surface.

"My late wife's room," Kincaid said, with no discernible emotion in his voice. "No one comes in here."

Obviously, Selina thought, but said nothing. The room could pass as a storage closet in a museum. The woman's penchant for French continued in the pastoral tapestries strewn haphazardly throughout the room.

"Everything's very nice," Selina murmured absently, suddenly wishing only to be curled up and asleep in that bed. It was then that her attention trailed to the seemingly innocuous tapestry lying across the bedcovers. Her heart stopped. Aubusson. The pattern was different, but the coloring was the same. She could almost see Gideon's blood seeping along its threads.

"Something wrong?" Kincaid asked.

Selina started at the genuine concern in the man's voice, then realized she must look ashen. "I . . . I'm fine," she managed. "Just tired."

He seemed to accept that. "Anything in this room is at your disposal." He frowned as a thought suddenly occurred to him. "Prescott didn't bring in your bags, did he?"

She quickly reiterated her story about their having been routed on the wrong train.

"Lenore was a little taller than you, maybe a little . . ." He hesitated, studying her body much too intimately, "more rounded here and there."

She blushed. "I never professed to be attractive, Mr. Kincaid."

"That isn't what I said." His voice was husky. Abruptly he straightened. "Use whatever you need." He then gestured toward a doorway at the rear of the room's left wall. "It leads to the bathing room. There's another entrance from the kitchen.

If you want to freshen up, help yourself. If you're hungry, there's food in the pantry. We'll talk tomorrow about how you're to proceed with Celia." Without so much as a good night, he turned and left the room.

Selina, still unnerved by the rush of déjà vu the tapestry had wrought in her, forced her legs to move and crossed to the bed. Using only the tip of her thumb and forefinger she jerked the Aubusson onto the floor, then swiftly booted it under the bed.

Somehow, just having it out of sight calmed her a little, though now she had to deal with the disquieting thought of using Lenore Kincaid's things and wearing her clothes, knowing there was no way to avoid it. Drawing in a deep breath, she crossed to the vanity and sat down. Lifting the silver-handled hairbrush, she slammed it back down when she noticed a blond strand clinging to the soft bristles.

As much to distract herself as to find some nightclothes, Selina set about exploring the room. She opened drawers, doors, even peeked behind the muslin curtains. The tallboy spilled over with lovely gowns, expensively made. Silks, satins, ninons. She caressed the fine materials, even as she considered how totally impractical they were. Surely the woman hadn't worn such finery to engage in day-to-day housework.

Two riding skirts and several blouses seemed the former Mrs. Kincaid's only concession to living on a cattle ranch. Selina dug deeper into a pile of clothing rumpled near the bottom of the tallboy.

"Finally," she sighed, shaking out a wadded-up housedress made of simple cotton. At least she would have something to wear after she washed out her own dress. But so far nothing in the room even hinted at the character of the man who had been Lenore Kincaid's husband.

She searched further and found a flannel night rail in the bottom drawer of the vanity. She frowned as she lifted it out, noticing something hard and rectangular in the folded material. Unfurling the flannel, she discovered a book bound in red velvet.

Curious, she opened the cover, studying the inscription penned on its first page. *December 14, 1872— To my beloved daughter, Lenore Langston, for her sixteenth birthday. Papa.*

Lenore's diary.

On impulse Selina turned to the last entry, noting only the date. July 25, 1883. Just under three years ago. The year the woman died. Selina closed the book.

Lenore had kept this diary for eleven years, years that included her marriage to Morgan Kincaid. How better to learn something of the man than through the eyes of his dead wife?

Selina's conscience prickled. How could she justify such an invasion of privacy—to read the private thoughts and yearnings of another human be-

ing, one who was no longer alive to permit or deny
reading privileges to anyone. Perhaps if she asked
Kincaid . . . She caressed the elegant cover,
worn with use and age. It occurred to her then that
Kincaid probably was not even aware of the book's
existence.

Deciding a bath was her top priority for the moment, Selina rewrapped the book in one of the pei-
gnoirs and returned it to the drawer. She would
read the first few entries later, then decide whether
or not to read further.

Clad only in her petticoats, she gathered up the
things she would need for her bath and hurried
into the bathing room.

She stared at the zinc bathtub, again astonished
by how lavishly Kincaid lived on this isolated
ranch. Homes in the heart of San Francisco would
suffer by comparison.

Filling a huge kettle with water from the pump,
she set it on the stove to heat, then quickly rinsed
out her dress. While she waited for the water to
boil, she shampooed her hair with invigoratingly
cold water, then wrapped her damp tresses in a
towel. It was good to have her familiar chestnut
color back. She hoped the light had been too dim
for Kincaid to notice its changeable hue.

She pumped the zinc tub nearly full with cool
water, then added the heated contents of the kettle
from the stove. "Heaven," she pronounced, eyeing
the waiting bath.

Eagerly she tugged open the tapes of her chemise. The entry door from her bedroom creaked open. Her hand flew to her bosom, covering the exposed cleavage. She relaxed only a little when she saw that her visitor was Celia.

"Is something wrong?" Selina asked, as the child merely stood in the corner of the room regarding her sullenly.

"I want you to go back where you came from."

"I know this is difficult for you. Please believe it's just as hard for me. Coming to a strange place . . ."

"My father paid you, didn't he? You wouldn't be my mother unless he paid you. You wouldn't marry him unless he paid you."

"I was offered a home here," Selina said slowly, "food on the table, a roof over my head . . ."

"Money?"

"No, no money."

"But now that you've seen him you'll want money, won't you?"

Selina took a step closer to the child. "Does his scar bother you so much?"

The girl's eyes widened with an emotion akin to fear. But it wasn't fear. And it frustrated Selina that she couldn't quite put a name to it.

"My father was the most handsome man in the world," the girl said, her chin jutting forward, as though daring Selina to challenge the point. "But . . . after it happened he wasn't so handsome anymore. My mother . . ." She bit her lip, squeezing her eyes shut, as if trying to block a memory. Her voice wavered. "He was handsome. He really was."

Kincaid framed the doorway behind his daughter. "Go to bed, Celia."

The girl whirled. Selina could almost feel her pain to realize that her father had overheard, but the girl said nothing as she bolted away.

Seconds later, Selina heard Celia's bedroom door slam. "Please, don't apologize," Selina said as Kincaid raked a hand through his ebony hair.

"I don't intend to. You agreed to stay."

Selina clutched at the open throat of her chemise as Kincaid's gaze tracked from her hands to her face and back again. "Enjoy your bath, Mrs. Bodine." With a sardonic nod, he left.

Selina shot to the door and threw the bolt, then did the same for the kitchen entry. Trembling violently, she shed her underclothes and climbed into the warm water. From now on locking the doors would be the first thing she did whenever she came into this room. Long minutes passed, but at last the cleansing water soothed her.

By the time she finished bathing the water was uncomfortably cool. Toweling herself dry, she shivered as she pulled the flannel night rail over her head. Her hair tumbled free, dampening the front of the gown. The night air heightened the sensitivity of her nipples until they thrust out against the bodice.

Selina realized suddenly that she was famished. Peering out the kitchen entrance, she found her way to the pantry, delighted to find it fully stocked with an assortment of canned goods and staples.

A jar of apple butter caught her eye. Licking her lips, she smeared a totally unladylike portion onto a slice of sourdough bread and devoured it where she stood.

Her hunger appeased, she padded down the hallway toward the main entrance to the bedroom. She was trying hard to keep a renewed surge of anxiety at bay. What did she think she was doing in this stranger's home, presenting herself as Alberta Bodine, his mail-order bride?

A quick glance toward the front of the house told her the fire in the hearth was going out. Kincaid was nowhere in sight. She let out a grateful sigh, scurrying into the room, clicking the door shut behind her.

She was overtired now, uneasy. So much depended on her knowing Morgan Kincaid, on maintaining her deception. Assuring herself there was no other way, she opened the bottom drawer of the vanity and pulled out Lenore Kincaid's diary.

Selina lay on the bed, turned up the lamp, then opened the book to the first entry.

Dec. 14, 1872: Papa gave me my coming out party tonight. Sweet sixteen, he called me. I cannot

*believe how tedious it all was. Houston boys all seem
so childish, beseeching me for dance after dance.
My toes were positively crushed beneath their
clumsy feet. The night would have been a complete
disaster if not for Reginald, Sally's beau. He escorted me out to the garden and then the rascal
kissed me right on the mouth. Things grew even
more exciting when Sally found us together. She
turned positively green with envy. Especially after
Reginald sent her back inside. Then he kissed me
again!*

Selina had to smile. Lenore seemed a normal
adolescent, if conceited and unkind. Despite the
girl's shallow behavior, Selina felt a twinge of jealousy. Lenore's life at sixteen was in marked con-
trast to what her own had been. Lenore had been
encouraging boyish flirtations, while Selina had begun a five-year tour of Gideon's personal hell.

Selina read further, finding the entries sporadic
with varying gaps between dates. That explained at
least how the inch-thick volume could accommo-
date eleven years of a woman's life. Lenore seemed
to use the journal only for events she considered
memorable.

*Jan. 8, 1873: Margaret Brentwood's soirée last
night. All the men wanted to dance with me. Reginald was beside himself. I told him I didn't want to
see him anymore. He actually cried, right there in
Margaret's parlor. It was so embarrassing. I told
him to stop making a fool of himself.*

Selina shook her head, hoping Reginald and Sally got back together. She skipped ahead several pages, stopping at an entry bordered by stars.

June 19, 1873: Papa bought me the emerald brooch I've been wanting forever, after I reminded him that it was so difficult for a young girl to grow up without a mother!

Selina chuckled. The girl was impossible. She must have matured considerably before she met Kincaid. She couldn't imagine the man marrying such a ninny. She flipped through another block of pages, stopping when a name caught her eye. This entry, too, was embellished, this time by a number of tiny hearts drawn in the margin.

August 15, 1874: A new attorney joined Papa's law firm. Morgan Kincaid. He's only been in Houston two years. Papa's been trying to get him to join the firm ever since the man had the whole city in an uproar last summer defending some stupid half-breed. I caught a peek of Mr. Kincaid in Papa's office. He is very good-looking in a manly way. And he's so much older than these boys I've been forced to endure. He's twenty-six!

August 16: The man actually turned down my invitation to dinner! Of all the conceited so and so's!

Selina smiled. At least Kincaid had shown some initial sense. Then she sobered, her conscience niggling at her. She felt as if she were eavesdropping on Lenore's most private musings. She would read only a little further, and then she would put the book away. All she needed was a little insight into Morgan Kincaid, not a decade of Lenore's flirtations.

October 12: I made Papa order Morgan to come to dinner. Morgan was rude. He said I was a child. I'll show him.

November 8: I pretended to twist my ankle when I saw Morgan coming out of Papa's office. He carried me back inside and settled me into Papa's big leather chair. I winked at Papa, and Papa winked back. While Morgan went to get me the lemonade I asked for, Papa told me I should be ashamed of myself. But he was laughing! When Morgan came back, Papa left. This time Morgan finally said yes! when I asked him to dinner at the house.

Oh, his hands were so strong when he carried me. I felt no heavier than a cloud. And now when I walk I seem to float like one. Morgan is coming to dinner tomorrow night!

I must remember to limp. Just a little!

November 9: It was a dream! Morgan came to dinner and he and I and Papa sat around talking all night. (Well, I listened at least!) Morgan is just so handsome! I think I'm falling in love with him!

The words "falling in love" were underlined several times. Selina told herself to close the book, that she had read enough. But she didn't stop.

December 25: Christmas. Morgan gave me a magnificent necklace. He said he would like to take me to the New Year's Eve ball at the Brentwood's.

Anyone who's anyone will be there. Imagine how jealous all of my girlfriends will be to see me with the famous Morgan Kincaid.

Jan. 1, 1875: At midnight Morgan kissed me. "To bring in a new year as beautiful as you are, Lenore," he said. I've never been so happy. All quivery and warm.

"You can't read any more of this," Selina whispered aloud. "It isn't right." But she couldn't put it away. Not yet.

March 21, 1875: Alexandra Lambert's spring soirée. All the women were staring at me. They were just beside themselves with jealousy. I looked fabulous. And so did Morgan.

We went to his rooms afterward. He touched me. I told him I wanted him to stop, but I was lying. I didn't want him to stop. It felt so deliciously wicked.

Morgan undressed me. I should have felt so ashamed. But I didn't. I love him.

Selina slapped the book shut, her heart hammering. She felt as though she'd violated Lenore and Morgan both. Shoving the book back into its hiding place, she wished to heaven she'd never turned to the first page.

Morgan stood in front of the window in his bedroom, staring out at the darkened peaks of the mountains. He'd expected that his preoccupation with the widow Bodine would end with her arrival. They would exchange impersonal greetings, she would meet Celia, and, if she stayed, things would fall into an orderly routine of polite nods and study lessons.

How could he have been such a fool? Celia had objected to the arrangement from the first. He had repeatedly ignored his own nebulous wants; denied they even existed. But now the woman was here, and those wants had crystallized into a tangible, aching need he could still barely bring himself to acknowledge.

He had been standing in the shadows of the hearth when she'd darted into her bedroom like a frightened rabbit. He had not missed the curves of that lithe young body beneath Lenore's detested flannel night rail, the fullness of high, firm breasts.

He swore.

It had been so long since he'd been with a woman. He'd accepted his monklike existence because he'd had no choice, but now he would have Alberta Bodine in his home, as his wife.

One summer. If Celia didn't respond, the marriage would be dissolved. To his mind Celia's attitude foreshadowed the only possible result, no matter how fine a governess the widow Bodine had been. Come fall the woman would be gone.

All the more reason to stay away from her.

His loins tightened in spite of his resolve. Damn! Why did she have to be so young—so cursedly vulnerable? There had even been an instant when he could have sworn he'd seen a torment to match his own reflected in those wide brown eyes. But then it could have been a trick of the lantern-light . . .

He imagined the supple curves, the soft flesh beneath that night rail, and knew his noble intentions would be for naught. On his wedding night he would have her in his bed.

Chapter 8

Selina woke, trembling. Gideon's malevolent chuckle was so real that she feared opening her eyes lest his death become the dream. Struggling to clear her mind, she wondered if she would ever enjoy peaceful sleep again. Kincaid's harsh promise to "make use" of her body in bed had sparked dark memories of fetid breath and grunted obscenities. Determinedly she threw off the memories, even as she threw off the bedcovers and forced herself to rise.

Sunlight filtering through the southern exposed windows told her the day was already hours old. Why hadn't Kincaid roused her? She blushed heatedly, amending the thought, wondering instead why he hadn't sent Celia. Now the man likely thought her a layabout, when in truth her body had merely given in to exhaustion.

The pine floor was warm on her bare feet as she padded across the room to the bathing-room door.

Receiving no response to her timid knock, she slipped in and checked the dress she had rinsed out the night before. She frowned as she found the cuffs and hem still damp. Resigned, she returned to the bedroom and poked again through Lenore Kincaid's silks and satins, this time finding a serviceable gray cotton dress hidden at the back of the wardrobe.

When she'd finished dressing, she decided to take Kincaid at his word and make herself at home.

In the pantry she gathered the makings for an omelette. Adding wood to the stove, she started a fire, sauteed onions in butter, then poured in a mixture of scrambled eggs, cheese, and a little smoked ham. She'd always had a knack for cooking, though she didn't particularly enjoy it. There had even been times Gideon had permitted her in the Hardesty House kitchen. Such rare magnanimity on his part had not been to please her but rather to displease his mother. Marelda would fall into an attack of vapors, bewailing that cooking was a job for servants, that she would never survive the disgrace should anyone ever see the wife of Gideon Hardesty bending over a hot stove. Marelda worshipped her son, but the feeling had been almost entirely one-sided.

"Finding everything you need?"

She looked up, startled. "Mr. Prescott. I didn't hear you come into the house."

"It's Clay, remember?" The blond rancher strode into the room, tossing his Stetson onto the kitchen table as if he were a resident, not a guest.

"I thought you'd have left." She felt uncomfortable all at once, though for no reason she could put her finger on. After all, Kincaid had sent Prescott to meet her. Certainly, the two men were close friends.

He gave her an amiable shrug. "My horse is lame."

Selina turned back to the stove, uncertain whether she should encourage him to stay. "I was just fixing myself breakfast. Mr. Kincaid was kind enough to let me sleep late this morning after my long journey."

"That's Morg all right. Kind to a fault."

She spooned a portion onto her plate, assuring herself she had not really heard the sarcasm in Prescott's voice. "Have you eaten?"

"Hours ago. Smells awful good, though."

She had to be polite. "I've made plenty."

He sat down at the table. "I'd love some." He smiled easily, as though enjoying some private joke. "Just what did you think of your fiancé? Kind of surprised, I'll bet."

Whatever relationship existed between Kincaid and Prescott, Selina now knew it was not friendship. Prescott's flirting yesterday had been bad enough, but his smirking inference about Morgan's looks made Selina furious. "Yes, I was surprised,

as a matter of fact," she said sharply. "Mr. Kincaid was not at all what I—"

Booted footfalls announced another presence.
Morgan.

His rigid stance told her he had heard every
word.

She longed to finish her sentence, to say that
Morgan Kincaid was not the shy middle-aged
rancher she'd expected. He was bitter and hurting,
and with associates like Clay Prescott she could
well see why. But she couldn't say the words now,
not when he was standing there regarding her with
ill-concealed venom. The tension between the two
men was palpable.

"Would you care to join us, Mr. Kincaid?" she
asked hopefully. "There's plenty."

"Join *us?*" he mocked. "I wouldn't want to intrude."

"D-don't be silly," she stammered.

"I just came in to see if you were making out all
right, Mrs. Bodine. I can see that you most certainly are."

"Yes, Bertie and I are doing just fine, Morg,"
Prescott said, shoving a forkful of eggs into his
mouth.

Morgan cocked his head toward her. "Bertie?"

"It's, uh, a nickname. My mother used to—"

He cut her off. "When you finish your breakfast,
Mrs. Bodine, you'll find Celia outside by the corral. I'd appreciate it if you'd begin her lessons to-

day. Maybe we'll find out all this isn't necessary even before the preacher gets here."

She felt cold.

Clay's eyebrows arched with sudden interest. "You saying you might not be going through with the wedding, Morg?" His gaze shot to Selina. "May I be the first to stand in line to court you, madam?"

"Take the roan in the far corral, Prescott," Morgan bit out. "I'll have Stubby bring by your sorrel when it heals."

"I'd rather wait. Lancelot's my favorite mount." He continued wolfing down his breakfast even as Selina's appetite faded completely. Prescott's tone seemed smug, but she caught a false note.

"I want you off my ranch today, Prescott," Morgan continued. "And out of my kitchen now."

Selina felt her face heat with rising embarrassment. The feud between the two men was obviously a long-standing one. She found herself wondering what the scenario might have been had Clay Prescott ordered a bride instead of Morgan Kincaid. Prescott was certainly more agreeable, not an angry man with a troubled child on his hands.

Yet the prospect of leaving Wolf Trail sent a very real shaft of loss through her. How could that be when she'd been here less than a day?

She stood, shoving her chair back, facing both men squarely. Though her pulses raced, she kept her tone steady. "I would appreciate it in the future if the two of you would not discuss my disposition as though I were a prized heifer among your blasted cattle."

Morgan's gaze suggested first astonishment, then a measure of wary approval that almost made Selina smile. But since she was certain he would misunderstand, she merely swept over to the sink to begin washing the dishes.

"Thanks a lot for the meal, Bertie," Prescott offered, his voice still annoyingly amiable. "I enjoyed the company, too." He picked up his Stetson. "It's been a real pleasure meeting the future missus, Morg," he said. "Now, if you two will excuse me, I'll go check on Lancelot."

Kincaid waited until Prescott was gone, then came over to the sink. He stood there for nearly a minute, saying nothing. Selina worried at first that he was simply too angry to trust himself to speak, but quickly guessed that his silence was more rightly due to the fact that he didn't know what to say. He was as ill at ease as she was. Finally, he cleared his throat. "I trust you're finding everything you need, Mrs. Bodine?"

"I'm just fine, Mr. Kincaid. Honestly."

"That's good. Fine." He drew in a long breath. "Well, I've got a few chores to attend to. If you'll excuse me, I'll, uh, see you at dinner."

She nodded, though she sensed there was more he wanted to say, and knew there was more she wanted to say. Still, neither of them was willing to make the initial overture, for she was now certain he regretted the whole episode with Prescott.

After he'd left, Selina gripped the edge of the oak counter to steady herself. Morgan Kincaid had to be the most intimidating man she'd ever met. To calm herself she ate a little of the omelette, then washed up the dishes and headed out into the front room. Peering out the window, she spied Celia sitting on the top rail of the nearest corral. Kincaid had instructed her to begin the girl's lessons today, but Selina dare not approach her yet. She was still too shaken to risk the possibility of getting off on the wrong foot with the child.

She wandered over to the piano instead, raising the cover that protected the keys. The Baldwin was magnificent. How did Kincaid come to have so many lovely things here in this isolated land? The rough terrain would have made transportation difficult. The Northern Pacific route across Montana had only been completed in the last year. Everything would have had to come by wagon.

Kincaid must have loved his wife very much to go to such lengths for her comfort. The thought sparked a peculiar melancholy and an unwelcome, but compelling, urge to read further into Lenore's diary.

She shook off the notion, seating herself at the brocaded bench seat in front of the Baldwin. Morgan was nowhere about. Surely it wouldn't hurt to play for just a few minutes. She tried a little Mozart first, grimacing to find several of the keys out of tune. Even so, it felt good just to be able to play again.

Several minutes passed, the music soothing her, calming her as nothing else could. She was so absorbed in what she was doing that it took a while for the feeling to take hold, but when it did she knew she was being watched. Not missing a note, she turned to see Celia regarding her warily from the doorway.

The child squared her shoulders, though she said nothing. Selina turned back to the keys, digesting the child's silence. Evidently her vocal protestations played best before an audience, especially when the audience was her father.

More minutes passed. Selina switched to a lively version of "My Darlin', Clementine." She hid a smile as she heard Celia start to sing along.

Hands on her hips, Celia sauntered over. "My mother played, you know."

"You must miss her very much."

"That's none of your business."

"I think you may be a little afraid that I'm here to take her place."

The girl didn't answer.

"That isn't going to happen, Celia. My mother is dead, too. No one could replace her in my life. But I hope that, over time, maybe you and I could be friends."

More silence.

"Do you play at all?" Selina asked.

"I'd rather rope and ride."

Selina considered that a moment. "Perhaps we could strike a trade. You teach me to rope, I'll teach you to play."

"You couldn't rope!" the girl scoffed.

"And why not?"

"Ladies don't do that sort of thing."

"This *lady* once trailed a wolf pack for a summer with her parents." She grinned as the girl's eyes widened in awe, then worried again that she might have contradicted something in one of Bertie's letters.

But Celia seemed unperturbed, circling around to sit on the opposite end of the bench seat.

Selina suppressed a sudden flare of hope. She didn't want to become too enthusiastic and risk scaring the child off. "I wish the keys were more in tune. I think you'd have a better sense of the songs."

"I bet Charlie could fix it. Charlie can fix anything."

"Charlie?"

"One of the hands."

"Is he here now? On the ranch?"

"He's out on the range with Stubby and Pete and Stewie. They're getting ready for roundup." She stared at Selina's hands as they lingered on the keys for a bittersweet "Greensleeves."

"Those men all work for your father?"

"Them and Chino. He's the foreman. He's been helpin' Pa with a sick calf, but he'll be goin' back out on the range tomorrow too."

"Do you stay here alone sometimes?"

"Not usually," she said, suddenly on her guard. "Why?"

"You seem a little young to be left on your own."

"I know as much about ranchin' as anybody." She poked at one of the keys, adding a sour note to Selina's piece. "If Pa's ridin' out for more than a day or two, he makes Stewie or Charlie stay with me."

"And this Charlie can really fix anything?"

"Anything. He fixed up my treehouse out back."

"I'd love to see it."

"It's only for me."

"Oh. Well, that's all right. Everyone should have a private place." She hit another klinker. "I hope you're right about Charlie. But piano tuning is a rather specialized skill."

"Charlie plays the fiddle, and he was a blacksmith, and a carpenter, and he was even a cardsharp on a Mississippi riverboat once till some Yankee said he was bottom-dealing. Charlie learned how to swim that day."

Selina laughed with Celia, their eyes meeting. Celia turned away. "I'll ask him anyway."

"Would you like to play something?"

"I don't know how."

"Neither did I once, and now I'm pretty good, don't you think?"

"Maybe. What do I have to do?"

"Well, first there's the scales." Selina showed the girl how to begin. "Learning them can seem pretty boring, but once you have them down, it opens the world to you." They stood up long enough for Selina to retrieve some sheet music from the bench seat. "I'll show you how to translate this to the keys."

Celia thumped one of the ivories.

"That's a good one," Selina said. "You hit it whenever I nod, and we'll see what we get."

Selina sang as she played. *All around the mulberry bush the monkey chased the weasel, the monkey said was all in fun.* . . . She nodded to Celia, who played her key.

POP! *Goes the weasel!*

In half an hour she had the child giggling merrily and playing the tune herself. Then the front door opened and Kincaid strode in. Celia stood so abruptly, she almost went over backward. Selina's hand shot out to catch her. Celia jerked away. "Stupid piano. Stupid lessons. I won't play this thing and you can't make me!" She streaked out the door.

Kincaid stalked over to the divan, his back to the piano. "This isn't going to work."

Selina felt otherwise, but was leery of contradicting him. His daughter was obviously very troubled. There was more going on than any ordinary father/daughter squabbling. "I'd like a chance to help her. I know what it is to be unhappy."

"Was that before, during, or after your marriage to Norman, Mrs. Bodine?"

She stared at her hands, threading her fingers together anxiously. Norman? Who in the world was Norman? Selina quaked inwardly, cursing herself for not taking the opportunity this morning to search for Bertie's letters when she'd been alone in the house.

"I'm sorry," he said, maintaining his now familiar stance of not facing her directly. "I had no right to ask that."

She prayed he was in no mood to ask her anything at all until she could find those letters. He probed no further, but her senses remained on alert. She had to change the subject. "Are you hungry? I was thinking I should start dinner soon."

"You're here as a teacher for Celia, not a housekeeper. We've gotten along for three years on our own cooking."

"I don't mind." She headed toward the kitchen. "Will it just be the three of us?"

"Hoping Prescott can join us?"

Selina winced at the sudden harshness in his voice.

Keeping her own voice steady, she said, "I was

merely inquiring about the number of people who will be present at your dinner table, Mr. Kincaid. I know you have ranch hands . . ."

"They eat in the bunkhouse, when they're not out on the range. *Clay,*" he emphasized the name, "can eat with them."

"If you dislike him so much," she ventured boldly, "why did you send him to get me?"

"I didn't have anyone else available at the time."

Together they entered the kitchen. Her heart thudded. She feared more questions, yet some elusive part of her was glad he had followed. In spite of the inherent danger to her freedom, she wanted to better understand this man. She would just have to make certain that Bertie Bodine did not become the focus of their conversation. Toward that end, she said, "Mr. Prescott seems to be able to leave his ranch indefinitely."

"That should tell you something." Morgan grimaced. Gossip seemed at odds with his nature, but she found the comment understandable.

"Is that healing all right?" She gestured at his bruised hand.

"It's fine." His tone remained terse, but she was heartened by the fact that he answered at all. He sat at the table, staring balefully at the potatoes she piled in front of him.

"You said you were used to doing your own cooking."

He began peeling.

When the silence grew awkward, she sat down next to him. "We need to talk."

"It isn't necessary."

"I think it is. There are things we should discuss . . ."

A long-haired dark-skinned man sauntered into the room, tipping his hat toward her.

"Chino Black Hawk, my foreman," Morgan said.

Selina nodded politely. "I'm pleased to meet you."

"Mutual, ma'am," Chino said. He looked at Morgan. "I wanted to check with you on the pinto stallion. He's still too wild for Ceecy to ride. You should let me break him."

Morgan stood, chafing. "Why can't she just ride her mare? Damn, does she have to defy me on every—" He took a long breath. "I'll talk to her."

Chino nodded, touching his hat brim. "Real good meeting you, Mrs. Bodine. We'll have to talk more soon." He left them alone.

Selina didn't waste any time. "Has Celia always been so . . . difficult?"

He bristled.

"Mr. Kincaid, the more I know about her, the better I can help her."

He couldn't argue with that. "She was a happy little girl. She was five when we settled Wolf Trail. She took to life here from the first. My . . ." He touched the scar unconsciously. "When I . . .

when it happened, it seemed to shake her up a lot. But things really deteriorated after Lenore died."

"She was very close to her mother?"

"Aren't all children?" He rose abruptly and left, seeming to have had enough of the personal exchange.

She finished putting supper on, wondering if she'd pressed him too far. She didn't want him to send her packing. Wiping her hands on her apron, she returned to the main room, finding Kincaid at his desk, totaling columns of entries in a large ledger book. "I'm sorry—"

He didn't look up. "I don't need your pity."

She stomped her foot, furious. His head jerked up. She'd so startled him that he actually forgot to angle his gaze as he stared at her. "I don't feel sorry for you, Mr. Kincaid," she hissed. "You sent for me. We have a bargain. I have no complaints." Straightening, she brushed back a loosened tendril of her chestnut hair. "I am *sorry* that we were interrupted. We need to talk. I need to know what you want from me, and what I can expect from you."

"I made that clear enough in my letters," he said, obviously struggling to keep his tone even. "Celia needs tutoring on the basic subjects—English, history, arithmetic."

"Many men wouldn't think a girl needed to learn anything but cooking and sewing." A safe response, she thought—one that skirted the issue of his letters.

He slapped down his pen. "One thing is certain: Celia loves it here. Someday Wolf Trail will be hers. She'll need all the education she can get to run it." He paused. "It's not that I don't want her exposed to the more delicate arts. I was amazed to see her at the piano today."

Selina crossed to the Baldwin. "It is exquisite." She trailed a hand along the satin-smooth surface. "I just wish it were in better tune."

"Would a tuning fork help?" He fished through the bottom drawer of his desk and produced the device.

Selina clapped her hands with delight. "We could try."

He was more than willing to help her tune the piano himself. His cooperativeness surprised and pleased her. While Kincaid tightened wires, Selina listened for pitch, testing notes as they went along. "It's not perfect," she pronounced when they'd finished, "but it's better."

Morgan sat on the piano bench while Selina returned the tuning fork to the bottom drawer of his desk. Her heart pounded. At the front of the drawer lay a small stack of bound letters. The top one was postmarked San Francisco.

"Charlie could do a better job," Morgan was saying.

"So Celia tells me." At her earliest opportunity she had to read those letters.

"You must have had quite a little chat with her."

"Not too much. But it's a start." She came around to sit beside him on the bench. "How about a real test?"

He shot to his feet. She cursed her stupidity. Her preoccupation with the letters had prevented her from noticing she had seated herself on his blind side.

"I need a third hand for this piece, Mr. Kincaid," she said softly. "My mother and I used to play it together."

He kept his back to her. "I don't play."

"You only have to repeat the same chord. Please?"

With obvious reluctance he sat down on her opposite side, making certain to keep every inch of available space between them. In that instant she decided that if she accomplished nothing else this summer, she was going to get this man to be at ease around her regarding his looks.

Taking a deep breath to settle her new resolve, she took his left hand in hers, setting each finger on the appropriate key of the four-note chord, noting wryly how he tensed at the contact, and feeling grateful for it because then he wouldn't notice how her own hands trembled. "That's the part I used to play. I was a little younger than Celia. I had to use a finger from my other hand because I couldn't span the entire chord."

She played her part effortlessly, nodding, smiling as he played beside her. She found herself mesmerized by his hands. Tanned, powerful hands, but with a potential for gentleness. In spite of her efforts to suppress it, her pulses pounded. "You're doing very well, Mr. Kincaid," she said, praying she sounded matter-of-fact.

The right corner of his mouth ticked upward a fraction in a grin she had to characterize as sardonic.

"You think I'm patronizing you, don't you?"

"Do I?"

"Uh-huh. But for someone who doesn't play, you really are doing well, Mr. Kincaid."

"Thank you . . . Mrs. Bodine."

She finished the piece. He slid his hands to his thighs.

She looked at him. He looked at her.

"Clay calls you . . . Bertie? It doesn't suit you."

"He didn't like it either." She could have bitten off her tongue.

He stood up, stalking off a couple of paces. "Maybe you'd rather he had been the one to write Ladies in Waiting."

"No. No, not at all. I . . . no." She chewed her lip. "Bertie was, uh, a pet name. My mother had a favorite aunt. I've never actually been too fond of it myself."

He angled a glance at her. "So what would you have me call you?"

Her mind raced. She ached to have him call her Selina, but she didn't dare. It wasn't the most common of names. It might mean nothing to Morgan, but someone else could make the connection. *Allie . . . Albie . . . Abby . . .* Her mind tumbled the possibilities. "Maybe . . . maybe you could call me . . . Abby."

"Abby." He said it once, returning to the piano bench. He said it again. Softer. Like a caress. Her heart leaped.

He leaned forward, his lips brushing hers ever so lightly, sparking an unfamiliar heat that sifted to every part of her.

Mortified, she looked away. What must he think of her? What did she think of herself?

He straightened. "I'm sorry. That shouldn't have happened."

"It's all right. Really." She tried to sound convincing. "We are going to be married, after all."

"That's why I'm sorry. I'm not sure there's going to be a wedding. I'm not sure at all."

Chapter 9

An hour later Morgan stood on the bank of Ford Creek arcing a stone toward the tumbling water. Whatever had possessed him to tell Abby the wedding might not take place?

The kiss.

In that moment all of his altruistic motives had wavered. He had expected—wanted—to feel lust. But he had not expected the gut-level jolt to his senses when for that briefest instant she had kissed him back.

From their first encounter, nothing about Alberta Bodine had been as he had expected. Her quiet beauty had almost been his undoing. Her vitality, her intelligence, even her temper, stirred in him a simmering want that astonished him. And now he sensed in her an aching vulnerability that tugged at emotions he would have named dead and buried years ago with Willowsong. Against all reason he had wanted to pull her into his arms, to shield her, protect her.

Protect her from what?

He cursed. He was being a fool.

This was no love match. It was a business arrangement.

The kiss.

A fierce heat kindled anew in his loins. He muttered an oath, closing his fist over another stone. But he didn't throw it. He stood there, unmoving, his mind snared by the memory of haunted brown eyes.

Selina gasped, the heavy iron skillet clanging loudly back onto the stovetop. The towel she'd wrapped around the handle had proved painfully inadequate against the hot metal. "Serves you right, Selina," she muttered. "Since you burned the entire meal to a crisp anyway."

Sighing, she redoubled the towel and carried the ruined steak over to the sink. Maybe she should try and salvage the blackened beef. One of the hands could tool it into a new pair of boots.

At least her quick substitution of eggs and bacon had proved acceptable enough for Celia. The child hadn't had to go to bed hungry. As for Kincaid, the man hadn't come back to the house since delivering his quiet thunderbolt over four hours ago. It was now well past ten, the darkness beyond the windows as pervasive as Selina's mood.

She sagged dejectedly into one of the ladderback chairs at the kitchen table. No wedding would mean she could be leaving Wolf Trail as fast as the temperamental Kincaid could order someone to take her to the train.

"Why now?" she murmured. Just when she had begun to feel a little safe, a little secure; just when she thought that perhaps she didn't have to constantly look over her shoulder, her security was all threatening to unravel.

She pressed her fingers to her lips, remembering the feel of his mouth on hers. Why would he kiss her and then tell her there might not be a wedding? Had he found the kiss unpleasant? And why did that thought sting her so, when *she* was the one who wanted no intimacy in this relationship?

She caught the sound of the front door opening, and she tiptoed to the kitchen archway to peer into the outer room. Kincaid. She knew he had seen her, but he didn't so much as nod. Instead he strode over to the hearth to sit—his back to her—on the divan. Selina straightened, her mouth a grim line. Whether or not either of them liked it, this had to be resolved.

Marching over to the fireplace, she positioned herself between the man and the crackling flames, needing the warmth of the fire to ward off the sudden chill in her heart. Her future, maybe her very life, was in this man's hands. "I need to know," she ventured with a bluntness she didn't feel. "Is the wedding off?"

There was a long pause. "I don't know yet." He leaned forward, resting his elbows on his knees. "What makes a woman accept a stranger's marriage proposal, Mrs. Bodine?"

"What makes a stranger ask?"

"Touché."

"I didn't mean to sound flippant. It was as difficult for me to say 'yes,' I'm sure, as it was for you to ask."

Nervously she sat next to him on the divan. It was then she noticed the faint scent of whiskey. As she watched, Kincaid raised a bottle to his lips and took a short pull.

She resisted making any comment, but when he started to shift his body away from her, her temper flared past polite restraint. "Dammit, don't do that!"

He jumped, genuinely startled. "Do what?"

"Turn your head."

He faced her straight on, his body rigid. "You like looking at it?"

"Just stop it. It's there. Your turning one way or the other isn't going to make it go away."

"No," he said softly, "I don't suppose it is."

"That isn't what I meant. I just . . . I just wish you wouldn't be so sensitive about it, that's all."

"Right." He raised the bottle.

She caught his arm. He glared at her, but lowered the bottle to the floor.

"May I ask you something?" she said. Without waiting for a reply, she continued, "This all seems so difficult for you. Why did you send that first letter to Ladies in Waiting?" She might be leading herself into a trap of her own making, but she had to know.

"My daughter said she hated me."

His voice seemed deliberately toneless, but she hurt for him. The liquor had lowered his guard. "Have you ever asked her why?"

"You mean it isn't perfectly obvious?"

"You can't think she would turn away from you because of the scar."

"Why not? Others . . ." That stopped him. "I'll let you know what I decide about the wedding in a couple of days."

"Is there anything I can do to sway your decision one way or the other?"

He looked at her with a gaze that burned, seared through to her soul, making her blood run hot.

"No," he said finally. "Not a thing."

"That isn't fair, you know."

He reached for the whiskey. "Please," she murmured. "Don't."

He sat back. "Making a spectacle of myself, am I?"

"No." He looked so vulnerable, so lost, as though what he needed most in the world was for someone to hold him, to tell him everything would be all right. She knew the mood would vanish in the sobering light of dawn, but for now she felt compelled to be with him.

"I don't understand you at all, Mrs. Bodine," he said, his words slurring ever so slightly. "I'm sure San Francisco was brimming over with handsome, eligible men for a pretty lady to marry."

"I was tired of the city."

"How long will it be before you're tired of Wolf Trail?"

"I can't imagine ever being tired of this place."

"I wish I could believe . . ." He cleared his throat. "This is all for Celia, you realize."

"Of course."

"I don't know how to reach her anymore."

Her hand closed over the back of his. She meant the gesture to be reassuring, but the warmth of him stirred her blood like fire.

"Abby . . ." His voice was hoarse. He pulled her to him, his mouth crushing hers, his tongue driving into her mouth so suddenly she had no time to resist. She didn't want to resist. Her whole body quivered as his tongue met hers.

Her hands glided to either side of his throat, feeling his life pulsing beneath her palms. The stubble of his beard was rough on her skin. She didn't care. She tasted the whiskey. She didn't care. She twisted her fingers in his hair, snagging the leather strip that circled his head, then brought her hand down to trail her fingers along his jaw.

He jerked away. "Don't."

"Morgan . . ." Her voice was an unwitting plea.

He stood, his back to her, his body rigid. "Go to bed. Please."

She reached a hand toward him, then allowed it to drop back to her side. Tears stinging her eyes, she scrambled for her room, mortified. Why was he so angry? What had she done? And did his body pound with the same powerful emotions that now surged within her?

She collapsed onto the bed, sobbing into the quilted coverlet. She tried to convince herself she was upset, terrified, as she had been with Gideon, but she knew that in truth she had *never* felt this way before. Trembling, frightened, yet exhilarated. Excited.

From nowhere the memory came.

"Your father was the most outrageous flirt." Colinda Michaels beamed, twining her arm through that of the dark-eyed man standing beside her in the small book-crammed office on the upper floor of the Blakeley College Archaeology Building.

Jeremy Michaels grinned, leaning down to kiss his wife full on the mouth. He angled a glance toward his daughter. "If we wish you nothing else, Selina darling, we wish you love as warm and fulfilling as ours. No treasure on earth is more precious than to love and be loved.''

Her mother's eyes had glowed bright, her skin flushing. Jeremy Michaels clearly adored his wife, and the feeling was mutual. It was one of the few times fourteen-year-old Selina had felt like an outsider. But she had been happy for them, too, and certain in her adolescent way that, of course, she would one day find such love in her own life.

How thoroughly that dream had been shattered by Gideon.

Selina burrowed under the coverlet of Lenore's bed. She closed her eyes, too tired to think anymore tonight.

But sleep came fitfully, her rest disrupted not by specters of Gideon, but by a presence more disturbing still. She blushed the next morning, remembering. In her dream she had lain in this very bed, but she had no longer been alone. With her had been the cocooning warmth of Morgan Kincaid, a very different Morgan Kincaid. He had not been angry or bitter, or in the least concerned about his looks. He had instead been gentle, caring, and content with spending the night giving her worshipful kisses.

Selina blushed heatedly, leaping out of the suddenly too-suggestive bed. She dressed quickly in a riding skirt and blouse, determined to put the night and the man from her mind. Opening her bedroom door, she spied Kincaid at work at his desk. Every intimate detail of the dream flooded over her. She could not look the man in the face.

Grateful that he seemed not to notice her, she pressed the door closed and scurried through the bathing room to the kitchen. She took no time for breakfast, but instead bolted out the rear door of the house. Circling around to the front, she spotted Celia straddling a hay bale near the barn. Selina hurried over to the girl, calling as cheerily as she could manage, "Is it time for my roping lesson yet?" Anything to take her mind off the child's father.

Celia looked surprised but pleased. She stood, shaking out the lariat she was holding. "Here." She handed it to Selina. "Hold the coil in your left hand, and the honda . . ."

"The what?"

"The business end," came a male voice behind her.

Selina turned and smiled at Chino Black Hawk striding toward them. "I'm getting a lesson in being a cowgirl."

Chino's gaze trailed past Selina. "Does your father know about this, Ceecy?"

"Of course."

Chino looked dubious, but Selina sent him a beseeching look and he let the subject drop. Selina took up the rope again and tried several times without success to snare the corral post some twenty feet in front of her.

"That post keeps leaping out of the way," Selina said dryly.

Celia giggled. "It's okay. You're getting it. Just keep trying."

Selina made another toss. The loop dropped again to the dirt. This time she heard muffled guffaws somewhere behind her. She turned to see four unfamiliar men loitering near the bunkhouse. Clay Prescott stood with them, but when he saw her looking, he headed back inside the small building.

"They're relatively harmless," Chino said, signaling the men to come over.

"They work here too?" Selina asked.

"Sort of," Chino said, giving her a quick wink. "But it must be some kind of holiday for 'em all to be standing around doing nothing."

Three of the men stared bashfully at the ground as they ambled up to her, but the fourth strutted like a peacock. They all stopped a few feet away, the three tipping their hats politely, the fourth bowing low, sweeping his hat from his head with a grand flourish.

"Clarence P. Sims, madam," the courtly one announced, not waiting for Chino's introductions. "One-time riverboat gambler, violinist, blacksmith, sausage salesman, and all-round ladies' man. You may call me Charles."

"Charlie!" Celia corrected.

The man smiled indulgently at the girl.

"The piano tuner?" Selina asked.

"Ah, I see you've already been apprised of one of my considerable talents!"

Selina looked properly awed. "If you could tune the piano in the house, I would be ever so grateful."

"It will be done forthwith, madam." He stepped forward and raised her right hand to his lips, bestowing a genteel kiss. "Now I'm afraid you must suffer the presence of the peasants as well, milady."

"Stubby Landro, ma'am," said the bandy-legged cowboy on the left. "You'll have to excuse Charlie. He's a little full of himself."

"But then if he wasn't, nobody else would be," chortled the man next to Stubby. Shyly, he extended his hand. "Pete McCord, Mrs. Bodine. Most folks call me Two Fingers."

Selina accepted the handshake, noting at once how the man had acquired his nickname. He was missing two fingers on his right hand.

"Danged dally welter," Stubby said. "If he'd know'd how to rope a steer like a proper cowpuncher, he wouldn't have got them fingers sliced off."

"What's a dally welter?" Selina asked.

Chino gripped the lariat, using a fencepost to illustrate. "A dally welter ropes a dogie and *loops* the rope around the saddlehorn a couple times to hold him. Texans like to tie it off, so it's less likely to slip and . . ." He gestured toward Pete.

Pete shrugged. "I can rope with the best of 'em. And I'm still a danged dally welter."

"Danged fool," the fourth wrangler put in, introducing himself as Aloysious P. Stewart. "But most folks call me Stewie."

" 'Cause that's the only thing he knows how to cook!" Stubby said.

"Gut-rustin' sidewinder," Two Fingers confirmed. "Like to eat your insides out with that stuff he calls stew."

"See how you like eatin' coyote soup come roundup," Stewie grumped.

Selina laughed, thoroughly enjoying the gruff affection among these rough-looking men. "You're all cowpunchers?"

"That we are, dear lady," Charlie said. "So long as they don't punch back, it all works out all right."

"Don't pay these boys any mind, ma'am," Chino said. "Roundup's in two weeks, and they're gettin' a little loco. Morgan hires five or six extra waddies then, too. But these punchers hang around most of the year—ride fence, check the herd. Which," he added meaningfully, "they should be doin' right now."

"Aw, we just wanted to meet the new missus, Chino," Stubby said. He looked at Selina. "We hope we ain't scared ya off with all our palaverin'."

"No, not at all. I think you're all delightful."

The man pshawed loudly. "When's the weddin'

anyway?" Stubby asked. "We wouldn't want to miss it."

Selina blushed, uncertain of what she should say. She certainly wasn't going to be the one to tell these men the wedding might be called off. Gripping the rope, she changed the subject. "Since you were all so fascinated by my practice throws, I'm sure you're going to want to see this real one."

The men looked doubtful, but remained graciously silent.

Celia crossed several fingers on both hands.

Selina said a silent prayer, then let the rope sail, tugging at just the right moment, letting out a whoop of joy when it settled over the post.

The wranglers all hooted their approval. Impulsively, Celia flung her arms around Selina, then just as quickly stepped back. "You done pretty good."

Selina giggled. "Thank you." Seldom had she felt more satisfaction in any accomplishment. "Now how about our deal? Grammar lesson number one. I *did well.*"

"You *did well.*"

The cowboys said their good-byes and rode out. When Chino lingered, Selina told Celia to fetch the copy of *Oliver Twist* she'd seen on a shelf behind Morgan's desk. "Why don't you read the first two chapters to get us started? I'll make out a more detailed lesson plan later."

"I'll read in my treehouse," Celia said, scooting off.

"She's taken to you," Chino said. "That's good."

"It's what Mr. Kincaid wants."

"But you like her. It's not a job."

"I like her, Chino. I like her a lot."

He rested a boot on the bottom rail of the corral. "What about Morgan?"

Selina looked away.

Chino sighed, lifting his hat to run brown fingers through his mane of dark hair. "He's always been a hard man—but he's never harder on anyone than he is on himself."

"If you say so . . ."

"He saved my life, Mrs. Bodine."

"Here? On the ranch?"

"In Houston. Morgan was a maverick lawyer, taking cases nobody else would touch." His gaze shifted to the center of the corral, where he focused on nothing in particular. "I was arrested for raping and murdering a white woman. My first lawyer was drunk most of the time. The way he presented the case, I would've voted myself guilty. The judge sentenced me to hang."

Selina blanched.

"Morgan not only got the verdict overturned, he actually found the guilty man."

Selina's memory flashed to an entry in Lenore's diary. . . . *defended some stupid half-breed.* She closed her eyes, wanting to shake some sense into the foolish girl who had written such a thing about this sensitive man. "Mr. Kincaid quit a law practice to become a rancher?"

"He took some time off, and he and I trailed a herd north one summer about seven years back. I'd never seen him happy before. When the time came that he didn't want to be a lawyer anymore, he remembered this place."

"It is beautiful here."

He grinned, turning toward her. "I knew you'd take to it."

It was her turn to stare at the ground. "That may not count for much."

"What do you mean?"

"I shouldn't say, Chino, but . . . Mr. Kincaid isn't altogether certain he's going to go through with the wedding."

Chino bit off a curse. "He can be such a jackass sometimes. Don't you worry. I'll talk to him."

Selina caught his shirtsleeve. "No. Please."

His dark eyes were unreadable. "You want him to call it off?"

"No, it's not that. I . . . I really don't know what I want. We scarcely know one another. But . . ." She blushed. "There is something about him. He tries to hide it, but it's there, especially when I see how much he cares about Celia."

"So how did you feel when you saw the scar?"

She grimaced. "Angry mostly."

"That he hadn't mentioned it in his letters?"

Selina could feel Chino rising to Morgan's defense. She felt a flush of genuine tenderness toward the foreman. "No. Nothing like that," she assured him. "It was his theatrics." She told him how Morgan manipulated their first meeting. "I guess he wanted me to look horrified or something."

"He'd pretty much convinced himself that you would."

"I think he uses that scar as an excuse to put people off."

Chino smiled. "I knew I liked you."

She smiled back. "Good. Because it's mutual."

"Has he told you how it happened?" He snorted, answering his own question. "Of course he hasn't."

Selina held up a restraining hand. "Then maybe you shouldn't . . ."

Chino paid her no heed. "It was four years ago. A gun accident. We were doing some target shooting, blowing bottles off the corral rail. Something went wrong, and Morgan's muzzleloader blew up in his face."

Selina closed her eyes, imagining the horror of it.

"We're lucky it wasn't a full load. Lenore just stood there screaming. Celia was in shock. She was only six. Prescott and I got him into the house, but there was no doctor, nothing anyone could do to save his eye. Morgan took it pretty well at first. But Lenore never did."

"I doubt he'd appreciate your telling me these things."

"That's exactly why I'm telling you. He'd never say it himself, but he hurts, Mrs. Bodine. He hurts. You got that same look, when you think no one's watching."

She started, her eyes going wide.

"Don't worry, I won't tell. And Morgan's too busy lickin' his own wounds to see anybody else's. That's what you've got to remember. You help him stop hurting, you'll never be sorry."

He left her then and headed for the bunkhouse.

She stood there, trying to sort through what she'd just heard. That Morgan was hurting was hardly a revelation, but Chino's astuteness made her wonder just how well she was pulling off this charade after all.

"Are we alone at last?" a male voice queried.

She whirled. Clay Prescott. "Does Mr. Kincaid know you're still here?"

"I thought those waddies would never leave."

"I asked you a question."

"I don't tell Morgan Kincaid everything I do."

"Why do you hate each other?"

"I don't know if 'hate' is the right word."

"What would you call it?"

"Let's talk about something more pleasant, shall we?" Before she could protest, he grabbed her hand and pulled her into the barn. "I'd like you to meet Lancelot."

She glanced at the sorrel in the first stall. "He's beautiful. Now, if you'll excuse me—" She started past him toward the door.

He caught her arm. "You're very pretty. You'd be wasted on a man like Morgan."

"Take your hands off me."

"You're a widow. I'm sure you get lonely." He moved closer. "Morgan couldn't satisfy Lenore. You won't be any different."

"I said let go of me!"

"Can't. All I've done since we met is think about you, about the accident of fate that brought you to Kincaid instead of me." His words rushed together. "Come with me to the Lazy C. I'll give you everything you could ever want."

"No. Please, Clay, don't do this." She tried again to pull free, hoping she could extricate herself from this impossible situation without having to make a scene.

"Oh, Bertie, let me show you how good it could be." He brought his mouth down on hers.

Selina forced her hands between them, shoving for all she was worth. He only tightened his hold. She was about to slam her booted toe into his shin when she felt him being wrenched away from her. She stumbled back, watching as Morgan Kincaid slammed a fist into Clay Prescott's face.

"Get off my land, Prescott," Kincaid snarled. "Take any horse. Walk. Just go. Now."

Prescott rubbed his jaw, glaring at Kincaid but making no move to retaliate. "I was just leaving, Morg. Thanks for the hospitality." While Kincaid held himself forcibly in check, Prescott saddled a bay horse and rode out.

Selina bit her lip, desperate to know what Kincaid was thinking. His face was cold, expressionless. She took a step toward him, brushing back her tousled hair. "I hope you don't think I allowed him to—"

"I don't think anything, Mrs. Bodine." Very pointedly he turned his back on her and picked up two baling hooks, then stabbed them into either end of a sizable bale of hay. Muscles rippling with effort, he carried it out to the adjacent corral. He did the same thing with a second bale, and a third, ignoring Selina's every attempt to explain.

Finally, she gave up and trudged toward the house. Things were going from bad to worse.

Inside, the house was quiet. She was alone. Crossing to Kincaid's desk, she pulled open the bottom drawer and extracted Bertie's letters. She read each one through several times, memorizing details about Bertie's supposed experience as a governess and her late husband "Norman," but nothing in any of them seemed even remotely special. She was more perplexed than ever. Something about the persona Bertie had presented must have appealed to the man, but what was it? What had made Kincaid choose Bertie Bodine?

With a sigh she started to shut the drawer, only to have it snag on something in the back. She fiddled with the drawer without success, then jerked it open again to see what the obstruction was. A folded newspaper tumbled out. Taking care not to tear it, she pulled it free.

Smoothing it out, she was about to refold it and put it back in the drawer when a headline in the lower right corner of the front page caught her eye. *Rancher's Wife Found Dead; Foul Play Suspected.*

Selina's heart pounded.

Morgan Kincaid, a former Houston attorney, is said to have proof of his whereabouts at the time of his wife's disappearance. His foreman, a half-breed with the unlikely name of Chino Black Hawk, supports his employer's claim that Kincaid was at his ranch at the time of Mrs. Kincaid's death. Chino Black Hawk is well known to this reporter as a man who would do or say anything to protect Morgan Kincaid.

Selina couldn't believe the salacious slant of the article. She wondered if the reporter had since moved on to a job with the *San Francisco Examiner.* With a grimace, she shoved the newspaper back in the drawer. If she didn't want people to prejudge her, she wouldn't prejudge Kincaid. But doubts had been planted in her mind.

She slammed the drawer shut, shooting to her

feet as the front door opened. "Mr. Kincaid," she stammered, stepping away from the desk, "You've . . . you've finished stacking your hay bales?"

He looked at his desk, then at her, his gaze revealing nothing. "Chino tells me you were roping a fence post." He spoke as though their recent encounter with Prescott had not taken place.

"I thought Chino had ridden out."

"He waited. We had a little talk."

"Oh." She didn't dare ask what they talked about. "I enjoyed Celia's roping lesson."

"You don't have to humor her."

"It was *fun.*"

He scratched his chin deliberately, his gaze growing more unsettling. "Do you ride?"

"What . . . ?"

"Take a ride with me. Let me show you more of the ranch."

A ride? Alone with the man?

"Well?" he prompted.

"You don't have to do this."

"Do what?"

"I don't know what Chino said to you . . ."

"He said I was being a son of a bitch."

"Oh."

"Shall we go for that ride?"

She followed him out to the barn, studying the play of well-honed muscles beneath his denim shirt, the pantherlike grace of his long stride.

Inside the barn he saddled a buckskin mare and handed her the reins.

"She's beautiful."

"Her name's Moondust."

Selina mounted. She hadn't sat astride a horse since that last summer trip to the Sierra Nevadas with her parents. It seemed a long, long time ago. She patted the mare's neck, nodding to Kincaid. "We're ready when you are."

Kincaid swung into the saddle, kneeing his Appaloosa stallion into an easy, loping stride. The mare kept pace. As they rode, Selina reveled in the feel of the wind sifting through her chestnut locks that whipped as free as the buckskin's mane.

An hour passed, then two. The pungent smell of sage and wildflowers filled her nostrils.

It was late afternoon when Kincaid reined in above a deep-cut arroyo, pointing toward the several hundred head of cattle scattered across the plains beyond.

"Are those yours?" Selina asked.

"Mostly. All the ranches share the range. We gather the cattle in the spring, brand our own beeves, then turn 'em loose to fatten up until fall, when we drive the four- and five-year-olds to market."

He dismounted, letting the reins trail, ground-tying the stallion. Selina followed suit with the mare.

"So what do you think of Wolf Trail?"

She had to smile. His attempt at being congenial was so patently uncomfortable to him that even talking about his ranch rang false. "Maybe Chino should've come along," she said.

"I beg your pardon?"

"To instruct us on how to go about this business of getting to know one another better."

He looked at her, his mouth ticking upward in a lopsided grin. "This *is* rather absurd, isn't it?"

The smile transformed him, making him seem younger, more at ease with himself and the world. She memorized that grin, vowing to humor him more often. She could fall in love with a smile like that.

The thought brought her up short. She turned away, meandering over to sit under a giant cottonwood.

He followed and sat down beside her. "We're here. We may as well get something accomplished."

She picked up a stick, scratching absently at a pebble embedded in the dirt. Thank heaven she'd found Bertie's letters. Still, she felt ill at ease, fearful of making some mistake that would arouse his suspicions.

"Well?" he prodded, amiably enough. "What more should I know about Abby Bodine? You said your parents were killed? You didn't mention that when you wrote."

"I was an only child. Their deaths were devastating. It's difficult to think about even now." She jabbed the stone free. "You weren't exactly a font of information in your own letters."

"What do you want to know?"

"Ordinary things. Childhood. Family. Chino told me a little about Houston, but I think I'm catching a hint of Virginia drawl in those tones sometimes, especially now, when you're trying so hard to be . . . nice."

He looked at her, then away. "The war destroyed my family, even though some of us lived through it." He told her about Willowsong.

She had the vague impression he was leaving something out, but she knew his telling her even this much had been very difficult for him. "How sad that your mother died on a day that should have been so joyful for you." She leaned back against the tree, her shoulder pressing against Kincaid's. She waited for him to shift away from her. He didn't. "You still have your sister."

"Marcette set her sights on one of the richest, most powerful men in Houston, and didn't stop until she'd maneuvered him into a proposal."

"That makes me feel better at least."

His shoulder tensed. "What is that supposed to mean?"

"Your disapproving attitude about women is apparently a long-standing one, Mr. Kincaid. So I won't take it all personally."

He glowered at her.

Unfazed, she continued: "Did it ever occur to you that Marcette was just trying to cope with her loss in the only way she could?"

"You're too generous, Mrs. Bodine."

"You're too cynical, Mr. Kincaid."

He swore. "I tell you I'm uncertain about the marriage, and you go out of your way to antagonize me. If you want me to call it off, just say so."

Selina planted her hands on her hips, even knowing she looked ridiculous doing so sitting down. Her long-suppressed willful streak was showing signs of life. "If you wanted a female to fawn over you, idolize you, and otherwise bow to your every whim, Mr. Kincaid, you might have done better to mail-order a puppy."

His lips thinned. So did hers.

He swore.

She swore back.

His mouth twitched. He looked away. But it didn't do any good. His chest shook, and then he was laughing, laughing with a genuine warmth and amusement she wouldn't have thought possible. He was still chuckling when he said, "You've got a helluva mouth for a woman."

"Is that a compliment?"

He gave her a searching look. "Yeah, I think maybe it is."

"Then, thank you."

He laughed again, then seemed to catch himself,

as if he hadn't meant to feel at ease. "How are Celia's lessons progressing?"

"For a day and a half . . . just fine."

That cerulean eye narrowed suddenly. "You lied to me in those letters, didn't you?"

She felt a sudden pressure squeezing the breath from her body. "What . . . what are you talking about?"

"I mean you totally misrepresented yourself."

"Could you be more specific?" Her mind raced. She had to bluff this out. Bertie's letters had seemed so bland, so nondescript. What was the man driving at? Would whatever mistake she had made now cost her her freedom?

"I mean," he said slowly, "I've never met such an independent-minded woman. In your letters you seemed demure, reliable, dull."

"Dull?" She jumped to her feet, relief mingling with outrage. "You asked a woman to marry you because you thought her dull? That's contemptible." She pursed her lips. "And not a little insulting!"

"I wanted a teacher for Celia."

"You hardly needed a mail-order bride for that. Charlie could teach her!"

"He'd teach her to deal from the bottom of a deck."

"You never know when such a skill could prove useful."

"You're just not anything like what I expected. And nothing at all like . . ." He stopped.

"Lenore?"

"I don't want to talk about Lenore." He frowned, apparently annoyed with himself for letting the tone of their conversation deteriorate so quickly. "I'm sorry. It's never been easy for me to talk about her. She didn't like it here—at Wolf Trail, I mean. Sometimes I feel more than a little responsible . . ."

Unwillingly Selina thought of the newspaper article. "Clay told me she fell from a horse."

Kincaid's whole demeanor changed. He was enraged. "You and Prescott were discussing Lenore?"

"I . . . I just asked him how she died." Dear God, was Kincaid's sudden fury rooted in guilt? Had she made a deadly error in judgment regarding this man?

"What else?"

She took a step back.

"What else?" he gritted.

"Nothing. Nothing at all."

"When you were going through my desk you found a certain newspaper article, didn't you?"

She hung her head. There was little use denying it.

"I did not kill my wife, Mrs. Bodine." He lifted her chin, forcing her to face him. "Not even for sharing a bed with Clay Prescott."

Quick tears came to her eyes. "Oh, my God." Of course. It explained so much. "I'm sorry. Truly."

"Mrs. Bodine, if you believe I killed Lenore, would you really think it prudent to be here alone with me?"

"Please, don't frighten me, Mr. Kincaid. Please, don't."

"What were you looking for, anyway?"

"You won't believe me," she sighed miserably, "but when I put the tuning fork away the other day I noticed my letters. I wanted to know if perhaps I'd oversold myself. I wondered if maybe that's why you were having second thoughts . . ."

"You'll have to do better than that."

Her brows furrowed. "I don't know what you mean."

"I think you were trying to make sure I was solvent. You were looking for my ledger books, weren't you? Checking Wolf Trail assets?"

So he thought her a gold digger. She didn't know whether to laugh or cry. "I am sorry. I should have asked your permission. But I promise you, I was only rereading the letters. The newspaper was an accident. And I most certainly was not going through your accounts."

"Maybe."

Her shoulders slumped. At length she said, "I'll need to borrow the ticket fee when you have Chino drive me back to the train. But I'll pay you back as soon as . . ."

"You're not going anywhere." He raised a hand and tucked a stray tendril of tumbled hair behind her ear. "Chino's right. I can be a son of a bitch."

She studied his gaze, now dark with passion. She didn't move as his mouth descended upon her own, his lips so feather-light she was unsure for a moment whether he'd touched her at all. Then his mouth plundered hers, his tongue probing, possessive. His throaty groan fired a heat within her that struck through to the very core of her being.

His arms circled her, crushed her to him, driving the air from her body in a rush. Her own arms felt awkward hanging free. Then seemingly of their own accord they tracked a path upward along the rippling muscles of his back.

She shivered as his hot moist breath fanned her face. She did not resist when he undid the first few buttons of her blouse, gliding his hand beneath the soft material to capture the silky fullness of her chemise-covered breast. The nipple swelled against his palm.

She couldn't think; didn't want to think.

He kissed the slender column of her throat, whispering inarticulate words of longing that stirred her past the bonds of reason.

He molded his body to hers, his hips in line with the softness of her belly. She stilled, feeling the unmistakable evidence of his arousal. Her mind leaped to Gideon. She started to struggle.

"You don't have to be coy," he said huskily. "We'll have the wedding. Just let me . . ."

She struggled harder. "No, no, please."

"I want you. I want you now."

"Morgan," she pleaded, fighting a rising panic, grasping at anything. "Morgan, I can't. We're not married. Please."

He raised his head, searching her face for a long minute. With a low curse he released her. "I can respect that. I don't like it, but I respect it. Our wedding night it is."

She drew in a shaky breath. "It's getting late. We'd best get back. Celia will be worried."

He stalked toward the Appaloosa, saying nothing. She headed toward Moondust. She was trembling so badly it took her three tries to get her foot into the stirrup.

As she rode, her thoughts roiled, one atop the other. The wedding was on. But did she want to go through with it? Marry the volatile, virile Morgan Kincaid? An unpredictable man consumed by a fearsome bitterness. A man who expected her to be a wife in the most intimate sense of the word. What would his reaction be when he found out she couldn't share that intimacy? She shuddered, realizing she had no choice but to find out.

lancing
taken her
manager
ing his
ook at

apter 10

Morgan paced his bedroom like a caged wolf. He couldn't stay in this house tonight thinking of Alberta Bodine lying asleep in her bed across the house. He ached for her with a lust that astonished him. Over and over he told himself it didn't make any sense, that his feelings existed solely because he hadn't been with a woman for four years.

Yet it was more than lust, try as he might to deny it.

She had taken to Celia, taken to Wolf Trail, and shown signs of a spirit that aroused not only his passion but his temper as well. Abby Bodine was like no other woman he'd ever known, a fact which by turns fascinated, infuriated, and terrified him. She was a mail-order bride, a quirk of fate! How could he be drawn to her?

He stalked to the window, staring out at the looming shadows of the mountains, the memory of

finding her in Clay Prescott's arm
through him. Abby swore Prescott had
by surprise. Maybe. But the Lazy C
hadn't taken Lenore by surprise. Clench
fists, Morgan forced himself to take a hard l
what he was feeling.

Was it rage?

Or jealousy?

His loins tightened, ached, his body throbbing
with the urgency of how much he wanted her.

He would send a rider to the circuit preacher
and have the man here by week's end.

In three days she would be his wife. He poured
himself a drink.

"Abby . . ." He said the name. It did suit her.
Soft, sweet. "Abby."

His cynicism intruded. What if it was all pretense—to get his money, his name? What if she
withheld her favors?

His fingers tracked the scar. No. For once he
shook off the crippling doubts.

She was alone in the world. She needed a home.
He was well off. They would fulfill each other's
needs.

He belted down the fiery liquid, imagining.

Selina turned up her bedside lantern, reading further into Lenore's diary. Tonight the journal was a
welcome companion, an evolving clue to the mystery of Morgan Kincaid. She read it slowly, al-

lowing the woman's life to unfold as she had lived it.

March 18, 1875: I became a woman tonight. I asked Morgan to stop, but I really didn't want him to. It was so exciting, so forbidden! But now I'm ashamed. Morgan wasn't pleased to find me a virgin. I shouldn't have hinted at past lovers. I wept when he said we couldn't see each other anymore. It hurts so much. I have to get him to change his mind. I love him, but I fear he doesn't love me at all.

Selina shook off a sudden rush of heat as she remembered Morgan's kiss, assuring herself it meant nothing. An unwelcome physical response to Kincaid's natural male lust. Nothing more. Certainly not love. She forced her attention back to the diary.

April 25, 1875: Dear God, I'm so frightened. My monthly is late. Oh, the shame of it. I'm afraid to tell Morgan, afraid he'll be furious. He's avoided me ever since we made love. Even so I must get him to marry me. If he refuses, I'll have no choice but to kill myself. Papa would never forgive the disgrace. I cry all the time, all the time. A baby. Dear God, how can I have a baby?

Selina closed her eyes.

Celia.

May 18, 1875: God help me! I am with child. A discreet doctor confirmed it this morning. I told Morgan. He wasn't pleased. But he said he would

*marry me at once. I'm happy and sad and so very
frightened. My life has turned inside out. I know
Morgan doesn't love me, but he is an honorable
man.*

The spoiled self-centered young woman had become a frightened pregnant young woman, a
woman in love with the enigmatic Morgan Kincaid.

Selina started to turn to the next page, then,
startled by a sudden noise in the main room, hur-
riedly shoved the book under the mattress. She
crept to her bedroom door, listening. The sound
was not repeated. Kincaid? Or a log shifting in the
hearth? She decided to take no chances, and put
the diary away.

Sleep eluded her, her thoughts troubled, confused. Lenore had actually enjoyed lovemaking.
Bertie, too, had been blatant in her approval of
physical intimacy. Could it be that Selina's pend-
ing wedding night with Kincaid offered the stuff of
dreams instead of nightmares?

Against her will memories of another wedding
night skittered through her mind. She had once
dared hope that night would be a dream as well.

"Mrs. Gideon Hardesty," Gideon chuckled,
tugging free the pale blue silk cravat around his
throat. "Can you believe it?"

"No." Selina blushed, barely able to meet her
new husband's steady gaze. She had been a married woman now for all of four hours. It was late,

nearly midnight. The last of the guests had gone home and she had timidly followed Gideon up the winding staircase to his bedchamber.

She had never been in the room past dusk before. In the daylight the decor was intimidating enough, but now even the gaslit crystal chandelier could not soften the effect of Gideon's prize collection of medieval artifacts. A sinister morningstar mace with its lead spiked head glowered down at her from its honored spot above the black marble fireplace. Crossbow, halberd, and Burgundian dagger flanked the mace on all sides. She turned away only to have her gaze fall on the open doors of the iron maiden standing guard in the near corner.

Taking a deep breath, she told herself it was normal for a bride to be nervous on her wedding night. Gideon cared for her. He would be gentle, kind, just as he had always been.

"Many women would love to be in your place," he was saying, dipping a wedge of bread into a silver bowl filled with caviar. He took an overlarge bite, staring at her. She thought he was looking through her, a peculiar glint in his gray-green eyes.

Selina tried to smile. He'd never looked at her that way before. "If I haven't said so yet today," she ventured shyly, "I am so very grateful for all you've done for me, Gideon. And I'm anxious for this night to go well . . . for both of us."

The reassurance she had hoped for was not forthcoming. Instead he continued to stare at her,

even as he methodically undid the buttons of his
waistcoat. His voice had a strange rasp to it as he
spoke, and his words chilled her. "We're about to
see just how grateful, my dear."

Selina sat gingerly on the canopied bed, watching as Gideon stalked over to the mahogany tallboy and extracted a sheaf of papers.

"I want you to sign these," he said, no particular
emotion in his voice.

"What are they?"

"Just sign them," he purred. "Don't ask questions."

She took the papers, glancing over the first
sheet. "This is about the trust fund my parents left
me."

"I know what it is, my dear," he said, an edge
coming into his voice. "Sign."

"You mean sign the fund over to you?" She was
more baffled than upset, certain she was misunder-
standing his intentions.

He handed her a pen. "Your signature. On the
last page. Now."

"If you could just explain . . ."

"You're my wife. What's yours is mine. That's
all the explanation you need."

"But my parents left me that money. I intended
one day to open a natural preserve, like Yellow-
stone."

"I don't want geysers or grizzly bears. I want
money."

"Gideon, I don't understand this."

Perversely, he let the subject drop. "Your father accumulated so many fascinating treasures during his travels. You will give them all to me."

Her bewilderment continued. "I was going to let the museum have them. You know that."

"You will not defy me twice."

She stood, her voice cajoling. "I don't mean to defy you at all."

He slapped her.

She staggered back, stunned. And outraged. "Don't you ever hit me again!"

He advanced toward her, his face contorted. The benevolent façade had been drawn back to reveal a hideous reality. "I won't have to hit you. You're my wife. You'll learn to do exactly as I say, just like everyone else in this house."

Selina cowered on the bed, trying desperately to make sense of this escalating madness. But the stark reality of it only grew worse as the door swung open and Marelda Hardesty swept into the room.

"Gideon, dearest," she cooed, "I've brought your tonic." She was still wearing the long-sleeved black satin gown that had so appalled Selina at the wedding ceremony.

"Thank you, Mother," Gideon said disdainfully. "Put it on the table and go. This is my wedding night, after all."

Marelda tittered.

Selina stared at the floor, mortified.

"Of course, dearest, a man must indulge *all* of his appetites." Marelda bent low toward Selina as though to brush her cheek with a kiss. Instead she hissed, "Take care that you please him. It's your duty."

"Please, Mrs. Hardesty, don't leave me alone with him. Your son . . . your son struck me."

Marelda smiled the most malignant smile Selina had ever seen. "If it pleases him to kill you, my dear, I'll expect you to die." The woman kissed Gideon on the lips, then turned to go. With a sly wink to Gideon, she set the lock, clicking the door shut behind her.

"Now, my sweet," Gideon said, "where were we?"

"You're frightening me."

"That's the idea," he said. "It makes it more exciting." He picked up his discarded cravat, threading it through his fingers.

"I thought you were my friend."

He slipped the cravat around her neck, crossing the silk so that he held either end in his opposite hand. He tightened his hold ever so slightly.

Selina jammed her hand between the material and her neck. "Don't," she pleaded.

"Take off your dress."

Hot tears pricked her eyes. "Gideon, please."

"Take it off. Now."

"No!"

He pulled the cravat tighter. She slapped him. Something snapped in him then. In a rush he ripped the clothes from her body and threw her back on the bed. Selina had no chance, but still she fought him, fought him until she had no strength left. Like a searing lance his sex tore through the barrier of her virginity.

Selina screamed, sickened.

He thrust once, twice, then spent himself inside her. Wheezing, he flopped over onto his back, muttering vile obscenities.

Sobbing, Selina slid away from him. He made no attempt to stop her. Jerking her gown back over her head, she rushed to the door and unlocked it. She didn't stop running until she reached her own rooms. She spent the next hour purging her body of the stench, the feel, of Gideon Hardesty. But she couldn't purge him from her life. Her dream of a marriage of pleasant companionship to a man who had seemed so often her parents' benefactor as well as her own had instead thrust her into the pits of hell.

As the weeks passed her efforts to ally herself with members of the staff proved futile. They were all too frightened of Gideon's wrath. She was a prisoner in opulent surroundings, never permitted to go anywhere unescorted, never allowed to speak to anyone alone.

Thankfully, Gideon rarely availed himself of her

body. When she learned to accept his lust passively, his interest waned further still.

One restless night she stole down to the kitchen for a glass of milk. On her way back to her room she was tiptoeing by the closed door to Gideon's bedchamber when an odd cry caught her ear. Hardly daring to breathe, she padded closer. She heard Gideon's grunting noises, the sound she loathed more than any other on earth. Whoever Gideon's mistress was, Selina prayed she was paid well to endure his perverted pleasures.

The odd cry came again.

What if he was raping the woman? As terrified as Selina was, she couldn't let what had happened to her happen to anyone else. Ever so cautiously she eased open the door. Bile rose in her throat. She backed away, not stopping until she reached the sanctuary of her room. There she stumbled over to the basin, hovering there, retching until her emptied stomach hurt so badly she couldn't move. And still the hellish image stayed with her.

Soon after, she dared pass a frantic message to a visitor who had been a friend of her father's. In the note she wrote that Gideon was not all he seemed. To her horror the man went to Gideon. Gideon forced her to watch one of his perversions that night, promising that she would be a participant if she ever again said a word against him to anyone.

She never did.

* * *

Morning. Selina threw back the bedcovers. She had fallen asleep at some point last night, but she had gotten no rest. Jumpy and irritable, she was grateful to find Kincaid up and gone.

She tried to be polite when a transient cowboy stopped by the house to water his horse, but she was glad to see him ride out again. She managed to mutter a cursory thanks when he handed her a two-week-old newspaper he'd been carrying.

"I already read it front to back and back to front myself," he said. "Readin' material can be pretty hard to come by out here. Maybe you could pass it around amongst your wranglers."

Inside the house Selina gave the paper's front page a passing glance, noting projected facts and figures on the upcoming spring roundups. Pages two and three were crammed with personal anecdotes of life in the Judith Basin—births, deaths, accidents of note, even a shootout in Miles City that left the contents of thirty-three bottles of whiskey seeping into the floorboards of the Broken Bull Saloon.

She was about to leave the paper on the piano for Morgan when a story on the bottom of the back page caught her eye. Her heart hammered.

The search continues throughout the western territories for the murderess of prominent San Francisco business tycoon Gideon Hardesty. The reward for the capture of Selina Michaels Hardesty was

*recently raised by the mother of the murder victim
to the enticing sum of ten thousand dollars. When
last seen the murderess . . .*

Selina shredded the paper into tiny bits and
burned it in the hearth. For a long time she just sat
there, staring at the twisted flakes of blackened paper. She had actually begun to delude herself that
perhaps she was safe now. The newspaper had
brought her terror crushing in on her again.

She drew in several shuddering breaths. She
knew she had to calm down, had to think what to
do. Perhaps a ride would help clear her thoughts.
She decided to saddle Moondust.

She was still some twenty yards from the corral
when she spotted Celia sitting on the top rail, tossing a lariat toward the pinto stallion. The horse
reared, flattening his ears.

"Celia," Selina snapped, unable to check her deteriorating mood, "your father told me you're not
to go near that horse. Get down from there."

The girl reacted with her own flare of temper.
"He's mine and I'll do what I want."

"Get down. Now."

The child stood, defiant, her feet resting on the
middle rail. "You can't tell me what to do. You're
not my mother. You're not anybody!" She set the
lariat in motion, twirling it above her head. Selina
could see the disaster brewing. Precious seconds
streaked by as she lunged forward. The rope whistled toward the angry horse. Selina reached the

corral just as the loop settled over the beast's head. She had her foot on the bottom rail when the stallion reared, trumpeting his fury. Selina grabbed for Celia but missed as the horse bolted toward the far end of the corral.

Arms flailing, her right wrist tangled in the coil of rope, Celia shrieked with terror as she was dragged to the ground. Selina ducked between the lower rails and dashed into the enclosure. The horse thundered by, Celia's body bumping, twisting along in the dirt.

Selina charged the stallion, her arms raised. The horse stopped and reared. Selina sidestepped, running to Celia, tearing at the rope, terrified that the horse would trample them both or begin another wild run.

From somewhere far off she thought she heard the sound of a rider coming into the yard, but she dared not take even a second to look. The rough hemp bloodied her fingers as she ripped at the tangled knot.

A blur of motion shot by her.

Morgan.

Gripping a knife in his left hand, he sliced through the rope in one vicious motion, then lifted the small, still body of his daughter into his arms. Selina raced ahead of him and opened the corral gate. Celia's face was gray, her eyes closed. Selina wouldn't let herself think as she hurried after Morgan toward the house.

Gently, ever so gently, Morgan laid Celia in her bed. "She's not moving."

Selina heard the fear in his voice but kept her own desperate control. She couldn't, wouldn't, panic. Gathering clean cloths, she poured water into the basin beside Celia's bed, then began to undress the child. Morgan sat down at the opposite side. She was too preoccupied to look at him, but she knew he was not only distressed. He was furious. "She'll be all right," she heard herself say.

She forced herself to work slowly, methodically, relieved to find only scrapes and bruises. But the girl remained unconscious. She could have hit her head, twisted her back . . .

"Is she breathing?" Morgan demanded as Selina bandaged the worst of the cuts on Celia's hands and forearms.

"Of course she's breathing," Selina said, reassuring herself as much as Morgan. "She'll be just fine."

Morgan tucked the covers under Celia's chin. "Did you check for broken bones?"

"As best I know how," Selina said, brushing a stray tendril of Celia's blond hair away from the girl's waxen face. Celia shifted, then moaned, coming groggily awake. Her lips started to quiver as her gaze fell on Selina. "I'm sorry," she whimpered.

"It's all right, sweetheart," Selina said. "How do you feel?"

"It hurts."

"I know it does. Can you move your arms and legs? Does anything feel worse than a bump or bruise?"

Celia wriggled her body beneath the blankets, grimacing as she did so. "Everything moves," she said. "Everything hurts."

Selina gave her a sympathetic smile. "You get some sleep. You'll feel better after you rest."

The girl nodded, turning her head, only then noticing her father. A look of such terror came into the child's eyes that Selina winced. Terror and something else Selina couldn't identify. "I'm sorry, Pa," Celia cried. "I didn't mean it. I didn't mean it."

"Of course you didn't," Morgan soothed, but Selina could see he was as disturbed by Celia's reaction as she was. "You do what Mrs. Bodine says, now. Get some sleep."

Selina leaned forward, giving Celia a swift kiss on the forehead. "We'll look in on you in a little while, all right?"

Celia nodded.

Selina rose and followed Morgan out into the hall, pulling the bedroom door shut behind her. She watched him stalk to the center of the room. So far he had been holding his temper in check, but she expected the explosion to come any second. He did not disappoint her. Slamming a fist against the mantel, he bellowed, "Would you like to tell me how the hell you let this happen? I thought she was safe with you!"

Selina chose not to rise to the bait. She remained silent, and found herself fighting an overwhelming urge to comfort him, hold him and shield him from the hurt that was tearing him apart. He was trying to use his fury to conceal his agony—from himself as much as from Selina. He was not nearly so angry about what had happened as he was confused by Celia's very real dread when she had seen him just now.

"Dammit, Abby," he said softly, his rage now directed inward, "why is she afraid of me? I don't understand it. I've never laid a hand on that child in my life. I swear she looked like I was going to beat her."

"I don't know why," Selina said slowly, "but I do know it hurts her, too. And until she trusts one or the other of us enough to tell us about it, all we can do is be here for her."

He shook his head, his jaw set hard. "I can't wait that long." He started toward Celia's bedroom. "She's going to tell me now."

Selina intercepted him. "You can't force her. She'll only shut you out more." A look of such raw agony crossed his face that Selina had to dig her nails into her palms to keep from pulling him into her arms.

He straightened, adopting a look of forced resignation. When he spoke again, his voice held a note of defeat she'd never heard before. And then she was too stunned by the words themselves to dwell on how he said them. "The wedding is Friday."

She gasped. "That's two days!"

"So it is." He headed for the door. "I'll sleep in the bunkhouse tonight. If Celia needs anything, let me know." With that he was gone.

Selina sank onto the divan.

She recalled his face. Not exactly the picture of the enthusiastic groom. She sighed. No more than the bride. What was the matter with her? Wasn't the marriage precisely what she wanted? Now she wouldn't have to worry about being on the run again.

The flames crackled in the hearth, her blood heating to match its warmth. Morgan Kincaid's wife. For just an instant her fears of intimacy were eclipsed by a rush of anticipation so strong it shook her to the core. And even as she dismissed the feeling as absurd, she clung to the afterglow of pleasure it gave her, savoring it, startled to find herself wishing Morgan could make it real.

The next morning Selina carried a breakfast tray to Celia's room. Opening the door, she frowned when she found the bed empty. She grimaced and set the tray down, knowing exactly where to look. Hurrying out the back door, she tromped through knee-high buffalo grass to the massive cottonwood abutting the creek bank. "Are you up there, Celia?"

No answer.

Selina climbed nimbly up the wooden ladder, shoving aside the moth-eaten blanket that served as a doorway to the treehouse. Even the child's wary glower was a welcome sight. "You sure you're well enough to be out of bed?"

"I'm not sick."

"Do you want me to leave?"

"I can't tell you what to do."

"This is your private place. If you don't want me here, you just say so."

Moving her bandaged hands stiffly, Celia rearranged two of the several colored rocks on the crudely made shelf behind her. "You can stay."

Selina climbed inside. "I like it here. You can hear the water rushing by below."

"Pa doesn't like me to be here."

"Why?"

"He just doesn't."

Selina sat down, smoothing her skirt. "Maybe that's because when you come here, you're usually upset with him about something."

Celia seemed to consider that. "Maybe," she allowed.

"He loves you very much. He's worried about you."

"He wouldn't love me if . . ."

Selina tried not to betray her sudden hope. If the child confided in her, perhaps Selina could put an end to the painful estrangement between father and daughter. "If what?" she prompted gently.

"Nothing!"

Selina sighed, but did not press her. At least they had made a beginning. "I came up here to make sure you were all right. But I have another reason, too. I want you to hear the news from me. Your father and I are getting married tomorrow. I'd like to know how you feel about that."

"I can't stop you."

"Do you want to?"

"I don't know. You're not as bad as I thought you—" She stopped.

Selina laughed. "It's all right. I want you to be honest with me."

Celia moved more of her rocks.

"They're very pretty," Selina said.

Celia held out a fist-sized blue one. "It's an agate. It's my favorite. Pa gave it to me when I was just a kid. Before Mama died. Before . . ." She put the rock back and was silent.

"There's one more reason why I wanted to see you this morning. I want to apologize about yesterday."

"Apologize?"

"If I hadn't been so cross when I came out to the corral, you might not have challenged that horse quite so boldly."

Celia looked sheepish. "I'm glad you came when you did. I'd just missed him a couple of times before. If I'd caught him when no one was around . . ."

"Then we both learned a lesson, didn't we?"

The girl nodded.

"I know you're a little stiff and sore, but do you feel up to showing me how to toss a rope again?"

"Pa said to stay away from the pinto."

"I'm sure we could get a gentler horse to volunteer."

Celia smiled.

"Maybe we'll work in a piano lesson, too, all right? We could surprise your papa with a tune at the wedding."

They kept each other busy for the balance of the day. Exhausted, Celia went right to bed after supper. Selina set about reworking one of Lenore's gowns. She didn't think of it as a wedding dress, but for reasons she refused to fully explore she wanted the dress she wore tomorrow to feel as if it were her very own.

It was well past midnight when Morgan strode into the house. He hadn't been in all day. Selina looked up from the divan, nervously shielding the dress.

"How's Celia?" he asked, his voice a painfully familiar monotone.

"She's fine. She's a tough little kid."

"Just wanted to check before I turn in."

"You're staying in the bunkhouse again?"

"Unless you have a better suggestion."

His leer seemed deliberate. Blast the man! Why did he persist in building and rebuilding this wall between them? She didn't answer.

"Well, good night, then, Mrs. Bodine."

Her voice was rose-petal soft. "Good night, Morgan."

He froze, then walked to the back of the divan. She didn't miss the slight tremor in his hand as he raised it toward her. But he seemed to think better of it, dropping it stiffly back to his side. "Thank you for taking care of Celia."

She felt uncertain, shy. He looked so achingly lost. One word, one touch, and she sensed in that moment he could erase the specter of Gideon Hardesty from her life forever.

But no words, no touch, came. He straightened abruptly and stormed from the house.

Chapter 11

Selina sat in front of the gilt-edged mirror on Lenore's vanity, her fingertips brushing lightly over the silver combs she had just arranged in her hair. Morgan had left word the preacher would arrive before noon. That meant that in less than an hour she would be Morgan Kincaid's wife. Wife to a man who had no notion of the horrors she had gone through with Gideon Hardesty. Wife to a man who wanted—demanded—a willing woman in his bed tonight.

Her gaze fell on the diary. She'd read a little further into it last night, but had deliberately stopped short of the entry that marked Lenore's wedding day. She told herself she couldn't bear the comparison. But it was more than that.

She couldn't bear the knowledge. What if Lenore's wedding had not been the golden moment the girl wished for? Even given the circumstances of her pregnancy, Lenore had written gushingly for days about her impending marriage—how much she loved Morgan, how happy her father was to have him joining the family, how envious her friends were that she had snared the handsomest bachelor in Houston. Selina saw all too clearly that Lenore had attached a host of unrealistic expectations to her marriage and to Morgan himself, imagining the life of a fairy princess once she became Mrs. Morgan Kincaid.

In all of those entries Lenore had written very little about Morgan's expectations. In fact they had spent little time together, and there had been no more intimacy. *He is resigned to the marriage. When I ask if he loves me, he says emotions get in the way of sensible business arrangements. One day he will come to love me, though, I'm sure of it. And I know he looks forward to the child.*

How could Lenore be so eager to marry a man who clearly didn't love her? Her increasingly frequent references to Morgan's good looks made Selina uneasier still. Just how devastating had Morgan's gun accident been to Lenore? Had she ceased loving her husband? Selina considered thumbing ahead in the diary, but resisted the temptation. What bearing could it have on her own wedding, now so close at hand?

"What of your wedding *night,* Lenore?" Selina murmured. That entry was the one Selina dreaded most. But it was the one she most needed to read. Deciding she might as well get it over with, she flipped to the entry marked May 23, 1875. The account was short, haunting, only three lines at the bottom of the page.

Morgan and I are husband and wife. I dreamed of this marriage from the first day we met. And now . . . and now . . . I spent the night in tears.

A knock sounded.

"Who is it?" Selina called, her stomach roiling. *Tears.* Lenore Kincaid spent her wedding night in tears.

"It's Celia," came a small voice.

Selina shoved the diary back into its hiding place. "The door's open."

The child peered in shyly. "Your dress is real pretty."

Selina followed Celia's gaze to the pale yellow silk that lay across the bed. Selina had spent last night removing much of its excesses, including the bustle, turning the gown into one of simple lines. "Thank you."

"Pa made me wear a dress, too. But I hate it."

The drab brown cotton was rather sad-looking. "It's fine, honey," Selina said, resolving to rework another of Lenore's finery for the girl.

"I . . . have something for you." Celia held out a tiny package wrapped in brown paper.

Selina accepted the gift, Celia's thoughtfulness shaking her out of her mood. "Thank you." Selina tore off the paper, gasping as the blue agate slipped into her palm. "Oh, I couldn't, Celia. It's your favorite."

"You liked it. I didn't have anything else . . . I mean, I really wanted to give you a present."

Selina hugged the girl close, genuinely touched. "Thank you, Celia, very much."

A shadow filled the doorway. Selina didn't have to look to know. "Can I talk to you?" Morgan's voice held no emotion.

Celia darted past her father and out of the room.

Selina clutched the front of her robe. "Don't you know it's bad luck—"

He cut her off. "Don't bother. I just want to give you one last chance. The preacher's here, but I can send him away."

Selina noted his denim shirt and jeans. Was this his planned attire for the wedding? Or was it a subtle hint to back out?

She turned the agate over and over in her palm.

"Do you accept my conditions?" He held his profile at a more exaggerated angle than usual, and in spite of her own misery the gesture tore at her.

"I do." And in that moment she hated him, hated him for being so caught up in his own torment that he couldn't see how desperately frightened she was. And she hated herself for caring.

He left the room then, and she dressed quickly. She thought about finishing Lenore's account of her wedding night, but now suspected that such knowledge might only make things worse. People could change a great deal in ten years.

Taking in a deep, steadying breath, she opened the door and stepped out into the main room. Morgan was nowhere to be seen, but Chino and the other ranch hands were milling about near the front windows. She smiled, gaining a measure of confidence at least from their admiring glances.

"You're beautiful," Chino said, coming over to take her hand and escort her further into the room. "Morgan's a lucky man."

"I doubt he'd agree with you."

He ducked his head toward her, whispering urgently. "Please. Give him time."

"I don't have time, Chino. He expects . . ." She didn't finish, unsure exactly what she had been going to say. She forced a smile as the other wranglers came up to her—Stubby, Two Fingers, Stewie, and Charlie, each in turn bowing slightly as they passed. She doubted they'd ever all shaved before on the same day in their lives. Clean dungarees, gleaming belt buckles, and string ties made them all look thoroughly uncomfortable and unforgettably sweet.

The preacher, a nondescript little man with wire-rimmed glasses and close-cropped salt-and-pepper hair, stood off by himself. He was thumbing through a small leather-bound book.

Morgan strode down the hall from his bedroom. "This is Reverend Peters." But Selina made no response; she could only stare. The transformation stunned her. Gone was the denim. In its place Morgan wore a silver-gray jacket with a silk brocade vest and pants that seemed to have been tailored deliberately to flaunt lean hips and taut thighs. The ruffled blue silk shirt was unabashedly masculine spanning that broad chest. His ebony hair shone like a raven's wing, his strong jaw clean-shaven. The scar disappeared and she saw him as he had been, and knew how an impressionable young girl could fall in love with him at first sight. But even with the scar, the black eyepatch only added to the sense of tightly controlled power and grace. Selina suddenly was warm all over.

"I'd appreciate if you'd get this over with as quickly as possible, Reverend," Morgan said. "I have a ranch to run."

Celia scooted over to Selina, quickly shoving a bouquet of wildflowers into her hands. Selina clutched them to her breasts, giving the child a tender smile. Then Celia took her place behind her father, the ranch hands spanning out to flank the small wedding party.

The preacher cleared his throat. "Dearly beloved . . ."

The front door swung open. Clay Prescott sauntered in. Morgan stiffened perceptibly.

"Sorry I'm late." Prescott bowed low before Selina, lifting her right hand to his lips to plant a lingering kiss there. She would have jerked it free, but feared making things worse.

"Get on with it," Morgan growled to the reverend.

The preacher's hands fluttered upward to adjust his white collar. Evidently he had planned on an uncomplicated ceremony. The tension in the room was palpable. Again the man cleared his throat.

"Morgan Kincaid, do you take this woman as thy lawfully wedded wife, to have and to hold from this day forward . . ." The preacher droned on, Selina scarcely listening. Her whole world had narrowed down to the man standing so rigidly next to her. She had the strangest sensation that the tenseness in him was not anger, but what it was she couldn't have said.

Though he faced her in his usual manner and did not touch her, his gaze was steady, intense, almost fierce as he spoke the vows that would seal their marriage. "Alberta Bodine, I take you to be my lawfully wedded wife, in sickness, in health, for richer, for poorer, in good times, and in bad. I promise to love you, honor you, and cherish you all the days of my life."

Her knees shook.

"I swear faithfulness to you—with my mind, with my heart, and with my body."

The passion in that look was almost her undoing. If his arm hadn't come around her waist she might have fainted. Somehow she managed to stammer like words back to him. On the last she spoke in barely more than a whisper, ". . . with my heart and with my body."

She tried to shrink away then but his hold was granite-hard.

"I now pronounce you man and wife," the reverend intoned, "and pray that this union be blessed with many healthy children." The man smiled— relieved, Selina imagined, to be able to take his leave, which he did the instant Morgan handed him his fee. "Oh, you may kiss the bride, sir," he called back, disappearing out the door. "Sorry to rush, I have a funeral in Miles City."

For all the heat that had simmered behind the vows Morgan had just spoken, he only leaned forward and lightly brushed her cheek with his lips. "Welcome to Wolf Trail, Mrs. Kincaid."

Had there been a subtle warning in his calling her thus? Selina thought of the night ahead. Morgan seemed relaxed enough, almost congenial, but her own wild imagination kept recalling the words in Lenore's diary.

She had no time to dwell on it, surrounded at once by a crush of wranglers congratulating her. Clay Prescott, too, stepped up to her. "Do I get to kiss the bride?" He didn't wait for an answer. His arm snaked out, pulling her to him. She tried to keep a breath of space between them, but he would have none of it. He captured her mouth in a sloppy, insulting kiss that infuriated her. She drew back her right foot and kicked him hard in the shin.

Prescott yelped and leaped back, pretending to have stumbled. "Think I'll get me a drink."

The wranglers formed a line and each gave her a shy handshake except Charlie, who whipped a piece of paper out of his vest pocket. "Composed a little poetry for the occasion, ma'am, if you don't mind?"

"Poetry?"

Morgan had only strayed a few feet from her. "Must you?"

"Aw, boss, I worked all night on this."

Morgan grimaced.

Charlie cleared his throat, anchoring one hand in the space between the middle two buttons of his shirt. His voice boomed. "She came by rail in the mail, We wondered how she'd be. Now she's here; what a beauty!" He paused to wink broadly. "Ye got a sister fer me?"

Selina giggled. "Thank you, Charles. That was quite . . . unique. But, no, I don't have a sister."

"That's all right, ma'am. I got plenty more poems." He started fishing through his pockets.

"You'll have to excuse us, Charles," Chino said, catching Selina's arm and guiding her toward the hearth. "I've heard his other poems." He grinned. "I've just saved your life."

Selina smiled, but immediately sobered as she spied Morgan heading toward Prescott.

"Don't worry. Morgan wouldn't kill him in front of witnesses."

"That's not funny. They hate each other."

"Prescott was a fool to come here today."

"I know about Lenore and Clay. Morgan told me."

Chino's eyebrows arched in surprise. "So you *have* said a few words to each other."

"Very few."

"It'll get better. You'll see. By the way, I liked the way you handled Prescott. Very discreet."

"I tried."

He caught her hand, suddenly deadly serious. "I care about you, ma'am. I think you know that. But Morgan's the best friend I've ever had. I don't want to see him hurt."

"Do you think I'll hurt him?" Selina heard the surprise in her own voice.

Chino didn't have a chance to answer before their attention was diverted by a loud whoop from Charlie. "Is this a weddin' or a funeral? I say it's high time for a little singin' and dancin' around here. The piano's tuned up. I got my fiddle. Let's do her up good!" He settled the fiddle under his chin and began to strike out a merry tune Selina didn't recognize.

Selina welcomed the break. Her conversation with Chino was cutting too close. Gathering her skirts, she glided happily to the piano. She caught on to the melody and joined in with an enthusiasm she hadn't felt for days.

The wranglers swarmed close, clapping and laughing, singing along with Charlie's bawdy lyrics until Selina was doubled over with laughter. Even catching Morgan watching her did not dampen her high spirits. Only when she saw that Celia had moved away to stare forlornly out the window did Selina stop playing. "Celia!" she called. "Isn't it about time for your surprise?"

The girl paled. "Oh, no, I couldn't. What if I mess it up?"

"You won't." Selina stood and hurried over to the girl, curving her arm affectionately around her small shoulders. "I know you can do it!"

Reluctantly Celia crossed to the piano. Her fingers trembled above the keys.

"You can do it," Selina whispered.

Celia started, hit a wrong note, and stopped. Selina gave her shoulders an encouraging squeeze. "You're doing fine." Celia started again. Slowly she played "Greensleeves."

Selina watched Morgan regard his daughter, his features a study in pride and approval. He led the applause when she finished. "Great job, honey. Just great!"

Celia smiled shyly.

Morgan came over to Selina, his voice admiring. "I didn't know you'd gotten so far with her."

"She's a wonderful student. She loves to learn. What more can a teacher ask?"

Morgan stepped back over to his daughter. "How about an encore?"

Celia beamed, launching into a repeat of "Greensleeves." Impulsively, Morgan gathered Selina in his arms. "Dance, madam?"

She didn't resist, melting against him, mesmerized by the play of muscles beneath the hand she rested on his right shoulder, the heat of his left hand as it curled around her right. He moved with a fluid grace that surprised her, until she recalled his southern gentleman's background. She watched as his head lowered, his mouth tracking languidly toward her own. She tilted her head to meet him, then caught herself.

He stopped, his hands dropping away as if she were fire. "All right," he said, looking around the room, "I think I've paid you men to loaf long enough. There's fence to mend, steers to track. Roundup starts in a week."

To Chino he said, "See to it Prescott doesn't wait around. I want him gone. Now."

Prescott paused, wavering slightly on his way to the door. He leaned drunkenly toward Selina. "Are you going to peek under his patch?"

Her eyes went unwillingly to Morgan, who turned away. "I believe my husband asked you to leave, Mr. Prescott," she said loudly. Under her breath she hissed, "And if you ever say any such thing again I'll ram my fist down your boorish throat."

Prescott straightened, his eyes wide as saucers, wondering if he'd heard her right.

"Yes, *ma'am.*" He stumbled out the door and was gone.

Chino gave her a reassuring hug, then he, too, left the house.

Selina stood nervously, smoothing imaginary wrinkles from her gown.

Celia was still poking at the piano keys. "You can sleep in your treehouse tonight, Celia, if you like," Morgan said.

"Oh, can I, Pa?" she said, obviously delighted. "Thank you!" She raced into her room to gather up the things she would need overnight.

Morgan tugged on one end of his string tie, pulling it loose, then began to work the buttons of his shirt. "Hungry?" he murmured.

Selina seized on the suggestion. "Yes." She ducked into the kitchen, then realized she couldn't possibly eat a thing. She was too nervous. Instead she slipped through the bathing room into her bedroom. She stood there, her heart pounding so hard she was certain it was going to leap from her chest. Her legs gave way just as she reached the seat in front of the vanity.

"God, help me." She sat there, rocking back and forth, fighting an overwhelming urge to be sick. There's still time, her mind thrummed. Still time to bolt. If she went out the back door, she just might make it to the corral, to Moondust.

She tore at the buttons of the dress. She couldn't run away in the voluminous silk. Quickly she peeled down to her pantalets and chemise, then grabbed her riding skirt and blouse. She had one arm in a sleeve when she noticed the wrapped package sitting on her pillow. Curious, she picked it up. A wedding gift from the hands? No, they wouldn't have come in here.

Morgan.

Her heart still thudding against her ribs, Selina unfolded the wrapping. The silk peignoir spilled into her hands, the pale ivory shimmering in the lantern light.

Someone knocked. Selina jumped, then relaxed when Celia popped her blond head in the door. "I'm going out to my treehouse now. Good night, Abby." Her eyes lit up when she saw the peignoir.

"A present from your father," Selina said.

"It's so pretty. It looks just like . . ." She clamped her mouth shut.

"What is it, Celia?"

"Nothing." She started to back out the door.

Selina felt cold. "This was your mother's, wasn't it?"

"I never saw her wear it. Honest."

Selina dropped the night rail as though she'd been burned.

"Oh, please, I didn't mean anything!"

"I know. It's all right. You just go on outside. Enjoy your night." As the child rushed off, Selina could only stare at the filmy night rail. How could he give her such intimate apparel from his dead wife? And why did it hurt so much that he had? Refusing to puzzle it out, she jerked at her riding blouse, lining up the buttons, then twisted each mother of pearl circlet viciously through its matching hole. "Damn you, Morgan," she murmured. "Damn you."

She nearly leaped out of her skin when he rapped on the open door. He was already in the room when she turned around.

"Did I hear my name being taken in vain?" She caught the mild sarcasm even as his gaze settled on the crumpled peignoir. "You didn't like the color?"

"Maybe I don't care for its history," she snapped, her voice quavering.

A flicker of understanding skated across his features. "She never wore it. She threw it in my face, in fact. I'd hoped you wouldn't have the same reaction."

He seemed hesitant all at once. She might even have said shy, if the word didn't seem so ludicrous attached to such a devastatingly handsome man. And how very handsome he did look to her tonight. Dared she believe that this night might not be a nightmare after all? That Morgan could understand her fears, prove to her that she need never know such fear again?

But even as her hope flickered, she watched him grow suddenly wary, his gaze straying to the riding skirt on her bed. She felt the blood drain from her face.

"Going somewhere?" he asked softly, too softly.

"I . . . the wedding dress was uncomfortable."

"Don't lie, Abby. Were you running to any place in particular or just into the night? Any hole in the ground would be preferable to my bed, eh?" He was fighting a losing battle with his temper. "I only stopped by to remind you that this isn't your room anymore." He gripped her hand, all but dragging her across the house.

Her legs felt wooden. *Tell him, Selina,* her mind screamed. *Tell him you're afraid. Tell him. He will understand. He will.* But no words came.

He didn't release her until they reached his bedroom. For each step he took toward her, she took a step back, until she was flat against the wall between the étagère and his bed.

He swore. "You act like I'm going to rape you, for God's sake."

"Aren't you?"

His good eye narrowed with icy contempt. "We made a bargain. This night is part of that bargain. I've waited too long . . ." He shook himself, straightening. He was acting like a jackass. No wonder she was shaking like a leaf. "Look, Abby," he said, struggling to sound reasonable, though just being with her here in his bedroom was threatening to drive all reason from his mind. "Neither one of us is . . . inexperienced. As a widow I'm sure you're well acquainted with the marriage bed."

"My . . . my late husband was . . . was . . ." Tears rimmed her eyes.

"Was what? A good lover? Handsome? Out of his mind in love with you?"

"Morgan, please. Don't do this."

His voice was husky, his gaze darkening with mounting passion. "The way you looked today, you could've asked me anything." He staked his hands on the wall at either side of her, trapping her. "So beautiful. So damned beautiful." His lips brushed her cheek. "Don't ask me to free you from your promise. Don't dare ask me that, *Mrs.* Kincaid. I've been imagining this night ever since you walked into this house."

She trembled. "Please."

He pushed away from the wall and stalked over to the étagère, where he extracted the half-full bottle of Cyrus Noble and poured himself a drink. "Join me?" He held up the bottle.

She nodded numbly, sinking into the chair beside his bed. Her fingers quivered as she accepted the glass. She raised it to her lips, gulping it down. Her throat burned, her eyes watered. Gasping, choking, she held out the empty glass for a refill.

"Oh, no, I don't want you falling asleep." He took the glass, then caught her wrist and guided her to the bed. "I won't hurt you, Abby," he said. "I won't. It'll be good for both of us. I promise."

She heard his voice, but couldn't discern the words. Her ears rang, and her head was now buzzing with the effects of the liquor. He was easing her back on the bed. His fingers were working the buttons of her blouse.

She struggled feebly. "Don't make me," she whimpered. "Don't." She gripped the sheets, holding herself rigid. *Give it time,* Chino had said. *Morgan won't hurt you.*

But Morgan didn't know about Gideon. No one knew. Except Marelda. And Marelda didn't care. Even when Selina had tried to tell, no one had believed her. The things he had done to her . . .

She bucked upward. "You won't humiliate me again. You won't!"

"Shh, it's all right, Abby." Morgan watched her eyes, cursing under his breath to see that haunted look back again. He forced himself to go slowly. "I won't hurt you. I never meant to scare you. Please, believe that. I want you, Abby. I want you to want me." The words were halting, his own fears riding him.

He eased the blouse off her shoulders, tugging at the ribbons of her chemise. His fingers shook. *So clumsy, Morgan. Don't you remember how it's done?* Damn. He shut his mind to Lenore's taunts.

He knew how to please a woman. He would prove it. Now.

He parted the sides of the chemise, exposing her breasts, his sex throbbing, demanding. Such lovely breasts, dark tips, nipples thrusting. "I want you, Abby. I want . . ." He kissed her throat, her cheek, her mouth. "You don't know how long it's been."

Tears slid from her eyes.

"Don't cry. Dammit, don't cry." His body burned. Gently, so gently, he eased away the last of her clothing and his own, then raised himself above her, the aching core of him teasing the entrance to her womanhood. "Want it," he pleaded. "Want me." He waited, holding himself still. "Say yes, Abby. Say yes."

Gideon's specter hovered all around her. "Don't touch me. Don't hurt me, Gid—"

He silenced her cries with his mouth, his tongue plundering, exploring. She writhed, moaned, unaccustomed to the sensual assault. There was something . . . something wrong. Gideon wouldn't be kind. Where was the pain?

"Let me be inside you, Abby," Morgan whispered. "Let me. Now. Say yes, Abby. Say it. Please." For this woman, for this moment, he dared risk his pride. God help him, dared risk his heart.

Selina twisted, sobbing. She saw Gideon's face

above her. "I can't bear to look at you, can't bear to have you touch me."

The body above her went rigid, ceasing even to breathe until the silence in the room deafened her. Then the words came. "So we have the truth at last, sweet Abby. I do repulse you."

The strangled voice didn't register at first, the words meaningless as she cowered away from him. By the time she understood, he was gone.

Chapter 12

Morgan sat by the hearth, his whole body trembling.

Can't bear to look at you.

She had tried to lie, but when the moment had come for them to lie naked together, to be lovers, she had not been able to carry through the pretense.

With an oath he shot to his feet. He couldn't stay here, couldn't face her, not now. In the morning she would no doubt regard him with tolerance and pity. He could abide neither.

Hadn't he planned to be gone during roundup anyway? He would just leave a week early.

He headed for the barn, a steely coldness seeping into him, through him, sinking ever deeper with each step he took until it had woven its icy chrysalis around his heart.

* * *

Selina lay awake long after Morgan had stormed from the room. If she had set out to hurt him, she couldn't have cut him more deeply. She shuddered as she recalled her own words. *I can't bear to look at you, can't bear to have you touch me.* She had not been speaking to Morgan when she said them, but to a whiskey-induced apparition of Gideon Hardesty returned from hell.

But how could she explain it to Morgan without exposing her charade? She realized, now that it was too late, that she had made a grievous mistake. Physical intimacy need not go hand in hand with pain and degradation.

Morgan had not hurt her; had made no threats. He had been patient, even kind, in spite of his body's fearful arousal. He had waited, asking, *wanting* her to welcome his lovemaking. And in return she had ripped at his very soul. Her tears came then, as she perceived the awful price he had paid for his tenderness.

Say, yes, Abby. Say yes.

She had hurt him, perhaps beyond forgiving, because she had savaged him where he was most vulnerable.

She sat up, wanting to go to him, not knowing what to say. What could she say? That she'd seen a ghost?

Maybe it wouldn't matter. Maybe he'd discovered that intimacy in marriage with a woman he scarcely knew wasn't a very good idea after all. But she knew there was more to it than that. He had spoken of wanting this night since first he'd seen her. In spite of all his blustering, this marriage had not been only for Celia's sake. Morgan Kincaid was a lonely man, isolated by his own bitterness. Rather than risk courtship and rejection he had proposed marriage to a stranger, a stranger whom he could wed and bed, but from whom he could remain emotionally distant.

He could touch and be touched without risk to his heart. But he did have to risk his pride. And that he dared take that risk told her more than any words ever could. *Want me. Want me as much as I want you.* Locked inside the Morgan Kincaid he presented to the world was a man who longed to be held, caressed—loved, physically loved.

And she had failed him.

She pulled on her robe. She had to find him, at least try to explain.

That Morgan did not recognize her own pain made no difference. She made no attempt to rationalize why she cared. She had felt drawn to Morgan from the first moment by the hearth. Whether or not anything could ever come of it—their separate tortured pasts standing so hard and fast between them—she couldn't, wouldn't, predict. She only knew she couldn't bear that he was somewhere hurting right now because of something she had said.

She found him in the barn, saddling the stallion.

"Roundup's in a week. I have to get ready." His voice was totally expressionless. He was not looking at her.

"I'd like to talk—"

"Nothing need be said, madam."

"I didn't mean what happened. You misunderstood . . ." This wasn't going to work. It was too late. Like a tangible thing, his hatred hovered there between them.

"This was a business agreement. I was a fool to think sex could be a term of such an agreement. You'll have your way." He tied down his saddlebags. "The marriage will be only for the sake of appearances. I'll not trouble you again with my physical appetites."

"It's not . . . it wasn't . . ." She reached a hand toward him, but his glare made her drop it back to her side. She wanted to sob, to scream, to hurl herself at him, but she didn't dare. In her present state she would tell him anything, everything, to convince him she hadn't meant what she'd said. And that she couldn't do.

"Good-bye, *wife.*" He swung into the saddle.

She sank to her knees, giving herself up to the sobs that wracked her as he thundered away. "I'm sorry, Morgan. I'm so sorry."

Selina was certain the marriage was over. Five days went by and Morgan did not come home.

"He's just getting ready for the roundup," Celia said cheerily as she practiced a new piece on the piano. "He'll be back in another day or two. He always takes me with him on roundups."

Selina kept her doubts to herself. She'd never seen the child so happy. "I take it you like herding cattle."

"It's fun to see all the new calves, to watch the wranglers ropin' and ridin'."

"And you get to spend a lot of time with your father."

Celia missed a note. "Maybe I should go work on my history lesson." The girl gathered up her books and disappeared into her bedroom.

Selina frowned. Perfect. Alienate the whole family. Why hadn't she kept her big mouth shut?

Celia was blossoming, coming out of herself, but there were still dark times when Selina was certain the child carried some terrible secret burden. "I know that kind of pain, Celia," Selina murmured. "And I'm not going to let you keep it to yourself." Selina herself had no choice; she must bear her secret alone forever. But she was going to see to it that Celia realized whatever was wrong, whatever was bothering her, could be explained, understood, or forgiven if she would just trust someone enough to speak of it.

On the afternoon of the eighth day of Morgan's absence Selina stood in front of a small pen in one of the larger corrals feeding fresh hay to the now fully recovered offspring of King Patrick. But even the sight of the frisky calf did nothing to buoy her flagging spirits.

Celia had been moping about since dawn, beginning to share in Selina's fear that Kincaid had ridden off to join the roundup without leaving word for either one of them. "If that man has dared leave his daughter behind . . ."

The sound of hoofbeats snagged her attention. As if on cue, Morgan rode into the yard. Her heart thudded just to see him. She hoped he had forgiven her, but his brusque manner proved quickly that he had not.

He didn't even bother to dismount, but rode the stallion over to where she stood. He tipped his hat with forced politeness. "Mrs. Kincaid."

She straightened, managing a wan smile. "Celia is going to be happy to see—"

He cut her off. "I'll be gone a month, maybe longer. I've hired a few extra men. They're already out on the range. You and Celia can manage for yourselves for a while. I'll send back a man to stay until roundup's over." He wheeled the horse to ride out.

"Papa!" Celia cried, rushing out of the barn. "Papa . . ."

Selina could tell Morgan wanted to leave, but the plea in Celia's hazel eyes stayed him. He dismounted.

Celia was suddenly bashful. "Papa, didn't you come back to . . . to take me with you?"

Morgan lifted his hat to run a hand through his dark hair. "Not this time, sweetheart. I'm sorry."

"But you promised!" the girl shrieked, her normal reserve with her father crumbling in the face of being denied something so important. "What did I do wrong? What did I do? I left the pinto horse alone!" She was sobbing.

Morgan gripped her arms gently, his tone soothing. Selina sensed an undercurrent of regret in his voice. "It can't be helped, Celia. Not this time. I'm sorry." He shifted his head in Selina's direction, though he did not look at her. "You'll just have to stay behind this year."

Selina understood it then. Her lips thinning, she marched over to him. "You're leaving her here to keep me company, aren't you?"

He still didn't look at her. "You can't stay here alone for a month. Celia knows her way around the ranch better than you do."

Selina could see the conflicting emotions playing across Celia's expressive face. The child wanted desperately to accompany her father, but she didn't want to hurt Selina's feelings by saying she didn't want to stay with her. Distraught, the girl raced back to the barn and disappeared inside.

Selina planted her hands on her hips. "I hardly think it makes sense to put the responsibility for my security on the shoulders of a ten-year-old."

Anger flashed briefly across Morgan's face, but he wrestled it down to speak in that maddeningly toneless voice she had come to know too well. "One of my men will be making sure you're safe. If I had any worries, I certainly wouldn't leave Celia. I just thought, since I brought you here for her sake, that you should be spending time with her."

"This roundup is all she's been talking about."

"There'll be other roundups." He gathered the stallion's reins.

Selina shot a glance toward the barn. Celia was peeking out from the edge of the huge doorway. She ducked back inside, but not before Selina had caught the imploring look in her sad eyes. Resolved, Selina turned back to Morgan. "What if I went along?"

"Absolutely not."

"I wouldn't get in the way. And it would let Celia . . ."

"I said no."

"Why?"

"It's no place for a woman."

"No place for *me*. Isn't that more accurate? You don't want me there."

"All right," he snarled, the sudden contempt in his face shaking her to her toes. "I don't want you there."

If Celia's happiness had not been at stake, Selina could not have challenged that hate-filled look. But because it was, she pressed on. "You asked me to come to Wolf Trail because of your daughter. I'm telling you that it is desperately important to her that she go with you on this roundup."

"Son of a—" He slapped his hat against his thigh, the motion so sudden the stallion snorted and shied.

Selina saw her advantage and rushed on. "I've camped before. I know what it's like to sleep outdoors. I can cook, wash clothes, whatever's needed."

"A roundup is not a camping trip!"

"Damn you!" she cried. "This is not about roundups or camping or anything else. This is about our wedding night."

"Don't." His jaw tightened. "Don't! That night was a mistake—a lesson I'd already learned. I just forgot it for a while. I told you it won't happen again."

"Fine. Then it's settled."

"What's settled?"

"Since nothing more is going to happen between us, I don't see any problem about my going along. You won't even know I'm there."

He looked at the barn and back again. He swore. "Fine. Come along. Let Celia come along. But if I hear even one comment about the heat, the bugs, the weather, the snakes . . ."

"I like snakes."

"Why doesn't that surprise me?" He stomped toward his horse. "I'll sleep in the bunkhouse. Both of you be ready to ride at dawn."

Chapter 13

Her mouth set in a grim line, Selina jerked the coiled lariat out from under the fifty-pound sack of flour in the back of the Wolf Trail supply wagon. Looping the stiff hemp over her shoulder, she trod toward the makeshift rope corral that held the extra mounts brought along by every ranch involved in the roundup.

She'd been doing her best to make herself useful in the three weeks since she and Celia had joined the roundup here in Flatwillow valley. She had spent much of her time helping Stewie with the cooking chores. Still, she'd also made a point of acquainting herself with the more adventurous tasks involved in herding together the thousands of cattle that had wintered on the vast range of the Judith Basin. New calves and mavericks had to be sorted and separated; questions—sometimes disputes—of ownership settled among the half dozen outfits involved in the massive operation; then the bellowing beasts were wrestled to the ground and their hides were seared with a red-hot iron brand.

The call of "roll out" would come before dawn, and there would be no turning in until well past dusk. But Selina never tired of watching dozens of bowlegged, stiff-jawed cowboys wrangle with the intrinsic bedlam of reluctant cattle, dust, heat, and the constant stench of singed hair.

The work was hard, the conditions primitive, the privacy all but nonexistent. Yet she reveled in being here. So far removed from any trappings of civilization, she could even imagine herself safe from Marelda. Even the fact that the Lazy C crew was on hand did not dampen her enthusiasm, since Clay Prescott so far had been wise enough to keep a respectful distance. The idyll of her time in Flatwillow could have been perfect. She let out a wistful sigh. Could have been. If not for Morgan Kincaid.

Each day of these three weeks she had endured the man's pointed ostracism. On those rare occasions when she'd actually seen him, his only acknowledgment of her existence had been a cold, silent stare. And though invisibility was precisely what she had promised him, she could tolerate his ignoring her no longer. He was going to notice her today. Or else.

She marched toward Moondust, tethered under a sprawling willow several yards from the other horses. "It's you and me today, girl," Selina said, patting the mare's silky neck. "We'll show him, won't we?"

Quickly, before her courage fled, Selina saddled the mare and hooked the rope over the saddlehorn.

"Goin' somewhere, Mrs. Kincaid?"

Selina whirled to see Chino striding toward her. Tiny dust clouds billowed alongside him as he slapped dirt from his leather chaps. Concern was etched on his swarthy features.

"I'm going riding," she said, not quite meeting his eyes.

The look of concern escalated.

She turned back toward the horse.

"Can't let you do that, Mrs. Kincaid."

"And why not?"

"Promised Morgan I'd look out for you."

Her heart took a funny leap. "He asked you to do that?"

"Not exactly."

She knew she had not hidden her disappointment. "You have your responsibilities with the roundup, Chino. I don't believe I'm one of them."

He stepped close to wrap one gloved hand around Moondust's trailing reins. "I know I haven't had a chance to talk to you much, ma'am. But maybe we should take a little time right now?"

"I don't think that would be a very good idea."

He went on as though she hadn't spoken. "I was real glad to see Morgan bring you and Ceecy along."

"He was coerced." She held her hand out for the reins. "If you'll excuse me . . ."

Chino frowned. "I guess I ain't goin' about this right. You just tell me to mind my own business, and I will. But I really would like to talk to you."

She dropped her hand back to her side.

"I'm not askin' for the particulars, ma'am, Mrs.—"

"Abby."

"Abby." He smiled. "I had a feelin' things weren't exactly rose blossoms between you and Morgan. He's been touchier than a caged bull in a corral full of . . ." He coughed. "Sorry."

"Maybe I should have someone take me back to the ranch house. At least then Morgan might come to camp often enough to spend some time with Celia. She was so looking forward to all this."

"Ceecy's doin' just fine and you know it. Every manjack around has taken her under his wing. She's havin' the time of her life. As for Morgan, he's been around."

"The camp? Recently?" Selina herself hadn't laid eyes on him for ten days. Even then he'd been on horseback, barking out orders about keeping a better tally of Wolf Trail beef.

"You may not know where he is, Abby. But he knows where you are all the time."

She bristled. "Because he has you spying on me?" The hurt look that came into Chino's brown eyes made her instantly contrite. Yet the hurt was mixed with more than a little embarrassment.

He tugged gently on Moondust's reins, leading the mare away from the camp. Selina had no choice but to trail along beside him.

"There's somethin' you gotta understand about Morgan, Abby," he said. "If you didn't matter to him, he wouldn't be nearly so ornery."

"The man hates me, Chino."

"No. If he hated you, he would be polite."

"That doesn't make sense."

"Neither does your goin' off with that rope you got slung over Moondust's saddlehorn. What were you planning to round up anyway?"

She felt her face heat.

"You don't have to throw a steer to get him to notice you."

"I couldn't care less if he notices me!" She tried to sound indignant but knew she had failed miserably.

"I got me a reputation as a real good scout, ma'am," Chino drawled. "That means I know how to read sign." He angled a glance down at her. "I've seen the way you look at him."

"I can't imagine what you're talking about."

"It's all right. Your secret's safe with me."

She blanched. "What secret?"

"That you're in love with him."

She stopped dead. "That is the most absurd, ludicrous, outrageous falsehood I have ever heard in my life!"

He chuckled. "You're two of a kind."

"That man and I? Alike? That . . . that self-absorbed, short-tempered—"

He gripped her shoulders, his face now deadly earnest. "I've told you this before, but I'll say it again. Morgan's my best friend. I love him like a brother, and I want him to be happy. But right now, he's hurting. Morgan can be mean as a snake, when he's hurting."

"Well I'm tired of being the one he sinks his fangs into."

"So bite him back."

"Do what?"

"Quit tryin' to be nice to him."

"But you said . . ."

"If he acts like a jackass, treat him like a jackass."

"I thought he was a snake."

He laughed. "I do like you, Abby. I really do." He lifted the lariat from the saddlehorn. "So I'm sure you'll understand why I'm not going to let you do anything stupid."

"There are other ropes."

"Abby . . ." He wasn't laughing anymore.

"All right. I just thought if I brought in a lost steer or something he might at least thank me."

"And if you came back lookin' like Two Fingers, he'd have my head on a plate. You wouldn't want that to happen, now, would you?"

She pretended to think it over, then had to laugh herself. "I'm glad you're here, Chino. Morgan doesn't intimidate me quite so much when I see that at least he has the good sense to have a best friend like you."

"Just believe me when I say he cares a helluva lot more than he lets on. He's just gun-shy about trustin', that's all. Lenore cut him deep."

"I understand that," she murmured. "But Lenore was hurting a little herself. She didn't want to be here."

"Morgan told you that?" Chino looked doubtful.

Selina brought herself up short, frantically searching her memory. Then she remembered the day by the cottonwood. "Actually," she said, "it was the day he took me riding. The day you told him he'd been acting like a . . . a son of a bitch."

"Then you two are getting along even better than I thought," Chino said cheerfully, handing her the mare's reins. "I'm gonna do a little trustin' myself. I trust you're not goin' off to do anything foolish."

"I promise."

"Promise me something else?"

"If I can."

"That you'll talk to him."

"He avoids me, remember?"

"Pin him down. Get him to admit whatever's stuck in his craw this time."

She fingered the reins. "I'm afraid I already know."

"Then get it talked out."

"I doubt talking can fix this, Chino."

"You won't know unless you try."

Sudden tears pricked her eyelids. "I may have hurt him more than . . ." She squeezed her eyes shut. "He won't talk to me, Chino. He won't."

"Then we'll force his hand." The foreman's face was suddenly alive with mischief. "Morgan's due back late tonight. When he gets here, I'll wake you. There'll be a full moon. You ride about a mile west to that big circle of boulders. Lay down on the ground like Moondust threw you."

Selina started to protest, but Chino plunged on. "I'll see to it Morgan finds you. Then he'll have to talk to you."

"He'd probably get Moondust to finish the job."

He ignored that. "Will you try it?"

Her whole plot to rope a calf had been to gain Morgan's undivided attention. How could she refuse a seemingly less dangerous plan with the same end? She nodded, then dared allow a spark of hope to kindle inside her.

For the remainder of the day she went through the motions, giving Celia a distracted English lesson, helping Stewie with supper—wishing it were nightfall. Even the part of the day she enjoyed most, when the wranglers gathered around the evening campfire to swap tall tales, palled as she awaited Chino's signal to ride out.

"I branded a calf today," Celia was saying, a proud grin on her dirt-streaked face as she sat cross-legged in front of the crackling flames.

"Good for you!" Selina said, forcing her concentration back to the conversation at hand.

Charlie was playing a mournful tune on his harmonica while Two Fingers Pete took his turn at trying to top an outrageous tale about a vengeful ten-foot grizzly told complete with bloodcurdling sound effects by a wildly animated Stubby. Only Selina's finger jabbed into Stubby's ample ribs convinced him to give a wide-eyed Celia a broad wink, or the child would never have been able to sleep again in her life.

"I can go one better than that." Pete snorted disdainfully as he rolled a cheroot. "Roundup always puts me in mind of an outfit I worked for down Wyoming way a few years back. Neighbor of my boss had the most peculiar cows. Every spring them fertile little ladies would be givin' birth to twins, even triplets. Time after time. It was plumb miraculous."

"Morgan should look into getting cows like that," Selina put in eagerly. "Think of the extra profits per animal."

"Oh, yeah, think of it," Pete said blandly, scratching a lucifer on his backside. He lit the cheroot, took a deep drag, then continued: "What was even more amazin' was at the same time the neighbor's cows would be so blessed, my boss's cattle was barren a lot of the time."

Selina felt herself blush as she started to catch on.

"Well," Pete continued, "me and the boys went over and had a little chat with this gent, real personal like. And you know, his cows stopped havin' twins and triplets after that."

He grinned at Selina, who responded with a good-natured laugh. "You're a good sport, ma'am," he said.

"That's me, all right," she said wryly. "You know, I have a little story to tell myself."

"Oh, please, do, Abby," Celia cried. "We'd love to hear it."

The cowboys looked dubious.

"It all began in Mexico," Selina said, allowing an edge of mystery to come into her voice. She wasn't going to let these wranglers better her. "I was maybe twelve years old at the time. My parents and I were exploring the site of some Aztec ruins. People living in the area had warned us that the surrounding caves were haunted, but of course my father didn't believe in such nonsense. Still, to placate me, we each took turns standing watch while the other two slept.

"It was past midnight, and I was on guard. That's when it started. The most hideous wailing

I'd ever heard. And it was coming from the caves. I woke my parents at once. By then the wails had turned to screams. I wondered if maybe the caves were some secret portal . . . to hell."

The cowboys' jaws dropped.

"A strange leathery fluttering began then, seeming to come at us from all sides. We left everything behind and ran. I stumbled and fell to the ground, certain I was about to be eaten alive."

"What happened?" Celia demanded.

"I blacked out. When I woke up, my mother was trying to get me to drink a little water. The sun was coming up, but the sky was still dark." Her serious tone shifted, her lips curving into an impish smile. "It seems that thousands of bats left the cave to feed every night, then returned to roost for the day. Papa said it was the wind whistling through the tunnels that made those horrid sounds. We all felt pretty foolish."

The cowboys pshawed loudly.

"But then," Selina continued with a twinkle in her eye she allowed only Celia to see, "even Papa could never explain the imprint of a monstrous clawed hand on a canteen he'd left inside the cave."

Stubby cleared his throat nervously. Pete's cheroot dangled in the corner of his mouth until it burned his lip. Stewie swallowed the tobacco he'd forgotten to chew for the last five minutes. Even

Charles seemed reluctant to head out for his turn to ride night herd.

With a triumphant grin Selina bid them all good night and marched off toward her own blankets. She was passing the supply wagon when she sensed a shadowed presence beside it. She started. Morgan stood barely three paces from her, his hooded gaze unreadable. Then abruptly he spun away and disappeared into the night.

Morgan settled himself against the cold stone at his back, trying to fix his attention on the rising moon, but nothing could snag his attention for long. His thoughts continually shifted to the chestnut-haired woman who was his wife.

He had hoped staying away from her would help. But it hadn't. Couldn't. And now seeing her tonight holding his men spellbound with her ghostly tale of creatures in the night, he could only marvel again at why such a woman would need to resort to the mail to find a husband.

Three weeks she'd been on roundup, and not once had he heard an angry word or complaint by her or about her from anyone.

"She sure is somethin', eh, boss?" Chino said, ambling up from behind him.

Morgan didn't look up. "Who?"

Chino laughed. "Two of a kind. You know damned well who I mean. I never seen the like. Abby's bug-bit, saddle-sore, and dusty as the Cimarron Trail, but she's always got a smile for every-one. Lenore would've committed murder by now."

"I don't recall asking your opinion."

"You never do. 'Bout women."

"You're such an expert."

"I've known my share. But I didn't track you down to talk about my love life. I think it's time we talked about yours."

"You're my foreman and my friend, but even you can push me too far, Chino."

"Somebody's gotta do it. You ain't gettin' no-where yourself."

"I'm not going to say this again—mind your own business."

"Uh-huh. So how many calves you think we got here so far?"

Morgan relaxed. "Probably three thousand. We'll likely double that before we're done."

"That means Wolf Trail'll be runnin' about twenty-five thousand head this year."

"Think we're overstocked?"

"I don't know. You've said it yourself some-times."

Morgan studied the sea of beef, listening to low-ing cattle, the steady, lulling tones of the night herders singing familiar trail songs. "That's Celia's future out there, Chino. I've got everything I own tied up in those cows."

"Those new Oregon shorthorns are lookin' real good. Better beef."

"But they're not as range-savvy as the Texas stock. I just hope . . ." He let the words trail off.

"It'll work out. Just like things will work out with Abby."

Morgan shook his head. "You're about as subtle as a dust storm, you know that?"

"At least your temper's settled back to the simmerin' stage."

"You got a point to all this?"

"She's your match. You just won't admit it." He started back toward camp. "Ceecy likes her quite a bit too. I mean, you do care about the woman, don't you, boss? Just a little?"

"I feel responsible for her," he said grimly. "That's all."

"Sure. Well, I was just wonderin'. It is pretty dark."

"What the hell does that mean?"

"Nothin'. Just that it's dark, and I seen Abby ridin' west on Moondust about ten minutes ago."

Morgan shot to his feet. "She did *what?* Why the hell didn't you tell me? She can't be out there alone!" He caught Chino's arm. "Why didn't you stop her?"

"I tried. She seemed pretty upset about something. Said she couldn't talk to me about it—that it was private." Chino gave Morgan an exaggerated shrug. "I told her to be careful."

Morgan swore, then straightened, eyeing Chino

with sudden suspicion. "Just how hard did you try to stop her?"

"What did you want me to do? Put a rope on her?"

"If that's what it took, yes."

"She's your wife, not mine."

"So you thought it best if I went after her?"

"Seemed more proper somehow."

Morgan continued swearing as he headed for his mount.

Behind him, Chino grinned.

The ground was cold. Selina stared at the full moon far above, wondering how much longer she should lie here and wait. What if Chino hadn't convinced Morgan to follow her?

Moondust nuzzled Selina's throat. In spite of the dreariness of her mood, Selina giggled. "Go away, girl," she whispered. "You're going to spoil everything." She gave the horse's head a gentle shove and the mare moved off a few paces to tug on a clump of buffalo grass.

Selina lay still another few minutes. "He's not coming." She sighed. "Why should he bother? The man despises me." She shuddered, surprised by the depth of the melancholy that sifted through her. Why did Morgan Kincaid's opinion of her matter so much? Certainly his patent dislike enhanced her chances of being set on her own again at the end of the summer. But there was more to it than that.

She refused to consider how much more, telling herself she was already twice the fool. First, to care what he thought of her at all. And second, to be lying on the ground in the middle of nowhere waiting for him to effect a rescue she didn't even need.

She was about to get up when she heard a twig snap. Her heart leaped. He did come! Mustering her courage, she moaned softly.

"My God, are you hurt?" a husky male voice called.

Her heart froze.

Clay.

She struggled to sit up, her limbs stiff from the cold. "I'm fine. Fine."

He came over at once and gripped her shoulders, restraining her gently. "Take it easy, you might have a broken bone or something."

"How did you . . . ?"

"I saw you ride out. I got worried, so I followed you. Did you get thrown?"

"Yes . . . no . . ." She couldn't bring herself to blame Moondust. "I . . . I was walking. I tripped." She tried to push Prescott away, his nearness reminding her all too clearly of the time he had kissed her in the barn.

He seemed to guess her thoughts. "I won't hurt you."

"Then let me go."

"As soon as I'm certain you're all right."

She could hardly tell him she'd set up this entire

scene to entice Morgan to her side. Uneasy, she lay back.

He was solicitous, but remote, as he tested her arms and legs for motion. "I . . . it was no accident that I saw you ride out, Ber—, ah, Mrs. Kincaid. I've been wanting to get you alone."

She fought down a sudden rush of fear, her eyes widening. "You let me up this minute or I'll scream!"

"Damn." He held up a hand, rushing to explain. "That's not the way I meant that. It's just that you're always with Ceecy or Chino or one of the hands. I wanted . . . needed to see you alone. So I could apologize. For everything."

In the dim light of the moon she searched his face. "You mean that, don't you?"

"I've been a bastard, I know. Morgan and I haven't exactly been friends. But that doesn't give me the right to use you to get back at him."

"He told me about you and Lenore." She doubted he could miss the censure in her voice.

He shifted uncomfortably. "A mistake I'm not proud of. She was lonely and angry. She turned to me because I was here. And because, like her, sometimes I didn't think I belonged in this wilderness either." His face twisted. "She just wanted Morgan to pay attention to her."

"He loved her," Selina defended, though she knew it wasn't true.

"No. He cared about her. But he didn't love her."

"Well, why should he?" she shot back. "She turned her back on him after his accident."

Prescott's smile was sad, and she had the oddest impression he felt sorry for her. But she told herself that was absurd.

"It wasn't the scar," he said. "He never accepted her loving him. She told me once it was like he had a wall between himself and the whole world. The scar was just a good excuse for them both."

Selina was stunned by his insight. "You don't hate him at all, do you?"

"Let's get you back to camp, shall we?"

Clay Prescott was finished with his revelations for the night. Leaning heavily against him, Selina allowed him to help her to her feet. She must have lain wrong on her right ankle, for it was numb, balking whenever she tried to put her weight on it.

"You two been meeting like this often?"

Selina gasped, jerking up to stare into the glowering countenance of Morgan Kincaid. Clay's arms were still firmly twined around her.

"She's hurt, Morg," Clay said quickly.

"I'm sure." He turned to leave.

"Morgan!" Selina cried. "Please . . ."

He continued walking, heading toward his stallion some fifty feet away.

"Blast it all!" she spat. "Why didn't we hear him coming?"

"We were preoccupied," Clay said. "I'm sorry. I didn't mean to make things worse between you."

"Worse?"

"It's no secret he stays away from you," he said, not unsympathetically. "He's no better with you than he was with Lenore."

"You'd better go."

Clay hesitated. "You sure?"

Selina followed his gaze to where Morgan stood unmoving beside the Appaloosa. "I'll be all right."

Clay released her and headed for his horse. She watched his gaze shift from her to Morgan and back again, as though debating whether or not it was really wise for him to leave her alone with Morgan. Then Clay mounted and rode out. He did not look back.

Selina waited until the darkness swallowed him, then limped painfully toward Morgan. "Clay followed me out here." Drat! Why had that sounded so defensive?

"I didn't ask."

She stiffened. "No, you wouldn't." She whirled toward her mare. She'd only taken three steps when her ankle gave way. She cried out. Strong arms circled her before she collapsed. She stared up at that rigid jaw.

"Did he kiss you?" he hissed, his breath hot against her cheek. "Did he turn your blood to fire?

Did he . . . ?" His lips came down, hard, bruising, his hands roving the curves of her body—roughly, insultingly.

She didn't fight him. Neither did she respond. She had to know how far he would go. Just that abruptly he stopped, shoving her back. His whole body quivered as he visibly drew rein on the rage that had spurred his lust.

She straightened her clothes, trembling. "That was the behavior I accused you of on our wedding night. I was wrong then. But I'm not wrong now. That repulses me."

He stared at his hands as though not believing himself what he had just done.

"I know how it must have looked," she said, fighting back tears of embarrassment as well as sheer frustration. Things could have been entirely different if only Morgan had arrived ahead of Clay. "I promise you he was only concerned that I might have been hurt. Nothing else happened."

"Of course not," he sneered.

Blast the man! Chino was right. Morgan wasn't capable of seeing anyone else's pain when he was so busily nursing his own. "Is this the same benefit of the doubt you gave Lenore?" If she kept him angry, perhaps she could also keep him honest.

"Don't." His voice carried a note of warning.

"Or didn't you really care what she did?"

The fury in him was awful to see, and yet she was able to detach herself from it. Just as on their wedding night, she sensed that other part of him, the hidden part that wanted to be held, that hurting, aching side of him that felt betrayed—no matter how unwarranted—at finding her with Clay. Just as he had found Lenore with Clay. "You knew about their affair and you did nothing to stop it. Why?"

"Get on your horse and get back to camp."

"Not until we sort some things out between us." He might never have admitted he loved Lenore, but Selina perceived for the first time that he had. Or he at least had needed desperately for her to love him. And when she had ceased doing so, he had been hurt and confused. He blamed the scar, but she had to wonder if somewhere inside him he believed he deserved her betrayal, even drove her to it.

"There's nothing to sort out. You have already made your feelings perfectly clear." The undisguised pain in his voice told more than the words. He turned and stalked toward a small boulder. She followed, still limping slightly, but feeling the blood beginning to circulate once again in her foot.

He sat down, his manner rigid, unyielding.

She bit her lip, trying to decide what to say. She dare not rouse his suspicions, yet neither could she have him go on tormenting himself that he was at fault for their wedding night. Haltingly, the words came. "I . . . it wasn't you, Morgan. It was nothing you did or said."

"I don't want to hear this."

"Yes, you do. You want to know that it was my doing, not yours."

"Oh, no, madam. I wouldn't think of blaming . . ."

"Dammit, Morgan! Shut up, and listen to me. For one damned minute, *listen!*"

His lips thinned dangerously, but he said no more.

"I was scared to death that night. But you couldn't see it. I think because maybe you were a little scared yourself." He looked away, and she knew she was saying it all wrong. Damn, what was she going to do? How could she convince him without telling him about Gideon?

Tears streamed unheeded down her cheeks. "I . . . it was after my husband died." The words began to tumble out, truth melding with lie until she didn't know or care what she was saying. All that mattered was that he believe her, believe too that she would never have deliberately hurt him.

"I was visiting a friend. It was dark. I walked past an alley. A hand . . . a hand . . ." She was in Gideon's bedroom, reliving it all. "He grabbed me. He threw me down; tore off my clothes. I tried to scream. He hit me. He was so big. I couldn't move . . . I couldn't move . . . He . . . he . . . oh, God—" She was sobbing.

Morgan's arms were around her, holding her fiercely against him, his words indistinct but profoundly gentle. Only the warmth of his sheltering body prevented her from sliding over the edge of hysteria.

"I'm sorry, Morgan. I'm so sorry." She said it over and over, knowing part of her was apologizing for what she could not explain. That no matter how much was truth, she was still lying to him, and because of that using him.

His lips brushed her forehead, her cheeks. "Don't cry, Abby. Don't cry. You're safe here. You're safe." He held her, rocked her. No wonder she'd had the look of a hunted fawn. Raped. A flood tide of rage ripped through him, rage at least partly directed at himself. He had indeed seen her pain, but he'd ignored it to nurture his own. "Is this bastard in jail?"

"I . . . he's dead. A man . . . a cowboy happened by. There was a gunfight." God, where was this fantasy coming from? In spite of his hold on her she began to tremble violently. "Can you forgive me?"

"I should be asking you that." He shifted his palms to cup her face, his thumbs brushing away the tears that glistened on her cheeks.

"You didn't know," she said.

"I could've asked, instead of bullying you." He trailed his fingertips from her temples to her chin. "I just assumed your reluctance was because of . . . my looks."

"No. Never that, Morgan. I promise you. It was
the . . . the intimacy itself. I still don't think—"

"Hush. I won't put any more pressure on you,
Abby. You tell me when you're ready. Then and
only then I swear to you I'll make you forget that
night ever happened." A sudden paralyzing doubt
swept through him, which he tried unsuccessfully
to shake off. What if he was as clumsily inept as
the first time?

"I don't know if I'll ever be ready, Morgan. I
just don't know." She was sniffling, and her vanity
was returning with her composure. She must look
awful. Funny she should care.

"I'll never force you," he said.

She looked up, puzzled by the tentative note
that had crept into his voice. But she dismissed it,
realizing he already had to be distressingly uncomfortable being so open with her. And as though he
had reached the very limit of being thus exposed,
he drew in a deep breath and said, "Thank you for
telling me. I know it was difficult. I'm sure you'll
agree it'll be best for now if we keep things status
quo between us. Strictly business." He let go of
her, seeming to deliberately put distance between
them. "We'd best head . . ." He stopped, his attention caught by a horse and rider thundering toward them.

Chino.

Selina felt a nameless fear clutch at her. Chino
would never have come here without a desperate

reason. As she watched, he hauled back on the reins, nearly setting his roan on its haunches. His words chilled her to her soul.

"Rustlers! Pete's dead."

Chapter 14

Dawn bled a dull red across the distant horizon. Selina prayed it was no omen as she urged Moondust into a gallop. The mare's hooves echoed the sharp staccato of gunfire ahead. A cold terror pulsed through her as she watched Morgan and Chino drive their mounts into the teeth of the battle. From what she could see, a half-dozen wranglers were firing into a boulder-strewn hillock, their own prone positions behind three-foot-high clumps of sagebrush precarious at best. Rising puffs of gunsmoke signaled return fire from at least four separate positions on the hill.

Selina reined in, her hand flying to her mouth as Morgan slid from his saddle, rushing toward a body that lay unmoving in the grass. Gently he turned the man over. Pete's chest was a mass of blood, his unseeing eyes staring upward at the brightening sky. Selina's stomach lurched, even as an aching sadness swept through her.

She watched Morgan's fists clench, his jaw tighten, and she was suddenly more terrified than she had ever been. Morgan could die here today, just like Pete.

She scrambled from her own saddle. Morgan yanked his rifle from its saddleboot, signaling Chino to circle around to the left. He hunched low, moving right, his attention riveted on the hillock. Heart pounding, Selina scurried after him. Nothing else mattered but knowing he was all right.

A bullet kicked up dirt six feet in front of her. She stopped dead. Morgan whirled, his gaze reflecting first disbelief, then fury. He reached her in three long strides, gripping her elbow, propelling her toward a steer-sized boulder some twenty yards away.

All but slamming her to the earth behind it, he ducked down beside her and snarled, "What the hell do you think you're doing?"

"Following you."

He swore.

"How many rustlers are there?"

He ignored the question, his voice grim. "Keep your head down. Do not move one inch until I personally come here and tell you it's safe."

"Only if you tell me what's happening out there." She wanted some kind of reassurance that he would be safe, though she knew in her heart he could guarantee nothing.

Exasperated, he hissed, "Chino said they hit at dawn. They tried to cut out about three hundred head. Pete caught 'em. He didn't get off a shot." A bullet sent chips of boulder spraying in all directions. Instinctively Selina ducked lower, but a muffled curse from Morgan made her look up. A blade-sharp fragment had raked a shallow gash along the side of his neck.

"You're hurt!" she cried, reaching toward him.

He swiped at the blood, glowering at her. "Do you see why I don't want you here? So help me, Abby, if anything happened to . . ." He sucked in a deep lungful of air, trying, it seemed, to settle his temper to a more workable level. He would need all of his wits about him to battle these outlaws. "I'm going to draw their fire," he said. "You stay the hell behind this rock. Do you understand me?"

She gave him a reluctant nod. She knew he was right, but she didn't like it. From behind the rock she would not be able to tell if he was all right.

"Morgan?" She couldn't let him leave with so much unsaid between them.

"Now what?"

"Be careful."

An unreadable expression skittered across his face before a mask of cold determination settled in. "Count on it."

He fired off two quick shots, then bolted from the security of the rock. Keeping low, he moved forward and to his right, heading toward the next bit of cover.

Selina could see clearly only to the rear. To check on Morgan would mean peering over the boulder. Behind her Wolf Trail and Lazy C wranglers continued to fire up the hill, laying down what she was certain was cover fire for Morgan, who was closest to the rustlers' position.

Clay kept up a steady stream of fire from behind a thick cottonwood, then seemed to grow more selective with his shots, the rifle tracking a steady path from right to left, as though following some movement she couldn't see. He fired again, the sound echoing with a sharp cry of pain. Daring to look, she stared, horrified, as a man tumbled from the boulders, levered himself up, then collapsed forward, his own weapon spilling from his hands as more bullets slammed into his body. His right hand twitched once, twice, as though seeking his gun, then he lay still.

"Three left," she heard Clay shout.

She was a spectator in a most deadly game. More bullets whipped past the rock that sheltered her. More frightening than the possibility of being hit by one of those bullets was the idea that one already could have hit Morgan.

Swallowing hard, she inched to her right, peeking out from behind the boulder. The acrid scent of gunsmoke was now heavy in the morning air. At first she saw nothing but grass and rock. Then she caught a glint of sunlight off something metallic. Her eyes widened. A gun barrel. Scarcely daring to breathe, she watched as the man holding the six-gun darted from rock to rock just yards from where she lay. A glance back down the hill confirmed her fear that none of the wranglers was looking in this direction. With the sun rising behind the hillock, she doubted any of them could even see the outlaw.

The man hadn't noticed her. His attention was riveted farther up the slope. Selina's heart somersaulted in her chest. Morgan! The outlaw would be coming at him from his blind side.

The rustler stilled, sighting his Colt on Morgan's back.

Selina stood, frantic. "Morgan!" she screamed. "Behind you!"

The outlaw whirled, firing a wild shot in her direction. She froze. In the next instant he stood straight up, a shocked expression coming into his eyes; then those eyes held no expression at all as he pitched forward, hitting the ground body-long, rolling limply to slap into the rock behind which Selina stood.

She stared at the lifeless body, heedless of the words Morgan shouted at her. Her stomach heaved. She turned to run, but an arm snaked out and rammed her back against the boulder. She gagged at the rancid smell of sweat and fetid breath.

"Well, well, what have we here?" a strange voice cackled. "It wasn't old Joe's lucky day, but it must be mine."

Selina cried out as the man's iron-hard grip around her middle drove the air from her lungs. She squirmed, kicked, but he held her fast, his stinking breath hot against her ear. "Kick me again, missy, and I'll put a bullet in ya." He jerked her arm behind her, twisting viciously. She couldn't even scream. It hurt too much.

"Drop your guns, gents," the man yelled, holding his gun barrel against Selina's head.

"Do what he says!" Morgan shouted, tossing down his own gun as he closed the distance between himself and the gunman.

"That's far enough," the outlaw growled.

Rage contorted Morgan's features. Selina wondered if it was meant as much for her as for the outlaw.

"Everybody out where I can see 'em," the man said. "Hands grabbin' sky."

One by one the ranch hands stepped from behind their cover, hands in the air. "You, too, mister," the outlaw said, glowering at Morgan.

Slowly Morgan raised his hands. Selina could feel his fury mount. If only she hadn't followed him . . .

"Come on out, Bull!" the rustler called. "We can ride out of here free and clear. I got us a ticket."

The last outlaw lumbered from behind a boulder

near the crest of the hill, a thickset man with
bushy eyebrows.

"Get the horses," the one holding Selina ordered.

"Sure thing, Baines," Bull said. He seized the
reins of two mounts and led them over to his com-
rade.

"We're going for a little ride, missy," Baines
sneered, licking his lips.

"Let her go," Morgan said, his voice deadly
calm. "You and your friend can ride out. Just let
her go."

"You expect me to believe that? We'd have more
bullets in our backs than you got beeves in this
valley." He chuckled. "Now, don't you worry,
mister, we'll be real nice to her. Real nice." The
man's hand tracked upward. Selina struggled. Her
eyes burned. She knew she was going to die.

"Drop the gun." Chino's voice came from somewhere behind her. Morgan had kept the outlaws'
attention as Chino had made his way around the
hill.

Too late, Bull tried to bring his gun up. Chino
shot him. The man sprawled in the dirt.

Baines held savagely to Selina, backing against
his horse, cursing. "She's dead!" he shrieked. "One
more shot by any of you and she's dead!"

Selina could feel his head snapping back and
forth as he tried to keep an eye on both Chino and
Morgan.

"I mean it!" Baines pulled back the hammer on the six-gun. "I'll kill her. Take her with me."

"Don't hurt her." Morgan held up a hand, gesturing for the others to stay back. But slowly he reached for his own gun, lying on the ground some four feet away.

"Leave it be!" Baines shouted. He took a shot at Morgan and missed.

Chino must have seen his chance. Selina heard him, felt Baines whirl to face him. In that instant Chino hesitated—held his fire, she knew, because of her.

Baines didn't hesitate, taking dead aim. Chino fell to his knees.

Selina screamed. Twisting, she raked her fingernails into the man's face, tearing, scratching. She flung herself away from him and stumbled toward Chino, vaguely aware that Morgan had fired his gun. She heard two shots. The outlaw grunted, then crumpled.

Chino lay on his side, holding his hand over the gaping wound in his abdomen. He bit off a grunt of pain as she pulled him against her, sobbing. His dark eyes were wide, gentle.

"Take care of Morgan, Abby. Take care . . ." He coughed blood, his body sagging limply against her.

She shook him, disbelieving, then stroked a hand along the side of his face. "Chino?" she whimpered. "Chino, oh, God!" She cried out, a wrenching, keening sound. "Chino! No! Please, Chino, no!" She sat there, rocking him, sobbing, sobbing.

"Abby, Abby, come on." It was Morgan, urging her to her feet. "There's nothing you can do. He's dead. Let him go."

"No!" She jerked away from him. "He can't be dead. He can't . . . he can't!" Her whole body shook. "It's my fault. My fault."

Clay was there, holding a gun on the wounded Baines. "Snake-Eye Jack," he said, drilling an unreadable look at Morgan. "Been a while . . ."

Selina didn't understand, didn't care. She cared only about Chino. He had died saving her life. This man who was like no other she had ever known, and who had become her friend, lay bloodied in her arms.

"Abby," Morgan said, "let go." This time he gently but firmly forced her to her feet. "I want you out of here."

She misunderstood. "Ride away? Don't come back?"

"God, no," he said, pulling her against him. "I mean I want you away from here. We've got graves to dig. Go back to camp. I'd like you to tell Celia about Chino. I don't know how she'd react if it came from me. And I want you to make sure she doesn't come near this place either. We'll hold a service later."

An odd quality in his voice made her look up at him.

She followed his gaze. Some quarter mile distant, the men were gathering under one of the cottonwoods near the creek. Stubby was holding Jack Baines, keeping him on his feet, the wound in his side bleeding freely. Clay was bringing up his sorrel. In his hand he carried a rope.

Selina staggered as comprehension ripped through her.

"Morgan, you can't!"

"Can and will. Now get back to camp."

"It's murder!"

"We have our own law here."

"Take him to Miles City. The sheriff—"

"We take care of our own."

"You were a lawyer," she reasoned desperately. "You swore to uphold the law."

"This *is* the law. You murder someone, you hang."

She backed away. "Sometimes I think I know you, just a little. And then . . . How many men have you hanged, Morgan? Clay was bragging about a triple lynching the day he brought me to Wolf Trail." She grew sick at the memory.

"This will be my first," he said coldly. "But I've looked the other way a time or two. And the rustling and murdering stopped."

"Until today."

He nodded. "And today we stop Jack Baines."

"He killed Pete and Chino, you kill him— What's the difference?"

"You damn well know the difference. You take a life, you forfeit your own."

Selina backed away. She, who was wanted for murder. Would Morgan see her hang as well?

The wranglers were milling about under the cottonwood. It had taken three of them to hoist the wounded Baines onto the horse. He sagged to one side, though he was still conscious.

Selina ran toward them. She couldn't let this happen. This wasn't justice, it was vengeance. Morgan followed, his attitude more cold and remote than she had ever seen. In fact, none of the men seemed even remotely bloodthirsty. In their minds they were performing a civic duty, like shooting a rabid dog.

"Any last words, mister?" Stubby asked.

Baines straightened, not a trace of fear in those cold black eyes. He sneered at Selina. "I'm sorry I didn't get a piece of you first, little lady. Would've been real nice, I'll bet." He spat, his gaze skating contemptuously over the rest of the gathering. "Would've liked to take you all with me to hell."

Morgan jerked his head at Stubby. "Get my wife out of here."

Stubby tried to lead her away. "Please, ma'am. It ain't purty."

She stepped around him. "Morgan, don't do this. Please. I beg you."

"We've got calves to brand," Clay said, nodding to Morgan. "Time's wastin'." For once the two men were in complete agreement.

Morgan stepped forward, gripping his Stetson in his left hand, seeming to look right through her. He slammed the hat against the sorrel's rump. The horse bolted, thundering off. An eerie silence followed as Baines for an instant swung free, then gravity performed its inexorable task. Too late Selina covered her ears against the hideous snapping sound she would never forget as long as she lived. But not once did she take her eyes off Morgan Kincaid.

Interminable minutes passed, the rope swaying, the limb above creaking, an almost tranquil sound. No one made any move to cut down the body. Finally Selina summoned the will to move and stumbled to a boulder, retching. She heard footsteps crunch through the dry brush, following. She didn't have to look to know.

She straightened, defiant. "I watched you when you hanged him, Morgan. Watched that damned blue eye of yours when you slapped the horse out from under him. You didn't feel anything. You don't feel anything for anybody."

Whatever he had been going to say was lost, a look of grim acceptance settling over him. She whirled away and rode back to camp alone to find Celia. Together they sat for hours, comforting one another.

"Chino was my friend," Celia said. "He was never mad at me. Never once. Not even the time I washed his saddle in the horse trough. It was a surprise for his birthday."

Selina hugged the child fiercely. "I'll never forget him either."

It was after dark when Celia finally fell asleep. Only then did Selina ride back to the battle site. She sat alone on a boulder, staring at two mounds of freshly dug earth. Pete, Chino, side by side. Another four graves were set some distance away.

Her thoughts drifted to Pete with his shy smile and tall tales. And Chino, who'd made her feel as though she belonged here from the first, made her believe she could reach the frozen heart of Morgan Kincaid.

Take care of him. "How can I, Chino?" she said aloud, weeping. "He doesn't want me to, doesn't want anyone to."

She started toward the grave, then stopped when she caught the sound of nearby footfalls. She waited, watching. Morgan. He gave no indication he was aware of her. He hunched down, head bent, gripping the wooden cross that marked Chino's grave.

Her shoulders sagged. It wasn't that he didn't care, but that he cared too much. And he was terrified someone would find out. Her heart ached.

She considered returning to camp. Then she recalled Chino's final request. Resolved, she walked over to the grave. Morgan looked up, startled.

An awkward silence followed. Finally Selina hunkered down beside him. "Last night was Chino's idea, you know."

Morgan cleared his throat, swiping self-consciously at the tears on his right cheek. "What are you talking about?"

"He told me to ride to the boulders and pretend to have fallen off my horse. He said he would send you to save me." Her voice quavered, but it felt good to remember, to talk about him.

Her words at least brought a ghost of a smile to Morgan's lips. "I thought it seemed a bit too convenient."

"He loved you."

He shifted uncomfortably. "I saved his life."

"You think that's why he was your friend? Don't you think anyone can care about you just because you're you?"

"Why don't you turn in. It's late."

She picked up a clod of dirt, crumbling it between her fingers. "I'm so sorry, Morgan. You don't know how—"

"If anyone's to blame, it's me."

"No. If I hadn't—"

"Two years ago," he continued softly, as though she hadn't spoken, "I caught a man rustling Wolf Trail beef. Chino and Pete were there. They were all for hangin' him. But that rustler got down on his knees, telling me how he had a starving wife and six kids. I didn't exactly believe him. But I let him go after he gave me his word he'd leave the territory." He looked at her. "That man was Jack Baines."

She let out a shaky breath. "People live whole lifetimes of 'what if's,' Morgan. Heaven knows I would change what I did this morning. And there are certainly other things in my life I would do differently."

"Like maybe not answer a certain letter?"

"Like our wedding night," she said quietly, then turned and walked slowly back to her horse.

He didn't follow.

She rode back to camp alone.

Chapter 15

Selina huddled in her blankets, afraid to stay awake, afraid to sleep, her thoughts consumed by the day's horrors. She had watched Chino die and had seen a man hang. Again and again she heard that hideous crack of bone, saw the man dangling lifelessly in the breeze.

And then it wasn't Snake-Eye Jack. It was herself, and it was Morgan slapping the horse out from under her.

"You're guilty."

"I didn't kill Gideon!"

"The law says you did. And I'm the law here."

She flung back the blankets and stood up. It was useless. She would not sleep this night. Striding over to Moondust, she gripped the mare's mane and pulled herself up. Twenty-four hours ago—a lifetime—she had ridden off, praying Chino's plan would bring Morgan to her side.

Now Chino was dead, and Morgan was more distant than ever.

Last night she had invented a lie layered with truth. And now that Morgan knew she had been raped, he still wouldn't come to her. His aloofness brought with it a pain different from any she had suffered at Gideon's hands. She had hated Gideon; despised him with every ounce of her being. Yet in a very real way he could abuse her body, but in the end he had had no power to hurt her spirit.

Morgan Kincaid had that power. And right now she was hurting more than she ever had in her life.

She slammed her heels into the mare's sides, seized by an overwhelming urge to run.

"Abby!"

Morgan's shout startled her. She hadn't seen him, but obviously he'd seen her. She put Moondust into a gallop. The mare's mane whipped back, lashing at her face. Selina bent low, urging her faster still.

In the darkness she didn't see the patch of brambles until it was too late. Moondust veered violently sideways. Selina tried to hold her balance, but couldn't, and felt herself catapulting through the air. The ground came up hard, slamming the air from her body.

She tried to rise.

"Don't move!" She heard Morgan's shout; heard the Appaloosa thunder to a halt nearby.

"Lie still," he called, leaping from the saddle. "Dammit, Abby, lie *still*."

She slapped at the brambles, feeling them tearing into the fabric of her shirt, the flesh of her arms. She fought harder to gain her feet.

Then he was there, holding her down, pinning her arms to her sides.

"Leave me alone!" she screamed.

"You're going to tear us both to bits. Lie still."

She clawed at him; slapped him. "Leave me be, damn you!"

He swore again, jerking her wrists down, his fists as iron-tight as any manacles. "Hold still, or I swear I'll knock you out. You're going to cut yourself to ribbons."

She tried once, twice, to jerk free, then realized it was useless. He was too strong.

He lifted her, upending her over his shoulder and carried her out of the thorns as though she were no more than a sack of grain. He didn't put her down until they'd reached a boulder. She could hear a stream tumbling by somewhere in the dark.

"You're bleeding," he said.

"So are you," she shot back.

He left her to retrieve a bandanna and bottle of whiskey from his saddlebags.

She tried to stand. "Where is Moondust?"

Morgan forced her back down. "She's fine. She's a tough little beast, and her hide's a lot thicker than yours."

She shoved his hands away as he made to unbutton her shirt. "What the hell do you think you're doing?"

"I see hanging around with wranglers has done wonders for your manners."

She pursed her lips together, but some part of her responded to the cajoling tone of his voice. Was the man actually teasing her?

"I have to see to those cuts," he said again. "Take the shirt off, or I'll do it for you."

She shed the shirt. "Satisfied?"

In the dim light of the moon she could not read the expression on his face, but she could feel his gaze heat. "Very."

She crossed her arms in front of her chemise-covered bosom.

"I can't get at the cuts that way."

She bit her lip, then slowly let her arms fall to her sides. He soaked the cloth with whiskey, then gingerly began to pat at the cuts and scrapes that lay up and down both her arms and across her back.

She hissed under her breath at the sting of the liquor on the open wounds.

"I guess this makes us even," he said.

She shivered.

When he'd finished with her cuts, he built a quick fire. "Better?"

Reluctantly, she nodded. "Shouldn't we get back to camp?"

"You're the one that was in such a hurry to leave it. Where were you going this time? Clay was still asleep."

She took a swing at him, but missed. "You're despicable!"

"I'm glad we're clear on that."

"Oh, just shut up. I've never met a man who makes such a business out of feeling sorry for himself."

He straightened and stalked off several paces. She knew he was angry again, but she didn't care. She had no interest in tact or subtlety this night. She was hurting, a raw, searing pain unlike any she'd ever known, and it had nothing to do with the welts on her body.

He tossed a blanket at her. "Get some sleep. We'll head back before dawn."

He sat down on the opposite side of the fire, lifting the whiskey bottle.

"If you drink one drop of that," she threatened, "I'll . . ."

He poured a little on his bandanna. "You'll what? Thrash me within an inch of my life . . . Mother?"

She grimaced. "You drink too often when you're angry. It's not good for you."

"Oh, excuse me. Yes, *Doctor.*"

"You can be such a bastard, you know that?"

"What do you expect from a man who makes a business of feeling sorry for himself?"

She slapped a hand against the dirt. "It's a good thing I don't have a gun."

He hefted the pistol from the holster on his hip and extended it toward her, butt first. "With my compliments."

She took it from him, but even the feel of the walnut handle made her skin crawl. She laid it down beside her. "I guess I won't kill you."

"Thank you."

"Not that you don't deserve to have a few holes in you to match that one in your head."

"You want to fight? We can fight."

Every frustration in Selina's life seemed to erupt within her, her body demanding surcease. "Let's just see you try."

He set down the whiskey and ambled over to her. She rose to her feet, her fists clenched. Never in her life had she ached for a physical battle as she did now.

Morgan seemed not at all wary or even particularly interested. "Well?"

She took a wild swing. He merely sidestepped.

With a cry of frustration she drove herself into him. He grunted with surprise and stumbled back. She landed atop him, doubling her fist and slamming it into his jaw with every ounce of strength she possessed.

He swore, catching her wrists as she sought to repeat the blow. She drove at him, struggled, twisted, trying to jam her knee into his groin. He curled instinctively, but still did nothing to retaliate, keeping her at arm's length until at last, exhausted, she collapsed against him, sobbing.

His arms encircled her. "It's all right, Abby. It's all right."

"No, nothing's all right," she whimpered. "Chino's dead and it's my fault. And you hate me. And you wish I'd never come here. Oh, Morgan, I'm sorry. I'm sorry."

His lips brushed the top of her head. "You've got nothing to be sorry for, Abby. Nothing. Hush, now."

She clung to him, suddenly desperate to have more than his embrace. She needed this man in her life. Whatever fate had brought them together, she couldn't bear to have it separate them again.

She kissed him. Desperately, hungrily. And when she felt him draw away, she pressed herself more intimately against him, until he gripped her arms and set her firmly away from him.

"I don't . . . don't want you to do something you'll regret in the morning," he said.

She was too upset to take any real note of the strange, reluctant edge in his voice. "I won't regret it, Morgan, I swear. Please, kiss me, hold me. Please. I know you don't . . . love me. I don't expect . . . I just need you to hold me, to . . . please . . . touch . . ." Her lips quivered, tears streaming down her cheeks. "Please."

"No. I won't do that to you. Not this way."

"Because . . . because I was . . . spoiled, ruined . . . by . . . by that other man. That's it, isn't it?"

"God, no. No, Abby. That isn't it. It has nothing to do with you. It . . ." He blinked savagely, his whole body trembling. He wanted her so badly, yet knowing she'd been taken by force made him doubly cautious. What if he made it worse for her? What if her fears returned and she pushed him away? He wouldn't take the risk, and for the life of him, he didn't know why.

He stalked away, grateful when she didn't follow. For long minutes he stood, staring off at nothing, feeling his whole world coming apart. For years he'd constructed an emotionless existence, but since the day he'd mailed that first letter to Ladies in Waiting that existence had begun to crumble. And when Abby had arrived . . . he'd been lost. He didn't know how to deal with the rush of feelings that tormented him constantly. He raged at his own doubts yet stood powerless to stop them.

He stiffened, pulling away when she caught his arm.

"I'm sorry," she murmured. "I didn't mean to make things worse."

He turned around, drawing in a deep breath. "We'd better get some sleep."

"My God," she whispered, peering up at him. "Did I do that?" She raised a hand to touch the path of the scratch marks that tracked across his face.

"They'll be gone by morning."

She caught his hand. "Come over here. I won't rest unless you let me wash them out."

He sat down against the rock. She noticed small rents in his shirt then, too. "Blast it," she said. "Those thorns took as much from you as they did from me. Why didn't you say something?"

"I'm fine."

He didn't object as she helped him strip off his shirt. Against her will she studied the wide expanse of his chest, the dark hair tapering down to the waistband of his jeans and disappearing beneath the denim. The quiescent bulge at the apex of his legs seemed to stir to life before her eyes. Abashed, she looked away, only to meet his searing gaze. Swallowing, she soaked his bandanna with whiskey and began to wipe at the cuts on his arm. Then she shifted her attention to his chest, gliding the cloth along the taut flesh.

"There aren't any cuts on my chest," he said huskily.

"I know."

She looked at him.

"Abby . . ." He started to say something, then stopped.

She washed down his arms, then his hands, then his fingers one by one. God, how she loved his hands.

She squeezed out the liquor, then dabbed gently at the marks on his face. "Damn. I'm sorry," she whispered.

He didn't say anything and she was suddenly aware of how stiffly he was holding himself as her ministrations brought her closer and closer to the scar. She eased the bandanna across his forehead and down his right cheek. He tensed further. She stood up, stepping over his outstretched legs to get to the other side of him.

She tried to keep up a steady stream of innocuous conversation, but she was nervous herself. It had to be done. She reached for the eyepatch. His arm shot out like a striking snake.

"No."

"Morgan, the cuts are all across—"

"No." It was almost a plea.

"It's all right." She worked the cloth across his scar and back up across his forehead. She was methodical now, detached. She had to be for his sake. She could feel the pounding of his heart, the fear.

"It's all right, Morgan," she soothed, curving her fingers beneath the thin strip of leather. "Trust me."

"Abby . . ." His voice was ragged.

She didn't stop, but lifted the strip away from his forehead, easing it over his head. She moved the cloth across the jagged flesh that covered his useless eye. "It's all right," she said again.

He was trembling, trying hard not to. He stared straight ahead, his jaw set hard.

When she'd finished, he snatched the eyepatch away from her, shoving it back in place at once. He didn't look at her. "Damn you."

"Morgan . . ." She didn't know what to say, how to ease his pain.

"Say it."

"Say what?"

His voice was harsh, bitter, agonized. "That you think I'm a freak."

"No," she said, more gently than she had ever spoken in her life. "*You* think you're a freak, Morgan. I love you." She stood, uncertain where the words had come from but not wishing them back. She left him then, lying there, stunned, speechless, as she returned to her blankets.

For long minutes Morgan wasn't sure he even remembered to breathe. *I love you.* As matter-of-factly as you please, Abby had just turned his life inside out. *I love you.*

No.

He couldn't believe it. Wouldn't.

He touched the scar, his jaw clamped tight to keep from screaming. He felt as if his soul had been laid open, as if she could see inside him, and know him for what he was—that she had seen the ugly truth, and it was only a matter of time before she despised him as he despised himself.

Even Chino hadn't known the full truth.

She wouldn't love him if she knew. No one could.

Yet her words, her voice, thrummed through his mind over and over as he slept.

I love you.

Chapter 16

Selina couldn't sleep, a condition she thought she should have grown accustomed to these past weeks. But this time her sleeplessness had nothing to do with nightmares. Dear God, she had told Morgan Kincaid she loved him. Loved him!

She lay there across the campsite from him, considering the significance of her three words. When Chino had teasingly accused her of being in love with Morgan, she had denied it vehemently. It seemed now Chino had known her better than she knew herself.

She did love Morgan. With her heart, her soul, her mind. She couldn't pinpoint the precise moment it had happened. She'd been too busy resisting the idea. But she didn't resist it now. She hugged it to her, reveled in the wonder of it—and the pain.

She had no doubt Morgan would reject her. He wasn't a man to open himself up to anyone.

For the briefest of moments when she had taken off his eyepatch last night, Morgan had been achingly vulnerable, his emotions surface-raw. The agony of having her see him that way had been so intense that even Morgan, a man who seemed to have devoted a lifetime to avoiding deep feelings, had been incapable of maintaining the illusion that he didn't care.

The irony was that the scar made no difference to her. She didn't even see it anymore when she looked at him. All she saw was Morgan, the man she loved. Perhaps the day would come when he would believe that, but for now she was certain her words would only drive him deeper inside himself. She didn't have to wait long to find out just how right she was.

Just past dawn Morgan came up to her, leading his stallion and Moondust.

"Morgan, I . . ."

He held up a hand. "Don't say anything. We weren't ourselves last night. Chino's death hit us both hard."

"Can't we just talk about it?"

He wasn't listening. "I did some thinking. There's a special stockmen's meeting in St. Louis in July. I'll be heading there when roundup is over. Then I may as well ride down to Texas to look over some new breeding stock. I won't be back to Wolf Trail until the end of summer."

It struck like a blow, though she showed no outward sign. The summer—their agreed-upon time limit. When he returned, she was certain, he would end the marriage.

"I . . . I'll miss you," she managed. "I meant what I said last night."

He looked away. "I have a lot of thinking to do, Abby. Please understand. You can't know how hard this is for me."

"What's hard?" Her voice shook. "Leaving for the summer? Or believing that I love you?"

"Both." He swung into the saddle, riding out ahead of her. By the time she'd arrived at the main camp, he was gone. "Said he had some business to tend to," Stewie said, his craggy features brimming with sympathy. "Meetin's and such."

Selina only nodded. She couldn't handle any more understanding looks right now. Morgan hadn't even said good-bye to Celia.

"He said he'd write," Stewie called after her, but Selina was no longer listening.

Celia took her father's abrupt departure in stride, not seeming to mind as much as Selina feared she would.

A week later the roundup drew to a close, but with Morgan gone, Selina's heart was no longer in it. She was glad to return to the ranch. At least there she could comfort herself with the piano and Celia's company. She and Celia grew closer daily.

Three weeks went by before the first letter arrived from Morgan. Addressed to Celia, it was woefully terse, noting statistics on cows, meetings, and stock reports. Selina wanted to shake the man. Couldn't he tell his own daughter he missed her?

Meanwhile, Celia excelled at her lessons. Although she continued her pretense of not minding her father's absence, Selina knew she missed him terribly.

One afternoon toward mid-July, Selina found Celia sitting on a corral railing looking entirely too interested in the pinto stallion. The horse snorted and pawed the ground in its usual spirited manner.

"I hope you're not considering anything reckless," Selina said.

"I probably should just let him go," the child said. "He's not happy here. But it sure would be somethin' to surprise Pa, if I could get him to trust me."

Selina's first impulse was to discourage this idea in no uncertain terms, but because the child had tied it in with pleasing her father, Selina couldn't quite bring herself to forbid it. "Maybe we're not trying the right approach," she said slowly. "Stallions are males, after all. Maybe the best way to his heart is through his stomach." Selina took out a carrot she'd stuck in her pocket for Moondust. "It's worth a try, anyway."

Celia took the carrot, giggling.

"You be very patient, young lady. It may be days before he'll take it. I don't want you getting hurt."

With a singlemindedness that astonished Selina, Celia set herself to the task of gentling the stallion.

Selina's own goal for the summer was less wearing. She spent her evenings reading Lenore's diary by firelight. She found the journal an even more bittersweet companion now that she had acknowledged her love for Morgan. She wondered if she and Lenore were doomed to share the same path, loving Morgan Kincaid—a man who could not or would not love in return.

Selina read the entries following Celia's birth. *The child, the child, the child. He loves her so! Sometimes I think it's because Celia is yet too young to understand. When she's old enough he'll likely turn his back on her, too.*

What a peculiar thing to write, Selina thought, then considered it more fully. Morgan really did find it difficult to deal with his feelings. To avoid them, he avoided the people who needed most to know he cared.

Entries detailing parties and business obligations went on for page after page. Lenore and her parties! If Morgan announced his disdain for a particular soirée, Lenore would attend with a business associate of her father's rather than stay at home. When Morgan took a leave from her father's firm to ride with a cattle herd Lenore was beside herself.

I scarce recall why I married him some days. But as my father says, I've made my bed . . .

How sad for them both. Lenore and Morgan were from two utterly different worlds. Lenore could no more appreciate why a place like Wolf Trail would please her husband than Morgan could understand why his wife thrived in Houston society.

Morgan grew more and more restless, Lenore more and more disenchanted.

March 3, 1881. Morgan quit Father's firm today, saying Papa was unethical, caring more about money than lives. When I ask if he's going to open his own practice again, he says he won't even consider it, that he's "fed up" with hypocrisy and doesn't even want to be a lawyer anymore! How will we survive? The Claytons and the Bartholomews have already removed us from their guest lists for any and all future soirées!

Lenore's difficulties seemed to accelerate after that.

March 12, 1881 We are leaving Houston. Morgan talks incessantly of his new paradise in Montana. Indians, lizards, wolves. I know I shall die there.

Selina stared at the last sentence, struck by the irony of it. She skimmed through the next dozen or so pages, unable to sympathize with Lenore's mounting self-pity as she bemoaned everything

about her new life at Wolf Trail, not once acknowl-
edging all that Morgan had done to make her life
as compatible as humanly possible with what she
had left behind.

Still, Selina didn't have to read between the lines
to acknowledge the patent unfairness with which
Morgan had handled his family's move to Wolf
Trail. Though Selina sensed that Lenore's affec-
tions were waning daily, at this point she still loved
her husband. Morgan could have salvaged their
relationship, but he had not.

*April 18, 1882 A new manager at the Lazy C
rode in today and introduced himself. Clay Prescott. He's devilishly handsome! He was even flirting
with me. I'm ashamed at how much I enjoyed it.
Thankfully, Morgan took no notice. Or is it that he
just doesn't care what I do?*

*May 10, 1882 Something went terribly wrong to-
day. Morgan's gun exploded. I fainted just looking
at him. Chino said there was nothing anyone could
do to save his eye. As usual, even this doesn't seem
to faze Morgan. He takes it in stride.*

*June 8 A doctor stopped by from Miles City. He
took the bandages off Morgan's wound. It was so
hideous, I ran from the room, retching.*

Selina shuddered. Just what Morgan would need
at a moment like that.

*July 14 Morgan wanted to make love tonight, but
I couldn't bear it. So many times when I wanted*

him, he seemed not to care. Now when he needs me, I can't . . .

Selina looked up from the page, imagining how Morgan must have felt to be turned away from his wife's bed. Another thought seared her: Though the circumstances were nothing at all alike, she had done much the same herself.

August 1 Clay has been so understanding. He is like a big puppy, unsure of himself one day, full of himself the next. I love to go riding with him. I must make certain nothing comes of it for Celia's sake. She adores her father so, though she has withdrawn lately from both of us. I suppose she senses the strain.

April 19, 1883 Clay and I became lovers last night. It was so good. He made no demands of me. I haven't felt so free in so long. I told him Morgan and I are no longer intimate.

Selina paced to the front window, peering out into the quiet darkness. Moonlight cast veiled shadows everywhere she looked. Where was Morgan right now? What was he doing? Who was he with? Did he think of her at all? Did he know that even in his absence her love for him grew daily?

She sighed, her thoughts sifting back to their wedding night. Might she have spared them both the pain of that night if she had read Lenore's diary sooner?

But then she knew the answer. It wouldn't have mattered. Morgan still wouldn't have known about

Gideon. And her memories of that horror were what had risen up to torment her that night.

Selina stood there, missing him, wishing for the courage to write to him. She wanted so badly to assure him her words of love had come from her heart, not pity. But she dared not. She had tried once to write, but had had to burn the letter when she realized she could not alter her handwriting enough to resemble Alberta Bodine's. She couldn't take the chance.

To her astonishment, she found it was at night in her bed that she missed Morgan the most. It was as though she didn't know her own body anymore. Strange longings woke her up from sound sleep, cravings she could not assuage with food or long rides on Moondust.

One night she had been utterly mortified to awaken to find her own hands caressing her breasts. She remembered the dream all too clearly. Morgan had been there, touching her, kissing her everywhere. She had denied him nothing, begged for more. She sat up in bed, tears streaming from her eyes. What was happening to her?

A short note from Morgan toward the end of August still made no mention of when he would be home. Charlie assured her often that he would have to be back before the beef roundup in the fall, but that did little to comfort her. If he wished to, Morgan could bypass the ranch altogether, joining

his herd on its drive to market, avoiding a return
to Wolf Trail for an additional six weeks.

Selina continued the routine she'd settled into,
teaching Celia, learning from her, taking long rides
on this ranch she now loved, and spending her evenings with Lenore's diary. She'd been reading it
more slowly than ever, postponing the inevitable
loss of her odd kinship with its writer. But at last
she reached the final three pages.

Her eyes fell on a separate note scribbled in a
margin. *I shouldn't write this. It shames me. I told
Morgan tonight, when he asked again to be intimate, that I found his attentions tedious. I wanted to
punish him for bringing me here, for ruining my
life. The look on his face crushed me inside. I didn't
mean to be so cruel. But I can't take it back. I
can't. He never loved me. He deserves to suffer.*

Selina sat there, sickened. She had been too absorbed in her own fears to see that Morgan might
have been as uncertain as she was. She longed for a
chance to make it up to him. Here in the familiar
shadows of her bedroom, she realized what her
body had known weeks ago. She wanted Morgan
in her bed, wanted—needed—him to give her body
surcease from the aching emptiness that pervaded
her soul.

Perhaps only by being apart from him these
months could she have discovered this truth about
herself. Without the subtle pressure they unknow-

ingly put on each other when they were together, she had been able to sort through so many things.

Now she was truly ready for him to come home. She could only pray that he would feel the same.

Only two more pages remained of the diary. Reluctantly Selina decided to finish it. Though a great deal of what was written in the book had been hurtful to the man she loved, she had learned much about him too. And through Lenore, she had learned things about herself as well.

July 15 God in heaven! Why am I punished so? I was so careful, but I am with child. Clay's child. Morgan will know it is not his. What am I going to do?

Selina sat bolt upright, stunned.

July 22 I cannot tell Clay. He urges me daily to leave Morgan. But how could I abandon Celia? Morgan would never give her up. I must make it through this alone.

Only one entry followed. Almost against her will Selina read on.

July 25 I'll take nothing with me but the little money I've set aside. God forgive me, but it's better if I just leave and start over somewhere alone. Tomorrow night I'll do it. I've told Clay I can't see him anymore. Morgan won't be back from Miles City until the day after tomorrow. Chino will watch out for Ceecy. As frightening as it may be, part of me actually looks forward to making my own way. I'll write Ceecy a note tonight, telling her how much

I love her, praying one day she'll find it in her heart to forgive me. For now, I'm just going to take a long ride alone, saying my good-byes to Wolf Trail.

Sometimes, when it's very quiet and the moon is full, I can even see why Morgan loves it here.

Tears streamed down Selina's cheeks. Lenore had taken her last ride that day. How sad that it had ended for her, when it could have just begun. Selina had seen Lenore grow, change, and finally accept.

Selina closed the book, feeling very much as if she had lost a friend.

A letter arrived the next day addressed not to Celia, but to Abby. Selina's hands trembled as she opened it. Did Morgan believe at last that she loved him?

Mrs. Kincaid,

The summer will be nearly over when I return September 1st. An important stockmen's meeting has been called in Miles City just two days following. You and Celia will accompany me. I hope it comes as no great shock to you, but while in Miles City you and I will be consulting a lawyer.

Selina sank onto a chair, feeling as though she had just been shot. It was over. Dear God, what was she going to do?

"What is it?" Celia asked. "Are you all right?"

Only then did Selina realize she must look stricken. She drew in a deep breath, determined to keep up appearances for the child's sake. It would be up to Morgan to break the news to her. "I'm fine, sweetheart. It's just word from your father saying that he'll be home . . ." She checked the date again, "Oh, my, he should be home tonight."

Celia jumped happily, then sobered, a habit Selina knew only too well. "I can't wait to show him my surprise! Can I stay up until he gets here?"

"Of course."

Later that evening Selina paced nervously, glad when the child drifted off to sleep on the divan. Why did he have to do this? Couldn't they at least have talked about it?

The sound of hoofbeats in the yard sent her heartbeat pounding. Morgan strode into the house, stopping short when he saw her standing by the hearth.

"Shh," she said quickly, holding a finger to her lips and gesturing to the divan. "Celia tried so hard to wait up for you."

He slapped off his gloves and hat, coming over to the fire, not really looking at her. "Is something wrong?"

"Wrong?" Selina asked, unable to keep the sarcasm out of her voice. "What could be wrong?" Had the man no sensitivity at all? She sighed shakily. What was the use? Just standing here looking at him was tearing her apart. "When will we be leaving for Miles City?"

"In the morning."

"Fine." She headed toward Lenore's bedroom.

"Where are you going?"

At his question, she turned. The strangest look came over him, as though he had just been greatly disappointed. But since Selina couldn't imagine about what, she said only, "Where did you expect me to sleep, now that you're home?"

"I see. Well, you needn't put yourself out. I'll be in the bunkhouse."

She twisted her hands in front of her, wanting to say something, anything, to get him to stay.

"If there's nothing else . . . ?" He was looking at her, but she could not read his expression.

"No . . . no, nothing."

"Then good night, Mrs. Kincaid." He threw open the door, nearly tearing it from its hinges, slamming it in his wake.

She sank onto a chair, stunned. How much easier his being away had made this for him, when the very opposite was true for her! Just seeing him had made her heart ache from wanting him. She had barely been able to restrain her urge to run to him, to fling herself into his arms and never let go. Yet in barely more than a day, he would let her go forever.

Chapter 17

Morgan wanted to leave for Miles City immediately after breakfast, but Celia would have none of it. Selina was certain he thought she had put the child up to something, but she wasn't about to spoil Celia's surprise. Morgan glowered at her all the way out to the corral, his gaze narrowing ominously when Celia climbed the corral fence and perched herself on the top rail. The pinto danced toward her.

"What's going on?" he demanded.

Selina shrugged innocently. "It's Celia's surprise."

Celia took a carrot from the pocket of her dungarees, then wriggled it at the pinto. The horse snorted, bobbing his great head playfully, then pranced over to the rail to accept the extended delicacy.

Selina grinned. "Oh, Celia, that's wonder—"

"Now for the real surprise! For both of you!"

Before Selina could react, Celia gripped the stallion's mane and threw herself onto the beast's back. The pinto stood placidly, curving his head around, waiting for another carrot.

"I'll be damned," Morgan said.

"I hope you have more to say to her than that," Selina hissed under her breath.

"I beg your pardon?"

"Can't you see how desperate she is to please you? Or don't you care?" That one hurt him. And in that instant Selina realized how Lenore had been able to savage him: because she had been so hurt herself. She was indeed following in Lenore's footsteps.

At least the comment mobilized him. He ducked between the rails of the corral and gathered his daughter from the stallion's back into his arms. "I'm real proud of you, honey."

Celia positively glowed. Selina turned away, lest either of them see the tears in her eyes.

Minutes later Morgan had the buckboard ready. Selina, her lips pursed, climbed into the seat, ignoring the hand he offered to assist her.

The ride to town, including a night on the trail, was accomplished in near silence, except for Celia's uncharacteristically animated chatter.

"We haven't had rain since June," Selina said to Morgan at one point, hoping to end their stalemate over who had made whom angrier.

His only response was a flat "I've kept in touch with Charlie."

They arrived in Miles City in midafternoon. Morgan tied up the team in front of the Yerby Hotel. At the registration desk he very pointedly requested two rooms.

"I'll be across the hall," he said, showing Celia and Selina to the room they would share.

"I'm hungry, Papa. Can we go out to eat?"

"I suppose we could," he said, apparently not relishing the idea.

His look suggested he would prefer to go alone with his daughter. Selina decided to make it easier for him. "I have a bit of a headache. If I feel better, I'll join you later."

"Whatever you say." Then they were gone.

Selina sagged onto the bed in her room. How long was Morgan going to continue this farce? They could've stopped at the lawyer's office first and gotten the divorce over with. What purpose did it serve to prolong the agony? And when in the world was he going to tell Celia?

Selina swallowed a sob. Perhaps he was telling her right now.

"This is fun, Pa," Celia said, sliding into a chair across from her father at Jensen's Café.

"That it is, honey," Morgan said, ignoring a few of the ruder stares among the patrons. He'd eaten a lot of his meals in hotel rooms this summer to avoid stares like that. But right now he concentrated on making Celia feel at ease in his company. The fact that Celia had even suggested they eat together spoke volumes for the progress Abby had made with her.

He would have to compliment her on that. The thought brought with it the sting of how badly they'd been getting along since his return. When he'd left in June it was to the echo of her telling him she loved him. Had their summer apart convinced her otherwise?

He made an exaggerated display of straightening his silverware. He'd spent the summer coming to terms about a lot of things himself.

"Celia, did Abby say anything to you about . . . being upset about anything?" He wasn't being fair, but then he wasn't feeling very fair either.

"Well, not exactly, but . . ." She chewed on her lip uncertainly.

"It's all right, honey. I can't help her feel better if I don't know why she's unhappy, can I?"

Celia's small face screwed into such a caricature of Abby when she was thinking hard about something, that it was all Morgan could do not to burst out laughing.

"The only thing I can think of," the child said slowly, "is that she acted kind of funny after she got your letter telling her you would be coming home."

He twisted his empty coffee cup, then tapped it

against its china saucer. Maybe he didn't want to
hear the answer to his next question. "She didn't
seem happy that I was coming home?"

"She didn't say that." Celia looked distressed.

"It's all right," he assured her quickly. "Don't
worry about it." He smiled. "You really like Abby,
don't you?"

Celia beamed. "She's wonderful, Pa. I'm so glad
you . . ." She stopped, swallowing guiltily. "I
mean, I guess she's okay."

"Something wrong?"

"Is she going away?"

"What do you mean?" He leaned back, allowing
the waitress to refill his coffee cup. He didn't miss
the way she deliberately avoided looking at him.

"She said it once, when we were doing lessons.
That she might have to leave in the fall."

"Sometimes things just don't work out, no matter how much people might want them to."

"Like with you and Mama?"

"Something like that."

"Mama was sad a lot, just like Abby."

Morgan stilled. "What?"

"Abby doesn't know, but sometimes I would
hear her cry in the night."

Morgan snapped open the linen napkin beside
his table service and settled it on his lap. Nothing
had been going right since he'd come back to the
ranch. Now he was finding out that Abby had
spent the summer in tears. Blast! He knew he

should have written more, but he hadn't even known what he wanted to say. He still didn't. His temper rose perceptibly as the waitress, now openly disapproving, stood at his elbow waiting for his order. "Steak and eggs all around," he said. When she didn't move, he said deliberately, "Is there something else?"

She leaned forward, not in the least abashed. "A couple of the customers are wonderin' if you could change places with the girl, mister. You know what I mean."

"You mean keep the more offensive side of my face toward the window?"

"Exactly!"

"You tell 'em to mind their own business!" Celia cried. "My pa can eat where he wants."

Morgan sat back, surprised but warmed by Celia's defense. "You heard the lady." He smiled as the waitress huffed off.

Celia bit her lip. "Are people always mean to you like that?"

"Only the ones with no manners. Where were we?"

She seemed reluctant to let the subject drop, but Morgan for once was intent on ignoring his scar. Finally, Celia asked in a small voice, "Are you sending Abby away?"

He took a drink of his coffee. "What gave you that idea?"

"I think that would be the only thing to make her so sad. She likes livin' with us."

"You think so?"

Unaccountably, she twisted the subject, "Would you ever send me away, if you got mad at me, Pa?"

"Celia, you're my daughter. I would never send you away."

"No matter what I did?"

Selina arrived at the café, wishing immediately she had not. She could tell she had interrupted something important. Morgan scraped his chair back, then pulled a chair out for her. Grim silence descended. Had he already told Celia? Is that why she looked so miserable?

"Are you all right, Ceecy?" Selina ventured. "You seemed so happy when you left the hotel."

"Some people were mean to Pa. About his . . . his eye. I mean . . ." Celia squirmed, panicking at bringing up a subject her father detested.

"I have an idea," Selina said brightly, reaching into her reticule. "Why don't you go to the mercantile and get yourself some candy? And maybe pick up a few licorice whips for me. All right?"

Celia nodded, grateful for the chance to flee.

"We'll meet you back at the hotel," Morgan called after her.

"I'm sorry," Selina said. "I didn't mean to interrupt."

"It's fine."

His nasty tone told her it was anything but.
Sighing, she asked, "When are we going to see this
lawyer?"

"As soon as you finish your lunch."

"I . . . I'm not hungry."

He rose. "Then we'll go now."

She wished she had the courage to talk to him,
but he had apparently spent the summer deciding
that sending that first letter to Ladies in Waiting
was the biggest mistake of his life.

She had to half run to keep pace with him as he
stalked down the boardwalk and across the dusty
main street of the small frontier town. Skirting
piles of fresh horse dung, Selina nearly tripped as
she stepped up to the walk on the opposite side of
the street. Morgan kept walking. She clambered
after him, scarcely noting the false-front buildings
she passed—a general store, saloon, the sheriff's
office.

She was twenty feet past it before it registered.
And when it did, she barreled headlong into Morgan, who had stopped in front of a doorway let-
tered: SAMUEL HENDERSON, ATTORNEY-AT-LAW.
She twisted away, staring back the way she had
come. Had she really seen it? There, on a huge
notice board in front of the sheriff's office, was a
reward poster with her name and likeness on it.

She shuddered. With her sun-bronzed face and
chestnut hair tumbled about her shoulders, most
people might not look twice. And yet . . .

"Abby, what is it?" Morgan demanded. From his insistent tone she guessed he had already asked the same question several times.

"I . ⌣ ." She looked up at him, praying she was masking at least some of the terror that coursed through her. "I . . . I'm afraid I feel that headache coming on again."

"Oh." It was obvious he didn't believe her. He opened the door to the attorney's office, the bell above the door jamb announcing his arrival to those within. "I'll bring the papers back to the hotel."

"I'm sure you will," she snapped, irrationally incensed that he did not perceive the fear she was trying so hard to conceal.

She had to get that poster, but she dared not grab it when there was any chance at all someone would see her.

Determined to wait for the right moment, she ducked into a tiny dress shop two doors down from the saloon, then peeked out the window to keep the bulletin board in sight. There were few passersby, but now two men were sitting on the bench outside the sheriff's office. She nearly leaped out of her skin when a voice behind her said, "Come for a dress for the ball, Mrs. Kincaid?"

"How did you know who . . ."

"Saw you with Mr. Kincaid earlier. He's a hard man not to notice."

Selina felt herself tense until the woman went

on, "He's so imposing, you know. Just seems to
take over a room when he comes into it. He used
to bring the first missus. Oh, I'm sorry. I do rattle
on. Please, let me show you some of my work."
The plump seamstress smiled warmly. "My name's
Elvira Smith."

She could hardly tell the woman she wouldn't be
at the ball, that her husband was even at this moment arranging their divorce.

"This is a busy time for me," Elvira said. "Lots
of ranchers' wives and their daughters come in for
the stockmen's ball. But Winifred Meyers couldn't
make it this year. She has such a tiny little figure,
even if she has the tongue of a viper." The seamstress bustled to the back of the shop. "I'm almost
glad she can't have this one," she said, holding up
a lovely emerald-green ninon and satin gown. "She
showed me a picture in a Paris magazine. Didn't
think I could do the job."

Selina ran her hand over the fine detailing of the
dress. "It's exquisite!"

"It would look so lovely on you, Mrs. Kincaid. I
just know it would. I'm sure the mister would love
for you to have it."

Selina decided it was better to take the dress and
avoid the gossip. Besides, the two men were still
firmly ensconced on the sheriff's bench.

Elvira fussed over the fitting, regaling Selina
with outrageous bits of town gossip. But Selina

could barely concentrate, her thoughts constantly returning to the reward poster.

Her dress wrapped and tucked securely under her arm, Selina finally escaped the dress shop and the loquacious Elvira. The two men were gone. As inconspicuously as she could manage, Selina tugged the poster free and stuffed it into her reticule.

"Going to the dance tomorrow night?"

She jumped. Clay was striding toward her, doffing his hat.

"I'm not sure," she said truthfully.

"It's quite the social event of the season. You really should talk Morg into it."

"Why would he need to be talked into going?"

"Morg? To a dance? Are you serious? Even before his accident, Lenore had to practically . . ." He stopped mid-sentence, looking past her. Selina didn't have to turn to know who had arrived.

"You've made another miraculous recovery from your headache, madam?" Morgan said.

"I feel much better, yes," she said, adding, "I was just coming to look for you."

"You found me."

"So I did." She linked her arm in his, feeling the tenseness in him.

Nervously, Clay bid them good day, then headed in the opposite direction down the boardwalk.

Selina gripped her package more tightly. "I hope you don't mind. I bought a dress."

"Buy whatever you like."

"Did . . . did you get the papers?"

He patted his jacket pocket. "I did."

Her eyes burned. "Would you take me back to the hotel, Morgan?"

"Of course."

He opened the door to her room, but made no move to enter. Selina stepped past him, looking quickly to make certain Celia was not yet back. She turned to face him. "We may as well have this out. Will you want me to leave immediately?"

"What?"

With exaggerated clarity she said, "Will you want me to leave Wolf Trail as soon as I sign the divorce papers?"

He straightened, a strange light coming into that cerulean eye. "I don't—"

Celia bounced into the room. "I got the candy!" she said, holding up a small brown sack. "And I even remembered the licorice for you, Abby."

Selina forced a smile. Morgan looked as if he wanted to say something, but wouldn't with Celia present. Instead he bid them both good night and left the room, his mood oddly buoyant. Evidently, the prospect of having the divorce so close at hand improved his disposition.

As Selina set about getting ready for bed, she

noticed Celia becoming more and more withdrawn. No doubt the child sensed her mood.

"Are you all right, honey?" Selina asked, dim-
ming the kerosene lantern on the nightstand between the two small beds.

Celia sat up. "I'm just a little scared, I guess."

"Of what, sweetheart?" Selina sat next to the
girl, stroking her cornsilk hair. When Celia didn't
respond, Selina prodded gently, "It's all right. You
can tell me."

"Is something wrong between you and Papa?"
she blurted.

"Why would you think that?"

"You seem so sad since he came home. Usually
you're not sad around Papa. Mad maybe, but not
sad."

Selina managed a wan smile. "It's very hard to
explain the feelings between your father and me,
Celia. I think even he and I haven't quite figured
them all out yet. But it's nothing you have to
worry about." She hated reassuring her, when it
would all come crumbling down tomorrow. But
she was not going to be the one to break this
child's heart. Ending the marriage was Morgan's
doing, and he was damned well going to be the one
to tell Celia.

"Pa said sometimes things just don't work out
the way people want them to."

"That's true."

"That happened to me once."

Celia was trembling so badly Selina grew frightened. She wondered if she should summon Morgan. Then suddenly she knew. This wasn't about her and Morgan. It was about Celia and Morgan. Right here, right now, for whatever reason, Celia was ready to share the awful burden that had for so long driven a wedge between her and her father. Celia was bestowing Selina with her ultimate trust on the night before Selina might be forced to walk out of her life forever.

"You won't like me anymore," Celia said, her voice quavering.

"Celia," Selina said, hugging the child fiercely to her. "I love you. Nothing you can tell me will change that."

The words poured out between hiccuping sobs. Selina closed her eyes, feeling the child's agony. When Celia finished, Selina was still hugging her. "You have to tell him," she said gently. "He'll understand."

"No!" she shrieked. "I can't! Promise me you won't tell him. Promise! He'll hate me!"

"He won't hate you."

"You hate me now, don't you?"

"I love you. I always will." She rocked Celia until the child fell asleep. Dear God, secrets.

Much later Selina fell into an exhausted sleep herself. When she woke the next morning, it was to find a note from Morgan slipped under the door.

He had things to attend to and likely wouldn't be back until evening. They would talk then.

Would he be back in time for the dance? Selina remembered Clay's warning that Morgan didn't attend such events, but she decided then and there that he was going to attend this one. If it was to be their last night together, she intended it to be one to remember.

She worked for hours getting herself ready, having a bath drawn, sending for a woman to do her hair. Celia joined in merrily. "You're going to be just like Cinderella," the girl said. "And Pa can be Prince Charming."

Selina couldn't help a rueful smile. Pure fantasy.

She stepped away from the full-length mirror, twirling in a full circle to catch her reflection. The emerald-green satin shimmered. A swathe of ninon crossed her bosom diagonally from the left shoulder, passing under her right arm and leaving her right shoulder exposed. Her hair was done up in an elegant French twist, her face framed with a sprinkling of curls that enhanced the delicate planes of her face.

"To think I once called you plain." Celia sighed.

"You really like it?"

"The dress is beautiful, just like you."

"Then maybe you'll like the one I had sent over for you." She crossed to the wardrobe and pulled out a near duplicate of her gown, except that its neckline was much more modest and its color was a deep blue to accent Celia's pale blond hair.

Celia was beside herself with glee, throwing her arms around Selina. "Oh, Abby, thank you, thank you!"

Selina delighted in helping Celia get ready. After adjusting the dress and fixing her hair they both sat back and waited for Morgan. The dance had begun at seven. It was already seven-thirty.

"You wait here," she told Celia. "I'm going to check his room." Selina crossed the hall. Her pulses pounding, she knocked on his door. No answer. She felt a little relieved. Perhaps his business had detained him. Certain she heard sounds of someone stirring, she knocked again. A low curse followed, as though someone had stumbled into something. She bit her lip, prepared for the worst.

She got it.

The door swung open. Morgan stood there, bleary eyed, unshaven, looking for all the world as though she'd awakened him from a deep sleep. She grimaced, smelling the whiskey. "I take it you're not attending the ball?"

He blinked, his eye still not adjusted to the light. The curtains in his room were drawn. "I don't attend public dances. Haven't you heard?"

She stepped past him into the room and slammed the door behind her. The noise jarred some of the haze out of him. He shook himself. "I never said anything about going to the dance,

Abby." He scratched the stubble on his chin. "At least, I don't think I did."

"You listen to me, Morgan Kincaid. Whether you like it or not, your daughter is going to have one last night of pleasant memories of this . . . this marriage of ours. And that means going to the dance. Now I am going down to the lobby. In ten minutes I expect you to be there looking like a human being instead of a grizzly bear." Her own composure wavered. "I want some decent memories for myself, too." Clenching her fists to keep the tears at bay, she stormed from the room.

Ten minutes passed, then twenty. The lobby was nearly empty. Selina blinked savagely, determined not to let Celia see her distress. "Maybe he meant for us to go ahead without him," she said. "He'll join us."

They were just about through the door when Celia grabbed Selina's arm and pointed behind her. Selina's heart caught in her throat. He was wearing the same fine gray silk he had worn for their wedding. He had shaved and even splashed on a bit of bay rum, no doubt to disguise the scent of the whiskey. His blue eye still looked faintly bloodshot if she peered too closely, but she was not about to complain.

This was her night, her Cinderella night. No matter what tomorrow might bring, she was going to have this night. She tucked her arm in his, not knowing how radiant her smile looked to him at that moment, how adoring her eyes. He stopped, holding her at arm's length.

"You are so beautiful, Abby. I think I could stomach a lifetime of balls, if . . ." He took a deep breath. Without finishing, he turned his attention to his daughter. "And you," he said, "look like a fairy princess."

The walk to the MacQueen Hotel took only a few minutes, but it was enough time for Selina to regain her composure. Nothing was going to spoil this night.

"I see you made it," Clay Prescott said, coming up to them. Morgan ignored his outstretched hand, instead hooking his arm through Selina's and guiding her toward the buffet table.

Selina accepted the punch he ladled for her, pronouncing it delicious. Celia was standing off looking a bit taken aback by all of the people and decorations. Selina gave Morgan a nudge. "Dance with her."

He grinned. "I think I'll just do that." He looked at her, long and hard. "You'll save your first dance for me?"

"I wouldn't miss it."

He hesitated. "Abby, there's something I need to tell you. About the lawyer—"

"Dammit, Morgan!" she swore. "How can you bring that up here of all places?"

"Because I don't think you under—"

Celia stepped up to them. "Oh, Pa, Abby, have

you ever seen so many pretty dresses?" She positively bubbled. "Yours is the most beautiful of all,
Abby."

"Thank you, sweetheart," Selina replied, stick-
ing an elbow into Morgan's ribs. Taking the hint,
he bowed low, asking his daughter to dance with
him. As they moved off together, Selina could see
Morgan's fatherly pride reflected in Celia's shining
face.

Selina poured herself another glass of punch.

"There you are!" Clay Prescott boomed. This
time he had a buxom brunette draped possessively
over his right arm. "Jessamyn Farber, meet Alberta Kincaid."

Selina managed a tight smile.

"Jessamyn lives here in town," Clay said. "Her
father owns the mercantile."

"How nice," Selina murmured, wishing they
would both go away.

"Clay's been telling me all about you," Jessamyn said, giggling coquettishly. "When he said
you were actually a mail-order bride I couldn't believe it. I mean you're so . . . pretty."

"Thank you." Selina felt suddenly uncomfortable.

"It's almost as though I've seen you before, but
I just can't place it."

Selina's heart hammered. Had the girl seen the
poster?

"Oh, I know what it is," Jessamyn tittered.

"You remind me of a storybook my mama read to me when I was a child."

Morgan and Celia had finished their dance, and Morgan was heading toward Selina with another glass of punch.

"You know the story I mean, Mrs. Kincaid," the girl said too loudly, "the one about Beauty and the Beast."

Morgan almost managed not to flinch. But Selina had seen it. She accepted the glass of punch he held out to her, a frozen smile on her lips as she stepped closer to Jessamyn Farber. Suddenly Selina tripped slightly, her hand shooting out, the deep red punch flooding the front of Jessamyn's pale yellow satin gown. "Oh, how dreadful," Selina gasped. "I am so very sorry. Do forgive me." She turned on her heel and looped her arm through Morgan's, guiding him toward the small band of musicians.

"I'm sorry," she said.

"For what?"

"That such idiots exist in the world."

"It's not your fault."

She gazed at him with such love in her eyes that she wondered at his inability to see it, aching for him to believe it. Impulsively, before her courage fled, she hurried over to the fiddler, whispering a pleading request. The lilting strains of "Green-sleeves" had already begun by the time she returned to Morgan's side. She smiled to Celia, who smiled back, then turned to Morgan.

"May I have this dance, sir?" she murmured, curtsying low.

Morgan bowed slightly, extending his right hand toward her. "My pleasure, madam."

She came into his arms. And then it was just the two of them, spinning slowly, light as air all around the dance floor. His arms tightened, his gaze searing into her own. She wished for the power to stop time, wished the dance would never end.

It took a while to register.

The silence.

The music had stopped, but she and Morgan had kept on dancing. She smiled shyly. For once Morgan didn't seem to mind being the center of attention.

Suddenly overwarm, Selina hurried to the buffet table, ladling herself yet another glass of punch. Celia was out of earshot, talking to another girl who looked to be her age. "I didn't realize how hot it was getting in here—and how thirsty I am." She was about to have another, when Morgan took the crystal from her. She frowned.

"Abby," he said, his smile wry, sweet, "you treated me rather critically this evening because I'd spent much of the day imbibing."

"As well I should," she said.

"Abby, this punch is not just fruit juice. You may not know it yet, but you're already feeling it."

"Oh." Her head did feel much lighter than she remembered. And she was feeling decidedly bold. "Why did you spend the day drinking anyway?" she scolded, waggling her finger at him as though he were a naughty child. "You said you had business."

"My business was getting drunk."

She moved closer, twining her arm in his. "Why?"

"Because I didn't want to come to this dance with you."

She was crestfallen. "Oh," she said in a small voice. "I'm sorry."

"Not that I didn't want to. I was afraid to."

"But . . ."

"Little remarks like Miss Farber's are not out of the ordinary."

"She's a little tart who deserves a good thrashing." Selina turned. "I'll just give her a piece of my mind . . ." But suddenly the room was spinning around her.

"I think you might want to wait a little while."

"Why would I want to do that?"

"Because you're drunk." He slid his arm around her waist, giving her the full support of his body without being obvious. "I think we'd best gather Celia and head back to the hotel."

"Do me a favor first?"

"Name it."

"Kiss me."

He frowned. "I don't think that would be a very good idea."

"Then I'll just have to kiss you." She placed her hands on either side of his neck, pulling his mouth down to her own. The kiss was soft, lingering; his arms swept her to him. A long minute passed, then she stepped back. "Thank you."

"You're welcome," he whispered hoarsely. "Now I really have to get out of here."

Her eyes trailed downward and she grinned lasciviously. "I should drink punch more often." She looked up, expecting him to be enjoying her newfound boldness, but instead he seemed suddenly fearfully intense about something.

"We're going back to the hotel, Abby. Now."

She acquiesced meekly. She couldn't very well navigate by herself anyway. She did her best to disguise her condition from Celia. Thankfully the child fell asleep the moment Morgan settled her into her bed.

Some of Selina's wooziness was starting to wear off, and reality came seeping back in. "The coach turns back into a pumpkin," she murmured.

"What did you say?"

"The ball is over. Do you want me to sign those papers now?" She spoke in hushed tones because of the sleeping child.

He looked out the window onto the quiet street below. "Yes," he said. "As a matter of fact, I do."

She stared at that rigid back. She had dared hope . . .

He went to his room briefly, then returned with a sheaf of papers. "You just have to sign the last page."

Her hand trembled. Tears blurred her vision so that she could scarcely see the line she was supposed to sign. She swiped at them, sniffling, not caring anymore if he knew how much he was hurting her. She didn't have much pride left when it came to Morgan Kincaid.

She held the pen poised, but something wasn't right. She peered more closely at the document. Flipping the pages, she looked at Morgan incredulously. "These aren't divorce papers!" She read the first line aloud. *"Last Will & Testament. I, Morgan Thomas Kincaid, being of sound mind and body . . ."* Her head snapped up. "Is this your idea of a joke?"

"Not at all."

"Then where are the divorce papers?" She jumped at her own strident tone, remembering Celia.

"There aren't any," he said, forced to whisper.

"You mean the lawyer hasn't drawn them up yet?"

"I mean there aren't any." He stepped close. "Unless you want there to be."

Her mind reeled. *"Me?"* She continued, more quietly, "You're the one who said—"

"Said what? When?"

"Don't you try to worm out of this. You put it in your letter."

"What letter?"

"The one and only letter you deigned to write to me this summer, telling me we were getting divorced."

"I never wrote any such letter."

"You most certainly did." She searched her memory. "You said, and I quote, that you and I would be consulting a lawyer in Miles City."

He grimaced. "So that's what all of this has been about?"

"All of what?" she demanded. Her previous light-headedness was giving way to a fearsome headache. She didn't want to have to think.

"I did not write anything about a divorce. I simply said we would be seeing a lawyer."

Her temper stirred. "Oh, no you don't, Morgan Kincaid." She hissed. "You know full well what saying such a thing would mean to me!"

"I swear, I didn't."

"That's why you were gone the whole summer, to stay away from me."

"I needed to sort things out. Abby, I haven't been able to think straight since I met you. And I'm not used to that."

"Think straight? I'll tell you about thinking

straight. You knew I thought these were divorce papers. I used that very word this morning, but you didn't correct me."

"Celia came in," he reminded her reasonably.

"So then this is thinking straight?" She waved the papers at him. "Your will?"

"It's a natural thing for a man to have. If anything happens to me, Wolf Trail goes to Celia."

"Well, of course," Selina said, "but . . ."

"But the will needed to be updated."

"Why?"

"Because I have a wife to consider now, as well as a daughter."

Selina sank into a chair.

He went on: "If I should precede you in death, you're to hold Wolf Trail in trust for Celia until she's of age. And there are provisions, of course, for you to spend your life there as well."

"My . . . life?" She blinked back tears. "But I thought . . . I thought you wanted me gone."

His gaze grew serious. "Thought? Or hoped?"

"Why ever would I hope such a thing?"

"When I came home, you spent the night in Lenore's old bedroom. The message seemed pretty clear to me."

"Oh, God." She fell silent, remembering her own bitter disappointment. "Then . . . then you don't want a divorce?"

"Do you?"

Tears spilled down her cheeks as she shook her head.

In an instant he pulled her against him. "Abby, I have just spent the longest summer of my life. All I could think about was how I'd wasted years of my life wrapped up in my own self-pity, years that began long before this." He gestured toward the scar. "I detested pity from anyone else, but I heaped it on myself."

She started to protest, but he continued relentlessly. "On our wedding night you were scared to death. But I was so caught up in my own misery I didn't see it." His hold on her tightened as he whispered, "I am so sorry, Abby. So sorry.

"I spent night after night dreaming of you, remembering the way you touched me, touched my face, that last night. The way you said you loved me."

"I do, Morgan. So much."

He kissed her, long and sweet, then caught her chin, tipping her face upward. "And I love you, Abby."

She clung to him, crying softly, swept up in a tide of overwhelming joy. "It's going to be all right, isn't it?"

He traced his thumbs along her cheeks, wiping away her tears. "Admitting we love each other doesn't make everything perfect."

"But I love you. You love me. Isn't that all that matters?"

He grew uneasy. "We still have things that need to be . . . resolved."

She sensed instantly what he was thinking. "You told me once that you could make me forget a certain night ever happened. I want you to do that. I was afraid before, but I'm not now. I want to make love to you, Morgan."

"That would be a little awkward." He gestured toward the sleeping child.

"We could go to your room."

He pulled away. And she knew he was right. Love didn't resolve everything.

He cradled her face between his palms. "Abby, I want it to be right. I want everything to be perfect for you."

"I don't need perfect. I need you."

"Abby . . ." He kissed her, fiercely, passionately, his body throbbing with need. He'd denied himself so long, so long. He crushed her against him. "I will make you forget that night. I will. I promise. But I want it to be in our bed. Not here. Is that all right?"

She nodded, terrified and excited all at once. He left her then, going back to his own room. She didn't move for the longest time, fearing that if she did, somehow the spell would be broken and these last minutes would shatter into a dream. Morgan loved her.

*   *   *

The modest two-day drive back to Wolf Trail seemed interminable. Selina fidgeted, fastening her gaze on the horizon as she willed Wolf Trail to appear. Beside her on the wagon seat she could feel the passion in Morgan, held in tight check because of Celia. Selina knew his need for what it was because she felt it herself. This was the magic her parents had known.

Late that night, when Celia was asleep, Selina tiptoed to Morgan's blankets. She sat there, listening to him breathe, and knew he was not asleep. Her hand shaking, she stroked his hair, trailing the back of her fingers along his jaw. There were so many things she longed to say.

With a groan he twisted toward her, then pulled her down atop him, kissing her hard, his lips tracking her face from her forehead to her chin. "I want you so badly, so badly."

Celia shifted in her sleep.

He stilled. "Poor kid. I think she felt like a fifth wheel all day. I tried to think of innocuous things to say, but all I can think of is having you in my bed."

"Funny thing," she murmured. "That's all I can think of, too." Nuzzling close, she soon fell into a contented sleep.

As they broke camp the next morning, Selina could barely contain her excitement. Tonight she would share a bed with her husband. Smiling, she helped Celia gather their blankets and cooking utensils—except for the still half full coffeepot—while Morgan readied the team.

Selina arranged the folded blankets next to her valise, settling her reticule atop the pile lest she misplace it. She frowned, noticing a bit of white showing through the opened catch of the handbag. She stilled, a sudden horror pulsing through her. The reward poster! She'd forgotten . . .

"Celia," she said, as nonchalantly as she could, "why don't you see if your father needs any help hitching up the horses?"

The girl hurried off.

Quickly Selina pulled the paper free, ripping it in tiny bits. Her heart constricting, she headed toward the campfire.

"What's that?" Morgan asked, striding over to pour himself a last cup of coffee.

"A . . . a recipe no one liked," she managed.

He slipped the bits of paper from her fingers. "I'm not hungry anyway."

"Me either." She didn't take her eyes from his hands.

He leaned toward her, brushing a kiss across her cheek. "Are you all right?"

"Fine," she lied. "Why?"

He shrugged. "I don't know. Sometimes when you think I'm not looking . . ." He stopped, then tossed the scraps of papers into the flames.

Selina swallowed a shaky sigh. "I'm fine, Morgan," she said. "Just fine. Really. Just anxious to get home."

He grinned. "Then I suggest we get started." He called to Celia, who clambered into the back of the wagon.

Selina forced the entire incident from her mind as she climbed onto the seat beside him. Now, when he had at last admitted loving her, she could allow nothing—nothing—to jeopardize the night ahead.

It was after dusk when they rode into the ranchyard. Selina was tingling with anticipation.

"Feel free to spend the night in your treehouse, Celia."

Celia clapped merrily. "Thank you, Papa!"

"You're entirely welcome."

"Thank heaven for treehouses," Selina said, trying to keep her voice light. What if something went wrong? What if the night became another disaster? What if he found her lacking as a lover? What did she know of pleasing a man in bed?

Hoping to defuse her mounting anxiety, she sat down at the piano and began to play. The piece began a little roughly, but then she settled down, and the music complemented her heightened sensibilities. Slowly, melodically, she played for him. For the longest time he just watched, his gaze heated, hypnotic. Then he slid onto the seat beside her, his mouth tracking a path from her temple to her chin, his breath hot, wet against her ear.

Finally she could bear it no longer. In mid-passage her fingers fell away from the keys. She moaned, melting against him. He lifted her in his arms, carrying her down the hall to the bedroom.

His mouth never leaving hers, he laid her down on the bed. "Abby, Abby," he moaned, his hands tracing the fine line of her cheekbones, the bridge of her nose, her lips. "I love you. I want this to be so good for you. Don't be afraid, my Abby, don't be afraid."

He undressed her slowly, patiently, pausing to worship every tiny part of her with his mouth, with his hands. Then he quickly undressed himself.

"I . . . I'm only afraid that I won't please you, Morgan," she whispered, her body aflame with the need his touch had wrought. She reveled in the splendor of his naked body lying next to her own, wondering how she could ever have feared this moment with this man.

"Abby, sweet Abby," he said, his voice hoarse. "I am almost insane with how much you please me. My body is tormenting me to take you now. But I don't want to rush it, rush you." He gathered her to him, and she could feel the heat in his loins. Still he did not hurry. Tonight, this night, he wanted only to pleasure her.

"Tell me what to do," she whispered. "Tell me how to make it good for you, Morgan."

"Just letting me love you makes it good for me, Abby."

"I want . . . I want to love you back. With my body as well as my heart."

He gasped as her hands grew bold, skating feathery rings across his arms, his chest. "You're doing just fine." He sighed. "Just touch me, Abby. Touch me anywhere. Everywhere. Please."

Her hands slid to his waist and down, teasing the heated core of his sex with the very tips of her fingers. To know that he needed it, wanted it, ached for it, for her, was all that mattered in the world. She caressed him, stroked him, drove him to madness.

He shifted atop her, staking his arms on either side of her. He held himself above her, not moving. "Say, yes, Abby! Say, yes."

"Yes! Oh, yes!" She cried out, opening herself to him, taking all of him, digging her fingers into the taut flesh of his buttocks, driving him even deeper inside her.

She twisted, moaned, holding him there, feeling him fill her, awed by the knowledge that their separate bodies were now one. She caught his head in her hands and slipped his eyepatch free. "Nothing between us, Morgan. Nothing." She pulled him down, kissing his mouth, his cheeks, his forehead. "I love you. All of you."

His mouth found hers and she tasted the salty sweetness of his tears, knowing he tasted her own.

And then he was moving, thrusting, driving her with him, hurling them both into the veiling mists of paradise.

Sated, replete, she snuggled into the crook of his arm. "Oh, Morgan . . ." A tear trickled down her cheek.

He tensed. "Did I hurt you?"

"No." She feathered her lips across his chest. "I didn't even know my body could feel this way." She cuddled upward, cradling his head against her breasts. "I knew I loved you, but sharing this night, this time . . . all that I am, really . . . I just never knew how much I love you."

"The feeling is entirely mutual, Mrs. Kincaid. Believe me."

"You're not . . . used to this sort of thing?"

He chuckled. "I would have died a much younger man had I endured such loving before now."

"Endured?" It wasn't exactly the term she was looking for.

"Indeed. I'm not certain my poor body will survive till morning."

She nipped at his arm. "Well, it had better. I want more nights like this. Every night would do nicely."

He feigned a terror-filled look. "How will I explain my sudden inability to walk upright to my men?"

"You'll think of something."

He kissed her, tugging his eyepatch back into place.

"You don't have to do that, you know."

"I know." His gaze grew serious. "There's something I need to tell you. Something in my past I'm not very proud of."

"We all have things we're not proud of, Morgan. You don't have to tell me anything."

"I want to. I need you to know about it, so that maybe you can understand a little better why for a long time I couldn't see what I had, even with . . ." He hesitated.

"Lenore?"

"I don't mean to upset you."

"You haven't. Lenore and I have kind of an understanding."

"I beg your pardon?"

"From . . . sleeping in her room. I can't explain it." Someday she would tell him about the diary, but this wasn't the time.

"You remember I told you about Willowsong."

She nodded. "You bought it back, but your mother died."

"During the war, when my sister and mother and I still lived there, I was feeling pretty guilty that my father and brother had been off fighting for four years, while I did nothing."

"What were you? Fifteen?"

"When you're fifteen, you're pretty sure you can

win the war singlehanded if some general would just be smart enough to stick a gun in your hand."

She propped herself up on one elbow, threading a hand through the dusting of dark hair that spanned his chest. "What happened?"

"I ran off to find Jared—he was six years my senior—and my father. It took a little doing, but I tracked them to Gettysburg. I thought my father would skin me alive when I came running up to him, proud as you please."

"He couldn't keep Jared out of the war, but he wanted to protect you."

"At the time I didn't see it that way. I'd lied about my age, stolen a uniform, and was ready to fight. Jared and Pa both grabbed me by the scruff of the neck and were intent on dragging me to their captain's field tent."

He paused. Selina felt his heartbeat quicken beneath her hand, and his breathing grew more shallow.

"We were cut off by a Union patrol. I tried to grab my father's extra gun, but he clipped me over the back of the head with it. When I came to . . ." His whole body tensed. "He and Jared were both dead."

"Oh, Morgan, I'm so sorry."

"If I hadn't been so damned stupid . . ."

"It was their choice. They wanted you to live."

"They wanted me to protect Willowsong. I didn't even do that right."

"You got it back." Her voice grew fierce. "You take one hard look at Wolf Trail and tell me your father wouldn't be proud of you. You've built it from nothing."

He pulled her atop him, planting a lingering kiss on her lips. "For such a long time," he said, "I never even felt I deserved to be alive. I just went through the motions. Ceecy shook me out of it a little. But it took you . . ." He kissed her again, savoring the taste of her, "to finally let me lay all those old ghosts to rest."

She smiled. "All I did was love you."

"And thank God for that."

Unbidden, she thought of her own ghosts. A sudden tremor rippled through her.

"What's wrong?"

"Nothing," she said too quickly.

"Abby," he said, his voice gentle, "you can tell me anything. Please, know that."

A tear trailed down her cheek. No, she couldn't.

"You're thinking about that damned beast who raped you, aren't you?"

"I can't talk about him, Morgan. I wish I could. Please don't ask me."

He sighed. "Damn. I promised you I'd make you forget that night, and here I am making you relive it."

"It's all right. It's not your fault."

"Abby." He lifted her chin, forcing her to face him. "This man *is* dead, isn't he?"

"Oh, he's dead, Morgan. He's very, very dead."

He looked at her, furious with himself for putting her through this, but needing to know more. "Abby, I'm going to ask you one more thing, and then I'll never bring it up again. All right?"

She gave him a reluctant nod. She wanted so much to tell him everything. But there was nothing he could do, nothing anyone could do, as long as Marelda was alive.

His instincts might be all wrong, but he didn't think so. "When . . . when you said, 'I can't bear to look at you,' you weren't talking to me, were you?"

She didn't answer. She didn't have to.

"You weren't talking to some stranger in a dark alley either, were you?"

Tears streamed unheeded down her cheeks.

He kissed them away, holding her. "It was your husband who raped you, wasn't it? More than once."

He felt her nod. "He beat you?"

She nodded again.

He held her tight, able to draw no rein on the rage that ripped through him. "Thank God he's dead. If he were alive, I'd kill him with my bare hands."

Chapter 18

Selina woke before dawn, but didn't stir lest she wake Morgan, sleeping so peacefully beside her. Three weeks had passed since they'd returned from Miles City—three weeks of passion beyond imagining. She never knew a human being could be so happy.

Morgan's eyepatch had slipped upward during the night and in the first new rays of dawn she looked at his scar, really studied it for the first time. It was a part of him, as much as his hair or his mouth or his hands. And though he would have been loath to admit it, it had shaped part of what he had become—just as her past had shaped her, and even now controlled her.

One day Morgan would learn the truth. He had shared his deepest pain with her. Would he forgive her for not sharing hers? Or would he think she'd been using him from the first?

He stirred, then raised up on one elbow to look

at her. With an indifference that warmed her heart
he tugged the eyepatch back into place. He seldom
noticed it anymore and had all but broken his
habit of shifting his profile when he spoke to her.

"Have I told you how much I love waking up
with you in my bed, Mrs. Kincaid?"

"You've mentioned it a time or two, Mr. Kincaid."

He pulled her on top of him, teasing her into
swift arousal. They made love, warm, sweet. She
prayed afterward his seed would take root in her
womb, partly because she could think of nothing
she wanted more than to bear Morgan a child, but
more selfishly because she nurtured the hope that
if she had his baby he could never let her go.

With a reluctant sigh she tugged free of his embrace and padded to the kitchen. Though she resisted the idea fiercely, she knew their idyll would
have to end soon. September was rapidly drawing
to a close. Morgan had already put off joining his
crew on roundup.

She glanced up from the stove as Morgan ambled into the kitchen and plunked himself down at
the breakfast table. His sleep-tousled locks fell
across his forehead, giving him such an unabashedly sensual look that it was all she could do
not to whisk him back to their bed.

"Woman," he began in that overserious voice
she had come to know of late, when he was about
to tease her royally, "it's come to my attention that

you are personally responsible for keeping a certain highly respected rancher from his official duties. Do you have anything to say in your defense?" He helped himself to more than his share of the stack of flapjacks she set on the table, ostensibly enough for three people, though Celia was apparently sleeping in this morning.

"I'm afraid I'll have to plead guilty, your honor," she said, trailing her fingers along the back of his neck, "and throw myself on the mercy of the court."

"No mercy," he said, taking yet another flapjack. "I'll have to sentence you to six weeks on roundup, spending night after night sharing my bedroll."

"Oh, your honor." She sighed, kissing him soundly on the cheek. "How can I ever thank you?"

He grinned. "I'll think of something." Without warning his arm flashed out, drawing her to him, pinning her to his lap. Suddenly intense, he whispered, "God, how I love you, Abby. I have never been so happy. Never."

She had to fight to keep her misting eyes from spilling over. "I love you, Morgan. I can never say it enough." A long, lingering kiss later, she pulled away. "I wonder what's keeping Celia? She can't have missed the smell of these flapjacks. They're her favorite."

"And I thought you'd made them just for me."

"The way you're eating them, they may well end up just for you," she scolded, rapping his knuckles with the spatula as he reached for the last of the stack. "But I did make them for Celia. You and I have been so wrapped up in each other, I'm afraid she's been feeling a bit left out."

"She said something?"

"No, but last night I promised to teach her a new tune on the piano." She blushed. "However, a certain one-eyed rancher kidnapped me and hied me off to his den of iniquity."

"That den was our bedroom, madam."

She smiled impishly. "That it was." The smile faded as she grew serious. "We really have been leaving her out too much. I shouldn't have disappointed her like that."

"Maybe the three of us can go on a picnic this afternoon."

"That's a marvelous idea!" Selina rushed at once to Celia's bedroom, but quickly returned, frowning. "She's not there."

"Did you check the treehouse?"

"This early?" Selina felt her first stab of concern, as she headed outside. In two minutes she was back in the house. "Morgan! Morgan, she's gone!"

He came rushing out of the bedroom, swiping the shaving soap from his face with a towel. "What do you mean, she's gone?"

She shoved a note at him. "I found it in the treehouse."

"You have each other now," he read aloud. *"You don't need me anymore."* He crumpled the paper in his fist. "Damn. I thought she was happy for us."

"She is," Selina assured him, hearing the guilt and confusion threading his voice. "But she wants to feel she belongs here, too."

"Well, of course she belongs," he snapped, then straightened, raking his fingers through his hair. "I'm sorry. I'm just scared to think of her all alone out there."

"I know. So am I."

He started toward the door. "I'll saddle the horses. You get some food together."

Selina bit her lip. "You think it will take that long to find her?"

His expression was grim. "Celia knows her way around this ranch as well as I do. If she's decided to hide, then God help us."

It took Morgan only five minutes to pick up Celia's trail, but it was soon evident they were not going to find her quickly. "She must have left in the middle of the night," he said, drawing up to let the horses blow. "Damn! I don't understand why she didn't come to us." He shook his head. In a voice that didn't quite mask the pain he felt, he amended, "come to you, at least. I can't really be surprised she ran from me. Maybe I'm surprised it took her so long."

"Morgan, don't," Selina said gently. "She's scared and she's hurting, and right now that's more my fault than yours. All summer I worked to get her to trust me, to believe how much I've come to love her. And what did I do? I ignored her when she needed most to feel included."

Morgan nudged his stallion forward. "If we're going to be able to apologize to her before nightfall, we'd best keep moving."

Selina followed, setting Moondust into a trot. Morgan followed Celia's trail until well after sunset, but at last had to concede to the descending darkness. Chafing, he set up camp for the night.

"She'll be all right," Selina said, trying to reassure herself as much as Morgan. "She knows how to take care of herself."

He snapped a twig and tossed it onto their campfire, but said nothing.

Later, Selina snuggled next to him as they settled down for the night. But for the first time since they'd come back from Miles City, they did not make love. Still, they needed the closeness. In the distance Selina heard the cry of wolves on the hunt.

"They're probably pulling down one of my heifers," Morgan muttered.

Selina laid her head against his shoulder, glad for a subject to divert her thoughts. "My parents and I followed a pack one summer in the mountains. My father recorded a lot of their behavior in a book he was writing. He loved them." She hesitated, but then went on: "I fell in love with them myself. They're very sociable animals. With each other, of course." Her voice took on a regretful note. "They're disappearing, you know. Wolfers, poison, settlers. It's sad."

"They eat my cows. It is not sad."

"They eat your cows because we've killed their buffalo. It *is* sad. They're beautiful animals."

He snorted, obviously unwilling to debate the need for predators among his livestock. Selina let him get what sleep he could. They were both worried about Celia, neither of them wanting to think too hard about a child they loved alone in the dark somewhere beyond their reach.

They rose at dawn and rode out, not stopping to rest the horses until well past noon. Selina all but fell from the saddle, her legs throbbing with weariness, but she would bear anything until she knew Celia was safe. Bending back to try to work the kinks out of her body, she spied a white bird perched high in a nearby aspen. She squinted. "I've never seen a white owl before."

Morgan frowned. "It's an arctic owl. I've never seen one this far south before. Chino would say we're in for a bad winter."

It was then they heard the scream—a child's

scream, coming from the ravine some fifty yards to their left.

"Celia!" Morgan vaulted into the saddle, driving his heels into the stallion's sides. Selina clambered aboard her mare. At the ravine's edge the stallion reared, his eyes rolling back in his head, refusing Morgan's command to plunge down the steep incline. Morgan leaped free, seizing his rifle.

At the same instant Moondust shied violently, nearly unseating Selina. She leaped off and scrambled up behind Morgan. At the bottom of the ravine she saw the reason for the horses' terror.

Wolves. A half dozen of them whined and yapped, circling the base of a massive willow.

"Celia?" Morgan shouted. "Celia, are you down there?"

"Papa!" she screamed. "Papa, help me!"

"There!" Selina pointed between the long, sweeping branches of the tree. "I see her." She murmured a swift prayer of thanks. "She's out of their reach."

Morgan took aim on the lead wolf, a large gray male. Selina jerked the barrel toward the dirt just as he squeezed the trigger. The bullet threw up dirt at her feet.

"What the hell?" he roared. "Have you lost your mind? I could have killed you!"

She met his gaze levelly. "Fire in the air. The wolves will run."

He was shaking with fury. "Celia is down there, for God's sake!"

"I know. But they haven't hurt her." Selina started down the brush-studded incline. Morgan reached her in two strides, yanking her savagely back. "I don't know what the hell has gotten into you, but I'm not going to be worrying about both of you. You stay right here. You understand me?"

Still livid, he fired two quick shots. The wolves bolted for the timber. "Don't move, Celia," he called, descending the hillside. "Not one inch till I get there."

Selina waited until Morgan was almost to the tree, then trailed after him. She saw it before he did: one wolf darting from the trees. The brown female set at once to worrying a hole some twenty yards from the willow. Morgan brought his rifle up.

Selina held up a restraining hand. "Please, Morgan. Don't." With extreme caution Selina edged toward the wolf. "I'll bet you've got a pup in there, don't you, girl?"

"Goddammit, Abby," Morgan thundered. "You take one more step and that wolf is dead, I swear it."

"She won't hurt me."

He cocked the rifle. "One more step."

Selina stopped, watching as the wolf continued to whine and snap at the entrance to the hole. With a final glare meant to root her to the spot,

Morgan turned his attention to his daughter. "It's all right, Celia," he said, peering up into the tangle of branches. "You're safe now." He reached upward and Celia leaped into his arms.

Morgan grinned with relief, but a shriek from Celia made him whirl. Abby was hunched down on all fours scarcely three feet from eighty pounds of muscle and fangs.

"Both of you be very quiet," she said. "We don't want to startle her."

Every instinct in Morgan's body demanded he empty his rifle into that growling beast, but he did not move. His fear for Abby vied with wonder as he listened to her speak in low, soothing tones to one of the most vilified predators on earth.

She knelt down, peering into the hole. The wolf whined piteously, scratching at the turf. "Your pup's in there, isn't he?" He'd probably crawled into the hole head first, then didn't have room to turn around. The she-wolf had tried tugging on him, but his yips of pain had sent her into a frenzy. Selina worked the sides of the small tunnel, getting both of her arms alongside the wolf pup. Gripping him by the scruff of neck, so he couldn't bite her in his fear, she managed to maneuver him back far enough so that he could turn around and bolt toward his mother.

The she-wolf licked the pup furiously, then nipped at him to set him moving toward the woods. For an instant the pack leader reappeared, giving them all an appraising stare. Then with a throaty howl he, too, disappeared into the timber.

Morgan sank to his knees beside his wife. "If you ever do anything that stupid again . . ." He didn't finish, pulling her against him. "Abby, your life is not just your own anymore. If anything had happened to you . . ."

"I'm sorry, Morgan," she murmured. "I didn't mean to frighten you. I can't explain it, but I wasn't scared. Not for one minute." Her gaze went to a very guilty-looking little girl. "But I think I know someone who was." She smoothed Celia's disheveled blond locks and gave her a fierce hug. "Are you all right?"

Though her lower lip trembled, Celia's chin jutted stubbornly. Now that the danger was past, her reasons for running away had apparently slammed back full force. She struggled free of Selina's embrace. "You wouldn't have cared if they ate me!" she cried. "You don't need me anymore, either of you."

"Celia . . ." Morgan began sternly.

"You told him, didn't you?" Celia said, looking accusingly at Selina. "You were with him all the time. I know you told him. That's why you both hate me."

"No, I didn't tell him," Selina said gently. "I promised you I wouldn't."

"What are you two talking about?" Morgan demanded.

Celia looked at the ground.

Morgan nudged her chin upward with his hand. "It's time we put an end to whatever this is between us. Whatever I did, we can talk about it. I know you blamed me when your mother died." The girl's face crumpled. "Ceecy, please . . ."

"You never call me that anymore."

"Call you what?"

"Ceecy," she said sadly. "Chino did. And Abby. And even Clay. But not you."

"What has that got to do . . . ?" He stopped, taking a long look at his daughter. "Celia," he said gently, hunkering down in front of her. "What is it? Please. You can tell me."

Tears spilled from her hazel eyes. "You said Ceecy was my special name. That you would always call me that, because I was special. But that day . . . that day you stopped."

Morgan stared at her, dumbfounded. "What day?"

"When . . . when the gun . . . when . . . your eye . . . when . . ." She began to sob.

He looked imploringly at Abby. "Do you know what she's talking about?"

Selina squeezed the girl's shoulders. "It's all right, Celia. It's time for the truth." She wanted the child to see that she had no influence over Morgan's reaction. Celia had to know that her father didn't, couldn't, hate her.

"It was my fault," Celia said, sniffling.

"What was your fault?"

"The gun," she whimpered. "The gun was my fault."

Morgan grew very still. "What are you talking about? It was an accident."

Her face was so pale that Selina feared the child would faint. The truth, locked inside for four long years, tumbled out in a rush. "I . . . I was playing by the hearth. You left your gun sitting there. I knew I wasn't supposed to touch it. But I did. I . . . I put one of my rocks down in it like I saw you do with the bullets. And I used the metal thing to put the rock in real hard."

"The ramrod," Morgan supplied, half to himself. He had already guessed the rest, but Celia could not stop.

"I heard the door open. I saw you pick it up. I wanted to tell you, but I was afraid you would be mad at me."

Morgan felt sick—sick for his daughter. "Oh, my God." He pulled her to him. "I deserve worse for not knowing you were in the house. I thought you were playing in the barn. You had that loaded gun in your hands . . . Oh, my God. Ceecy, you were six years old. It's not your fault."

"It *was* my fault, don't you see? My fault you have the scar. My fault Mama left you. My fault. My fault. My fault!" Sobs shook her small body.

"Oh, baby . . ." Morgan was crying himself. He rocked her for long minutes. Smoothing away her tears with his palms, he cupped her face, locking her gaze with his. "Ceecy, I promise you on my life, this scar had nothing to do with the problems your mother and I had. Those problems started a long time before the accident. And they never had anything to do with you. Your mother loved you very much. And so do I."

She flung her small arms around his neck, crying softly. "I love you, Papa. I love you."

Selina hugged them both.

Celia looked up at her father. "Is it okay if I love Abby, too?"

Morgan smiled. "That's just fine by me, sweetheart."

For a long time the three of them stood there, holding each other in a circle of family love.

Later, as they mounted to head home, Selina heard Morgan mutter, "Please, God, let this family be well and done with secrets."

She closed her eyes, thinking that her very claim to this family was based on the most fearful secret of all. And as she rode, she wondered with a mounting dread when it would all come crashing down around her.

Chapter 19

Selina stretched with feline grace, her fingers trailing wickedly along the taut flesh of her husband's belly. "I thought you said driving beef to market was hard work."

"It is." He gripped her hand, then cupped it suggestively over his crotch. "Damned hard."

"I hadn't noticed."

"Oooh, woman, you are asking for it."

"Uh-huh," she drawled. "I'm begging for it. Please? We'll be in Cheyenne tomorrow and then we'll have to make love in a stuffy old bed instead of under the stars."

"And won't that be too bad. Maybe we'll have to suffer through a hot bath, too."

"I'll scrub your back if you scrub mine."

"You drive a hard bargain."

"Mmm, there's that word again." She kissed him, slowly, hating to move, but knowing Stewie's shout of "roll out" would be reverberating any minute now through the main camp some three hundred yards away. It would be dawn in a couple of hours.

"Thank you for a lovely evening, Mr. Kincaid. I didn't feel much like sleeping tonight anyway."

"Me either. This was certainly the damnedest cattle drive I have ever been on."

"Do you think we could make it an annual tradition?"

"Sounds good to me."

She giggled, loving these moments with him most of all. He was so open and trusting now it was almost frightening. And nothing frightened her more than the prospect of losing it all.

Morgan saddled their mounts, then pulled her close and kissed her soundly. His voice was throaty. "Sometimes I think you're just a dream; that one day I'll wake up and find you're not there, never have been."

She held him. "If it's a dream, then I don't want to wake up either. I love you, Morgan. So much."

Cheyenne was a bigger town than Miles City, growing, bursting with life. Selina tried hard to feel inconspicuous, but ever since she'd seen the reward poster in Miles City she felt safe only at Wolf Trail or on the open range with her husband. As Morgan checked them into a hotel, she raced up the stairs to their room. She felt she could linger nowhere.

Morgan deposited their valise on the floor near

the bed. "I'll be down at the stockyards for a while, finishing up the details on the sale of the herd. Ceecy's still with Stewie. Maybe if I get back in time . . ." He eyed the bed suggestively.

She forced a smile.

He frowned, coming up to her. Taking hold of her wrists, he pressed his lips to her palms. "Is something wrong?"

She shook her head. "Just tired."

He accepted that, heading for the door. "I'll be back as soon as I can."

Selina lay down and stared at the whitewashed ceiling, trying to fathom why she was suddenly so edgy. She considered the subtle altering of her fear these past months. When first she'd fled San Francisco, her first and foremost terror had been for her life. She still feared Marelda's vengeance, but her all-consuming terror now centered on what would happen to her life when Morgan found out the truth.

Sometimes she knew him too well. While she believed he would protect her, even work to clear her name, the time had long passed when she could tell him the truth and have him understand why she hadn't confided in him earlier. Now, after what they had shared these past ten weeks, the truth would be a terrible blow to him. She imagined his old suspicions crowding him, wearing him down, until he convinced himself she had simply

used him to save her own life. He would believe
she hadn't trusted him. Or worse.

"Oh, Morgan," she murmured aloud, "it has
nothing to do with trust." She shivered, frightened,
not just for herself but for Morgan as well. He
would be an accessory, culpable for harboring a
fugitive. He could go to prison and lose everything.
No, she would just have to pray that somehow she
could manage to hide the truth for the rest of her
life.

She sat up, shaking herself. Morgan could be
back any moment, and she didn't want to have to
explain her tear-stained face. She rose to her feet,
hoping a bath would lighten her mood.

Opening the valise, she frowned to see that she
had forgotten to include the rose-scented bath soap
she liked so well. Her skin tingled. That Morgan
liked so well.

Deciding a wanton evening with Morgan was
just what they both needed, Selina decided to dare
a quick run to a general store.

Leaving the hotel, she met no one's gaze, keeping the brim of her hat pulled low. Even so, she
found her spirits reviving just at the thought of
Morgan trailing the perfumed soap across her naked flesh.

Minutes later, clutching her small package, she
crossed the street, heading back to the hotel. Morgan was probably already back and wondering
where she'd gone.

She quickened her pace.

It happened in an instant. From nowhere a hand closed over her mouth from behind. She tried to scream, but felt herself suffocating under the crushing grip. She was being dragged into a crate-filled cul de sac.

A vicious shove sent her tumbling between two high stacks of wooden boxes. "So we meet again, eh?" a vaguely familiar voice hissed. "Just like I promised."

She stared at him, an icy terror closing around her heart.

Zeke.

"Been looking for you for five months, missy," he growled. "Going up and down the countryside showin' your picture to anybody who'd look." His mouth twisted into a smile. "I was real smart, though. I cut the picture off'n a poster, tellin' 'em you was a long-lost cousin. I didn't tell none of 'em about the reward."

"P-please," Selina stammered, finding her voice. "I beg you. Let me go, and I'll see that you get money. I'll pay you myself."

"You got ten thousand dollars in that little bag of yours, missy?" he sneered.

"Of course not." Her mind raced. "But I have a trust fund. I can get it."

"When?"

She bit her lip, biting back tears. She had to keep her wits about her. "I can't get to it right now. Not as long as my mother-in-law is still alive. But as soon as I can clear my name, you can have five times ten thousand dollars. Wouldn't that be worth waiting for?"

He shook his head. "I want the money now. Later don't mean nothin'." He grabbed her. "Maybe I can even get me a little bonus."

His hand squeezed her breast, his mouth pressed down on hers. It was all she could do not to vomit, but she dared not scream. Zeke would tell anyone who came to her rescue the truth of her identity. She tried to claw at him, but he twisted her wrist behind her back.

"Get your filthy hands off my wife." Morgan's voice was death. He held his Colt in his hand.

Zeke threw his arms in the air, backing away, his eyes locked on Morgan's gun. "Wife?" he snorted, disbelieving. "She got you between the sheets? Is that the deal she made with ye? I'll bet you don't even know—"

"Morgan," Selina cut in, grabbing her stomach, "I think I'm going to be sick."

"Yeah, I'll bet, missy," Zeke said.

"Shut your mouth," Morgan snarled, "or this gun will shut it for you." He levered back the hammer. "Abby, get the sheriff."

She hesitated.

Zeke laughed. "You want *her* to get the sheriff? Yeah, missy, go on and git the sheriff. I'd like to speak to the gentleman."

"Morgan, I really am going to be sick." She didn't know what else to say. She had to stall for time.

Morgan reached for her. "It's all right. We'll take him to the sheriff together."

Zeke saw his moment slipping away. "You don't know what you got here, mister," he said. "And I'm not real sure I want to tell ya either. Wouldn't want to share. But, what the hell? Better half than nothin'."

He groped inside the pocket of the tobacco-stained vest he wore. Selina felt herself die a little, certain the man was reaching for a reward poster.

Morgan saw it before she did. A palm gun. He shoved her violently away from him.

Zeke fired, missed. Morgan didn't. Zeke fell heavily, tumbling back, several crates crashing down atop him.

Morgan ripped the boxes out of the way, kicking the small pistol from Zeke's beefy fist before he could spend the second cartridge. But Zeke's eyes were already glazing. He tried to speak, mouthing the words. "Money. Mine . . . want . . ."

Then he was dead.

Morgan looked at her, a strange curiosity in that blue eye. "Did you know this man?"

"Of course I didn't know him," she said. "Why would I know a creature like that?" Her voice quivered. "He . . . said he wanted money. I think

. . . think he knew I was your wife, that you'd have money from the herd."

He sighed. "That must be it." He hugged her; felt her trembling.

"Thank God you came when you did."

He released her, then bent to heave Zeke's body over his shoulder. "I'm going to the undertaker's. You go on back to the hotel and lie down. I'll have to stop by the sheriff's office, too."

Selina quailed inwardly, but said nothing. Later, pacing her room at the hotel, she worried every second that Morgan would return with a lawman to help cart her off to jail himself.

He strode in nearly an hour later, looking grim. "It's taken care of," he said.

She flung her arms around him. "It was so awful."

He held her for a long time, his words soothing. During moments like this, when she felt so close to him, she wanted so terribly to tell him the truth.

How tentative it all was, how tenuous. Her fear of discovery was back full force. And the one man in the world with whom she longed to share her fear stood here, holding her, but the words would simply not come. She couldn't take the risk— couldn't risk hurting him, losing him.

That night as he made love to her she thought she sensed something different, subtle, but there nonetheless, though he said nothing. She shoved away the thoughts, unable to bear even the tiniest doubt. She curled into his arms, her voice despairing. "Take me home, Morgan. Please, take me home."

Chapter 20

Even back at Wolf Trail, Selina had not felt safe since the incident with Zeke. She felt exposed, terrified, afraid to leave the ranch for any reason. It was almost as if she could feel some hidden menace sifting on the wind. Something terrible was going to happen, and there was nothing she could do to stop it.

She peered out the front window, glad at least to see no sign of the snow Morgan had forecast would fall before day's end. Though it had snowed hard in November, these past three weeks had been relatively mild. But the weather scarcely mattered. Neither storms nor blue skies seemed to affect her mood, which ebbed deeper into melancholy daily. For Morgan and Celia's sake she tried to shake it off, but thus far without success. They should be back soon. At dawn they'd left on a foray to find the perfect fir tree. They had asked her to join them, but Selina hadn't been able to muster even a feigned cheeriness.

With a resigned sigh, she turned toward the kitchen, twisting the pine cone she held in her hand, wishing she could conjure up even a little festive spirit as she went through the motions of decorating the house. After all, it was Christmas Eve.

She frowned as she caught the sound of a wagon pulling up in the yard. Morgan hadn't told her to expect anyone. She glanced out the window and saw the wagon pulling out again. Footsteps sounded outside. Selina felt a sudden chill that had nothing to do with the weather. She opened the door.

She gasped.

On her doorstep stood Alberta Bodine.

"Hi, there, sweet thing," the woman said, barreling past her into the room. "Been a while, huh?" She whipped off her muffler, shaking out a dusting of snow. "It's startin' up again out there. Gettin' colder, too. Driver said this storm's gonna be a beaut."

Terror-stricken, Selina stood there, gulping in air, trying desperately to slow the trip-hammer beat of her heart. "Why are you . . . ?" Dear God, she had to get rid of this woman, convince her to leave at once. "Morgan . . . Morgan is married. You can't . . . I mean . . ."

"Calm down, honey," Bertie soothed. "I got no

hard feelin's. You got him, you keep him—even if I
did find out ol' Kincaid is far from bein' a poor
dirt farmer." She propelled Selina over to the
hearth. "You look like you're catchin' your death.
Stand here with me and warm your bones."

"Bertie . . ." Selina felt for all the world as
though she were on the edge of an abyss and someone was about to push her over the edge. "What
are you doing here?"

Bertie plopped herself on the divan, working off
her boots. "I'm afraid me and my big mouth may
have got you in a whole heap o' trouble."

Selina felt the abyss widen.

"I seen your picture on a reward dodger, honey.
I knew there was somethin' scared about ya that
day on the train, but I never imagined it was as
bad as all that."

"You're here after the reward?" Selina sat on the
divan beside the buxom redhead.

"Oh, heavens no. I don't need money that bad. I
always get by. I got my pride." She bit her lip,
twisting the folds of her voluminous wool traveling
skirt. "But do you remember Willis?"

"Willis?" Selina shook her head, still reeling.
"No, I . . ."

"The medicine drummer on the train."

Selina felt the illusion of safety she'd been clinging to all these months shatter into a million irrep-
arable pieces.

"Well, I had a little too much brandy one night

after I seen your picture. I told him about meetin'
you that day. We talked some more and he got all
excited when I said I left the letters behind. He
was just sure as heck you woulda took me at my
word."

Tears tracked down Selina's cheeks. She didn't
have to hear the rest. Whatever variations there
might be, the end result would put her on the gallows for Gideon's murder.

"I had to warn you. Willis showed your picture
to that Miles City sheriff, what's his name, Jon
Lathrop. I guess he'd never really looked too hard
at it before. Anyway, I figure they can't be more'n
ten miles behind me, maybe less. I paid that driver
plenty to run them horses."

"So the sheriff is coming here," Selina said, almost to herself. She stood, feeling suddenly
strangely calm, detached. She knew what she had
to do. She might have faced Morgan with Bertie,
but she could not allow the sheriff to arrest her and
take her away in front of Celia. Her voice was
emotionless. "Morgan is an innocent bystander in
this. He didn't know any—"

She caught the sound of riders pounding into
the yard.

"Honey, I never meant for this to happen, I
swear."

The door banged open. Willis stomped in first,
snow clinging to the waxen ends of his handlebar
mustache. Behind him strode a barrel-chested gi-

ant of a man Selina guessed to be Jon Lathrop. He seemed embarrassed. He tried and failed to meet Selina's gaze.

"I'm afraid I'm here to arrest you, ma'am," he said.

"Bertie's been telling me," Selina said, as though they were discussing the weather. "I'll need to get a few things together, if that's all right?"

"No hurry, ma'am. I have no intention of dragging you out in this storm, and certainly not before I talk to Mr. Kincaid. Is he home?"

"He should be shortly." Selina felt as though she were going to be sick. She didn't want to wait for Morgan, didn't want him to see . . .

Willis rubbed his hands together in front of the fire. "Ten thousand dollars. Bertie, we have hit the jackpot!"

"Shut up!" Lathrop snapped. "I don't want to hear another word out of your mouth. You've made me sick from the minute I met you, and you are not improvin' my opinion one bit."

"In case I haven't mentioned it, Willis," Bertie said, her voice colder than Selina had ever heard it, "you and I are through."

Willis snorted. "You're both fools. I couldn't care less. I got me ten thousand dollars."

Selina walked stiffly into the bathing room, still not quite believing this was happening. She stood there, gathering a few necessities, thinking absurdly how sad it would be that she would not be able to wish Morgan and Celia a Merry Christmas. Her gaze trailed to the door that opened into her bedroom. The sheriff was waiting in the kitchen. Moving swiftly through the door, she grabbed a coat and scrambled out the bedroom window.

She hunched low, circling the house, her heart pounding, expecting at every step to be discovered. But she made it to the barn, where she made short work of saddling Moondust.

"It's you and me, girl," she said, patting the mare's thick winter coat.

Selina mounted and rode out. The snow was falling harder. She swiped at the tears that chilled her cheeks.

She was on the run again.

Alone.

"Think Abby will like the tree, Pa?" Celia chirped.

"She'll love it. You picked the best one." Morgan hefted the fir over his left shoulder. The snow had been falling lightly for half an hour now. He couldn't wait to get home, back to Abby. Spending Christmas with her . . . damn, but he loved that woman.

"Did you get her a present?" Celia asked.

He tugged off a glove, then reached into the inside pocket of his sheepskin jacket. He withdrew a small gold band. "That I did."

Celia gasped. "It's beautiful!"

"And what about you?"

She blushed. "I got her her own lariat."

He laughed. "She'll love it!"

His mood soured considerably when he saw Clay Prescott riding toward them, but then he felt a niggling alarm. Prescott was pushing his mount hard. Something was wrong.

"What is it?" Morgan barked.

Prescott wasted no time on their usual unpleasantries. "I was cuttin' back to the Lazy C. I swear I saw Abby ridin' off from your place not more than fifteen minutes ago, ridin' like the devil himself was after her."

Morgan vaulted onto his stallion's back, even as Prescott shouted after him. "I would've followed her, but then I saw you." He heard Prescott and Celia set their mounts into a gallop behind him.

Back at the ranch Morgan burst into the house. "Abby!" he shouted. He frowned as a red-haired woman got up from the divan. "Who are you? Where's Abby?"

"I don't know no Abby. Me? I'm Alberta Bodine."

Morgan stiffened, then turned toward Celia, who had stopped dead behind him. "Why don't you go bed down the horses, Ceecy?" he said. "I'll see to our guest." The sheriff and Willis stepped out of the kitchen, carrying slices of the gingerbread Abby had made for breakfast. "Guests," he corrected automatically.

"But, Pa, this lady just said she's—"

"Go on, now. I'm sure she's just having a little joke at our expense."

Celia left reluctantly. Prescott stood to one side, waiting to see what would happen next.

Morgan's gaze narrowed ominously on the woman who called herself Alberta Bodine. "Now who the hell are you? And where is my wife?"

"Your wife," Willis said, "is a murderess. And she's run off. But I'm still claiming my reward."

"I checked his story, Kincaid," Lathrop said, "and I'm afraid it's true. She's wanted for murderin' her husband down in San Francisco. Quite a ta-do over it. Biggest reward I've ever seen. Even the James boys didn't go for ten thousand."

"My wife didn't murder anyone. This is insane." Morgan stalked up to Lathrop. "You let my wife leave here with this kind of a storm blowing?"

"I didn't know she was gone till it was too late."

Swearing, Morgan slammed out to the kitchen, then gathered up the supplies he would need, taking an extra rifle and blankets. He stopped briefly at his desk, then headed toward the door. "Would you stay here, Prescott? Watch out for Celia? I don't know how long I'll be gone."

Prescott nodded. There was no need for explanations.

"I can't let you go, Kincaid," Lathrop said, stepping between Morgan and the door. "You ain't a deputy. And I don't reckon it's your plan to bring her back."

"I plan to see to it she doesn't freeze to death after being scared out of her wits." He straightened, his hand very deliberately shifting to the trigger of his Winchester. "You can try to stop me, Lathrop. But I wouldn't recommend it."

"You can't allow this, Sheriff," Willis whined.

Lathrop stepped away from the door. "It's gonna be a white hell out there in an hour. I don't envy nobody caught out in it."

"Well, I ain't lettin' no ten thousand dollars ride out of my life," Willis declared. "I'm gonna find her."

"Storm'll kill a dude like you, boy. Can't spend no money if you're dead."

Willis gave no indication he even heard. He stomped past the two men and went out into the storm.

"He'll last about an hour," Lathrop said.

Morgan, his own fears about Abby mounting, followed Willis. He didn't miss Lathrop's softly spoken "Good luck."

In the barn, Morgan could hear the wind beginning to howl as the storm picked up strength. Celia looked up from brushing down her pony. Her hazel eyes widened fearfully. "What's happening, Pa?"

"I'm going out to find Abby."

"What's she doing out in the storm? Who is that woman in the house?"

"Never mind any of that. It's not important

right now. What I need from you is your promise that you'll stay here with Clay. I don't want to have to worry about you, too." As he spoke he gathered more of the gear he would need for a long siege in the cold. "I may not be back for a while. Abby and I will have to hole up till this blows over. Do you understand?"

"You will find her, won't you, Pa?"

"I'll find her."

"But . . . will she be all right?"

He had to raise his voice to be heard above the wind. "She'll be fine. We'll both be fine. We may just have to have Christmas a little late."

Celia trembled. She was scared to death, though she was trying hard not to show it. "I love you, Pa."

He hugged her, gazing into her waiflike features, now pale with grown-up fears. "I'll find her. I promise." He hugged his daughter again, then tied off a lead rope to the pack horse. The storm could last a week, maybe longer. He mounted his stallion. Clay had seen Abby heading south. South to where? Was she trying to reach the train? He doubted it was even running in weather like this. The passes would be drifted shut.

With a final reassuring nod to Celia he rode out. As soon as he was out of her sight, he pushed the horses to the limit, needing to cover ground before the snow got too deep. The snow fell harder, the wind whipping it into a thousand tiny shards of ice

stinging his cheeks. He hunched low in the saddle,
pulling up the collar of his jacket. The wind
howled, keening. It was getting dark.

And it was so damned cold.

Selina couldn't see anything but white. Her fingers
throbbed painfully, but her feet didn't seem to hurt
at all anymore.

She had to find shelter—something, anything to
get her out of this wind. She had only one blanket.
What she really needed was a fire. She had to get
warm or die.

Moondust trudged on gamely for another hour
through drifts sometimes reaching her haunches.
Finally Selina guided the mare toward a copse of
trees. Maybe she could throw together some kind
of shelter of branches.

Dismounting, she immediately sank to her knees
in the snow. Somehow she forced her legs to move,
but they no longer seemed attached to her body.
One step at a time, she thought over and over and
over again, until at last she reached the cottonwoods. She collapsed onto her back, staring upward into a twisted mass of barren limbs. The
branches whipped wildly in the snowy blasts of
frigid air.

Cold.

So cold.

She struggled to her feet, then stumbled. Again
and again she rose, while all around her the wind

howled, relentless, unforgiving. By now Morgan knew it all—that she had taken Bertie's letters, that she had lied to him from the first day. Maybe he even believed she had killed Gideon.

Morgan. She closed her eyes. She'd always known it wouldn't last. But still she'd hoped.

She stumbled again. This time she could not summon the strength to rise. But it was all right. It didn't seem so cold anymore. The wind was fading, too. It was almost peaceful. Her hands and feet no longer pulsed with agony. Thank heaven. Now she could rest.

She would sleep.

She would dream about Morgan.

Even dream she heard him calling her name.

Then everything was quiet.

Morgan stopped to rest the horses. In some places the drifts were belly-deep. He called to Abby even though he knew she couldn't hear him above the shrieking winds. It gave him something to do. He had to keep looking, even when he could no longer see more than ten feet ahead. He thought of the line shack Clay and Lenore had used for their trysts. If Abby had seen it before the storm hit hard, she might have headed for it.

It was a long shot, but it was all he had. If he missed her . . .

"Abby!" He called her name until his throat was raw. Then he called it some more.

Time and again he jerked off his gloves to blow on his numbed fingers. He couldn't feel his face anymore. But he couldn't stop to build a fire. Without shelter, Abby would be dead by morning.

He stumbled across a creek bed and followed it. If Abby had found it, she might have done the same. The thought struck him that she might have turned back.

Turned back to the law?

No.

He rode on, forced to dismount more and more often, pulling on the stallion's reins with all his strength. Sometimes he would lead, tramping down a path for the horses. Then he would alternate the stallion and the pack horse. By nightfall both he and the animals were exhausted.

"Abby!" He dropped to his knees, feeling tears of rage and frustration course down his frozen cheeks, tears of grief as he imagined his life without her.

He dragged himself back into the saddle, forcing the horses onward. He wouldn't stop looking for her until he was dead too.

A miracle? An accident? He'd never know which. The stallion shied. He looked down, then dropped to the ground. "Abby." He turned her over, touched her face. She was so cold. With his teeth he yanked off one of his gloves, then touched his fingers to her throat. At first he felt nothing but cold, cold flesh. He blew on his hand, felt again. It was there. Faint, but there.

A pulse. She was alive.

Grunting, he heaved her belly-down over his saddle. He spotted Moondust near the cottonwood. With all three horses in tow, Morgan headed out. He had a new purpose now. He had found her. She was alive. But unless he got her warm—soon—she would die.

Muttering his first prayers in years, he stumbled onto his second miracle. The line shack.

He half dragged, half carried Abby through the door. One of his men must have used the place within the past week. There was still wood by the stove.

Oblivious to his own exhaustion he started a fire, then threw every blanket and buffalo robe over Abby. Then he went out to make certain the horses were sheltered. Without them they couldn't make it out of here.

His feet were numb as he struggled back to Abby's side. He shifted her closer to the stove, rubbing her hands, her cheeks. She didn't move, didn't even sigh.

He stripped off her clothes and then his own. Beneath the blankets and robes he held her naked body next to his own, knowing flesh-to-flesh contact was the best treatment for exposure to cold. He shivered violently. It was like cradling a block of ice.

"Dammit, Abby," he pleaded against her ear, "don't you die on me. Don't you dare die."

During the night she started to shiver, at times so hard and for so long that he feared she would die of exhaustion. But at dawn he woke from a stuporous sleep to find she was still alive. "You're going to make it, Abby," he said. "You hear me? You're going to make it."

She showed no signs of waking. He knew he had to get some food into her. Her strength was all but gone.

He managed to prepare some beef broth and forced her to take it in a small sips, stroking her throat until she swallowed. It took nearly an hour to get half a cup into her. He set up a routine, feeding her every other hour.

The next day she was no better. Nor the next.

All the while the storm continued unabated. The wind howled and screeched all around them, killing his ranch, killing his love.

Three more days went by. He never left her side, except to fix her something to eat. Cradling her against him, he willed the strength of his own body into hers, at times giving in to sobs of despair, terrified that she would die.

"Why didn't you trust me?" he whispered fiercely. "Why didn't you come to me? Don't you know I could forgive you anything?"

She moaned.

He stilled, uncertain whether or not he had just imagined it.

Her lips moved. "Mor . . . gan?"

He hugged her close, feeling her breath muffled against his throat as she again said his name. ". . . so sorry, Morgan. So sorry."

"Shh, rest now." He rocked her. "Rest. Save your strength. We'll talk later."

For the first time in a week he slept without the fear of waking up to find her dead. When he stirred hours later, it was to find her watching him, her brown eyes infinitely sad.

"You hate me, don't you?"

He shook his head. "That could never happen." He looked away. "Why didn't you come to me?"

"I was afraid."

"Of me?"

She winced at the pain in his voice. "Of what you would think of me, that you couldn't help but hate me if you knew."

He got to his feet and padded over to his saddlebags, then pulled out the folded piece of paper he'd taken from his desk. "I took this off our friend Zeke in Cheyenne . . . right before the sheriff came in to talk to me at the undertakers'."

Selina felt a hot flush of shame. A reward poster. Morgan had known. He had known for months.

"I told you about Gettysburg, about my father, my brother. I kept waiting for you to tell me about Gideon."

"I'm sor—" She stopped. The word seemed so fearfully inadequate all at once.

"Is it that you still can't tell me, Abby? Or that you won't?" He paused. "Maybe I should call you Selina."

Sad. He was so sad, so hurt. God, how she wanted to turn time back, make it right. But nothing could change what was.

She took a deep breath, then told him everything—about Marelda, about Zeke, about meeting Bertie on the train. All the while she knew Morgan was wrestling with the pain of believing she hadn't trusted him. "I didn't want you to lose everything you've worked so hard for. I didn't want you to go to jail."

He seemed not to hear her, his demeanor now chillingly akin to the stillness that blanketed the frozen land outside the cabin. "Did you kill Gideon?"

Tears stung her eyes.

"I don't care if you did," he gritted. "He deserved to die. But to help you, I need to know the truth."

"No, I didn't kill him—though why you should believe me instead of the newspaper accounts . . ."

"Do you know who did kill him?"

This was Morgan Kincaid, the lawyer. Detached, dispassionate. She wanted Morgan Kincaid, her husband, her lover. But he was gone. She shivered, wondering when or if the man who loved her would ever be back.

"Gideon," he prodded.

She closed her eyes. "Gideon would take bedmates. Buy them, actually. Pay them for their services."

"His mistress killed him?"

"Not a mistress." She shuddered, fighting a sudden wave of nausea as her mind brought back the hideous images. "One night I heard noises. I thought . . . I thought he was raping someone. So I . . . peeked into his room." She covered her mouth, fearing she would be sick. "He was with . . . a boy. He paid them. Fourteen-, fifteen-year-old boys. Paid them to . . . to . . ."

Morgan pulled her to him. "You don't have to say any more." He felt sick himself, that she should ever have witnessed such a perversion. But now that she had started, she couldn't seem to stop herself.

"One night . . . one night he made me . . . made me . . ."

"Abby . . . Selina, don't."

She sobbed against him, great hiccuping sobs that wracked her debilitated body. Morgan chafed to know the full story, needing every scrap of information he could gain in order to begin the process of exonerating her, but he feared pressing her when she was so emotionally and physically exhausted.

Easing her back on the blankets, he smoothed her sweat-dampened tresses away from her face. "I shouldn't have pushed you," he said. "I'm sorry. Rest now. Just rest."

"I want to tell you, Morgan."

"You'll have plenty of time to tell me the rest of it."

"No." She gripped his wrist. "I need to tell you now. Please. I may never have the courage again."

His mouth grim, he nodded. "All right."

She took a long, shuddering breath. "Gideon dragged me into his room one night to punish me." She shut her eyes, trembling, but she did not stop. "He made me watch . . . made me touch . . ." She swallowed hard to keep from retching. "After that, I didn't try to fight him anymore. He got tired of me, I guess, and left me alone."

"Do you know who killed him?"

"I . . . it was a delivery boy. I'd seen him once or twice before, bringing things to the house. Gideon had taken a fancy to him. But the boy would have none of it. That day . . . Gideon dragged the boy to his room. I came in just as he was scrambling out the window. He'd . . . he stabbed Gideon."

For the first time Morgan felt a spark of hope. "I'll hire Pinkertons. We'll find the boy. Until then, you'll stay here."

"I can't involve you, Morgan."

"It's a little late for that, don't you think?"

Tears slid from her eyes.

He kissed them away. "That didn't come out right. I'm involved because I want to be. Because . . ." He sighed. "Because I love you."

She trembled to hear the words; feared he said them only to comfort her. But then his lips found hers, and his hands, tentative at first, then bold, eager, shifted, moving over her, exploring the intimate curves of her body. She felt the rising heat of him against her thigh, her own blood flaming to life. She moaned, reaching for him, her need blazing against the fearsome cold without. Frenzied, primitive, their bodies linked.

She gave him all that she had, desperate to believe again that he loved her. Day blended to night to day again. The storm kindled anew, and again and again they made love.

Another week passed before Morgan risked venturing out. He returned just before dusk, looking grim.

"What is it?" she asked, looking up from the pot of stew she'd been stirring on the stove.

"The cattle," he said. "They're dying by the score. The drought last summer meant the last of the grass was gone in November." His shoulders sagged. "They're going to starve. Twenty thousand head, and every damn one of 'em could starve to death by spring."

She came over to him and slid her arms around his lean waist. "I'm so sorry."

He held her close for a long minute, then gently set her away from him. "I stopped at the ranch. I told Ceecy you're all right, and picked up more supplies. But I think it's best if . . ." He let the words trail off.

"You think I should stay here alone, don't you?"

"I can't investigate Gideon's murder from here. And if I try to ride back and forth between the ranch and this place . . ."

"Someone might see," she finished for him. Though she knew he was right, the prospect of being in the tiny cabin all alone was less than appealing. She did her best not to let him see how discomfited she was. Forcing her voice to be light, she asked, "When will you be back?"

"I don't know. When I hear something from the Pinkertons, I suppose. But don't worry, I'll have Stewie check in on you now and then, and I'll make sure you don't go hungry."

She gave him a wan smile. "There's one hunger food can't appease, Mr. Kincaid."

His blue eye darkened, and his palm cupped the right side of her face. His voice was husky. "Maybe there's something I could do about that."

She kissed him. "Maybe there is."

They made love, bittersweet, each seeking to give greater pleasure to the other. But even in the aftermath of the joining of their bodies, Selina sensed more than Morgan's physical withdrawal. It was as though he were girding himself for something beyond a temporary separation. He was preparing for a life without her.

She told herself it wasn't true, but the feeling persisted as she watched him ride out.

The next blizzard hit January ninth. It didn't stop snowing for ten days. Though she had no way to measure, Selina was certain the temperature plummeted some days far below zero. Wolf Trail was dying.

She waited, paced, worried, and imagined the worst. Three weeks went by before she heard crunching footfalls on the ice surrounding the shack. Stewie? Morgan? She raced to the door and flung it open.

Clay.

"You don't have to look that miserable," he said.

"I'm sorry." She stepped back to let him in, almost amused by how comfortable she now felt with the Lazy C ranch manager. It was her first human interaction since she'd unburdened herself of her terrible secret. "Did Morgan send you?"

He nodded, depositing a bulky burlap bag near the stove. "Supplies."

When he made no move to leave, she asked, "Would you like some coffee?"

"Thanks."

They sat opposite each other at the small rough-hewn table, sipping from tin cups. "Tell me what's happening," she said. "Has Morgan had any word from San Francisco?"

He gave her a wry smile. "He trusts me with you, or rather he trusts you, but he doesn't take me into his confidence about anything else."

"I'm sorry. It's just that I'm so eager to hear something, anything." She hesitated, but her curiosity forced her to ask, "What about the ranch?"

Clay minced no words. "The Lazy C is finished. Too much red ink, too little livestock. Wolf Trail's the same. And just about every other outfit from Montana to Colorado."

"You both can start over."

"We've wired a dozen banks. No one is lending ranchers anything. Morg saw it coming, but too late. Open range ranching is dead. The next bunch to come in here will put up fences and store winter feed."

"Morgan won't give up."

"He'll have to."

She didn't believe that, but there seemed little use arguing with Clay. "I know Morgan hasn't told you too much, but maybe . . . maybe you've heard about that man . . . Willis? And Bertie? Is Sheriff Lathrop looking for me?"

"The sheriff has his hands full right now. He never wanted to arrest you. It was that damned drummer." A look of grim satisfaction settled over

Clay's features. "At least he got what was comin' to him."

"What do you mean?"

"Froze solid as a glacier not more 'n a thousand yards from the main house."

Selina shuddered, realizing that might well have been her own fate. "What about Bertie?"

Clay coughed, his cheeks darkening. "She's, uh, she's been staying at the Lazy C. I mean, with everything all snowed in . . ."

Selina smiled. "You wouldn't want her to get cold."

"I doubt Bertie's ever been cold." He flushed. "I mean . . ." Abruptly, he stood up. "I'd best be getting back. I'm glad you're doing all right. I'll get word to Morg."

She hugged her sides against the blast of cold air he let in when he opened the door. "When you send word," she said, "could you tell him . . ."

"What?"

"Nothing. Never mind." She straightened. "Are you sure things are really that bad for Wolf Trail?"

"Worse."

"Then there is something I need you to tell Morgan. I have a trust fund. My parents left it to me. Gideon tried to get it from me, but my parents had a stipulation that even I couldn't have it until I turned twenty-one. I could send a wire."

Clay was shaking his head. "Forget it. Morg

wants you safe. You send for that money and you might as well run up a flag about where you are."

"But if he doesn't get the money soon . . ."

Clay gripped her arms. "Do I have to tell Morgan you're thinking of pulling something crazy?"

She bit her lip. "He has enough to worry about."

"Then you'll put all crazy notions out of that pretty head of yours?"

She nodded.

"Thank you." With that he left.

Selina waited until he was well out of sight. Then she pulled on her coat and hefted the supplies over her shoulder.

She couldn't let Morgan sacrifice his ranch for her. It meant too much to him. Somehow she would get the money from her trust fund, even if it meant risking an encounter with Marelda.

In minutes she'd saddled Moondust and was ready. Mounting, Selina sat still for long minutes, looking out over the glistening sea of white, knowing this might well be the last time she would see Wolf Trail, knowing too that if Marelda prevailed, she would never see Morgan again.

Chapter 21

Spring. A time for renewal, rebirth. But for mile after mile Morgan had found nothing but the stench of death. Carcasses were stacked like cordwood along cutbanks, arroyos. He estimated maybe twenty percent of his stock had survived. Not enough.

But even the death of Wolf Trail could be tolerated, as long as he had Selina. He'd heard nothing yet from the Pinkertons he'd hired, except an initial message weeks ago that Marelda Hardesty was one damned vengeful woman.

Selina would be anxious to hear any news, even bad news. He'd sent Clay with supplies over three weeks ago, telling himself it was safer. Clay wouldn't be followed. But in fact, Morgan had stayed away deliberately, giving himself time to sort through what he felt.

The conclusion was always the same.

He loved her, completely, mindlessly.

Just as she had understood a boy's mistake in battle, he understood why she had been unable to confide in him. And for his part, he'd reacted exactly as she feared he would—by pulling away when she needed him most.

The thought that she might have convinced herself that she loved him because she so desperately needed a place to hide gnawed at him more often of late, but it didn't alter his own reality. He loved her, and he would do anything—even give her up —to have her free.

But tonight he would see her. He'd tell her what was in his heart and let her decide what was in hers. Perhaps she wouldn't know until this whole sordid mess was resolved.

He would make love to her, though. How he had missed making love to her.

He was saddling up when a rider sloshed through the melting snow into the yard.

"You Morgan Kincaid?" the stranger asked.

Morgan nodded.

The man handed him an envelope and continued on his way.

Morgan tugged off his glove, ripped the brown paper, then frowned at the bank draft that spilled into his hands. The banks had all turned him down. What . . . ? He stared at the seal of the bank of origin—Union Savings Bank, San Francisco. A cold terror such as he'd never known twisted in his gut.

Like a man possessed he rode to the line shack.

Seeing Clay Prescott's sorrel tied to the hitch rail only added to Morgan's fury. He practically tore the door from its hinges as he slammed inside.

Bertie Bodine rarely blushed, but she did so now, peering out from under the blanket she shared with Clay Prescott. "Didn't you ever hear of knockin', honey?"

Morgan didn't even blink.

Prescott scrambled to his feet, ramming into a pair of pants. "Isn't this a little much, even for you, Morg?"

"Where's Ab— . . . Selina?"

Prescott's eyes widened. "What are you talking about?"

"You told me she was here, safe, when I sent you with supplies three weeks ago."

Prescott paled. "I thought you must have come and got her."

Morgan gripped Prescott's shirtfront. He was in no mood for anything but God's own truth. "What do you know about this?"

Prescott shook his head. "Nothing, I swear. She didn't say a word to me about leaving. I didn't think—"

"No, you never do. You didn't think with Lenore, either"

Prescott jerked free, suddenly as angry as Morgan. "Don't say her name to me, Kincaid. I loved her." He smoothed a hand over his blond hair. "You never believed that, did you?"

"She was my wife."

The feelings that had been dammed inside Prescott for years came spilling out. "She was lonely. And frightened. I was weak and available. She was like a child. All she ever wanted was your attention." He straightened. "She was going to have my baby. Did you know that?"

Morgan slammed a fist into Prescott's face.

Bertie had the good sense to do nothing.

Prescott did not retaliate. "It's the truth," he said. "For once, you're going to hear the truth." He took a steadying breath. "I found her when she was out riding. She said she was leaving—leaving you, leaving me. She was going to make it on her own. I begged her to stay, to divorce you and marry me. But she wouldn't."

Morgan sighed, feeling only a rush of sad irony. "She should have. I would've wished you both well."

Tears tracked down Prescott's face. "She slapped me. I pushed her. She hit her head on a boulder. She lived a few hours, sobbing about how much she loved you, how much she loved Ceecy. She wanted me to tell you she was sorry. But I was scared you'd shoot me where I stood if you knew. I left her there. And I've hated you and I've hated me ever since."

At length, Morgan said, "I'm sorry, Prescott. I really am."

Bertie hugged the blanket around her, edging close to Clay. "It's all right, honey," she soothed. "Bertie will take care of you."

Morgan rode out as if the demons of hell were on his tail, cursing every step of the way that the mountain passes were still drifted shut. He wouldn't be able to board a train until he reached Oregon.

The delay proved deadly. By the time Morgan reached San Francisco, every paper told the story on every street corner. Selina's trial had been over for a week. He crushed a newspaper in his fist, seething at the lies in every spurious inch of newsprint.

But there was one savage truth as well. Selina had been captured after sending off a bank draft. A coiled sickness settled over him. Tomorrow morning Selina was scheduled to hang.

He swore so viciously that passersby started and gave him a wide berth on the crowded bayfront. Bolting toward a offloading trolley car, he climbed aboard and corraled the driver, demanding to know which tram went by the prison.

"Want to see the hangin', huh?" The driver smirked knowingly. "Me, too. Wrangled the day off."

Morgan closed a hand over the man's throat. "If I see you there, I'll kill you."

Morgan left the ashen-faced driver struggling for air. As he rode toward the prison he forced his temper to settle to a more manageable level. He wouldn't be any help to Selina in this mood. He trembled. What if he couldn't help her at all?

No. She wasn't going to hang tomorrow, no matter what the cost—in money or blood.

The warden was a bespectacled man sporting a bowstring and an obnoxious attitude. He was taking a macabre pride in the spectacle scheduled for dawn in the prison courtyard.

"Sorry." He shrugged at Morgan's demand that he be allowed to see his wife. "No visitors for the condemned."

Morgan's hand slid over the palm gun he'd hidden under his shirt, but he resisted the urge to empty it into the warden's smirking face. His words were steel-hard. "As her lawyer, I'd better be escorted to her cell in the next five minutes, or it'll be you behind these bars."

The warden relented.

Morgan called on every ounce of self-control he possessed as he was led down the damp graystone corridor that led to the cage holding his wife. For her sake he had to be strong. But as the thick iron door creaked open and he was allowed into the tiny dank chamber, he nearly lost his resolve. Selina sat forlornly on a filthy straw mattress in the far corner, her chestnut hair hanging limply about her wan face. She didn't even look up, apparently assuming her visitor to be one of the guards.

The name he still whispered in the throes of their most passionate lovemaking tore from his lips. "Abby . . ."

Her head shot up. Her eyes at first were blank, then disbelieving, as though she thought herself in the grip of some desperate delusion. Then softly she smiled. "I prayed I would see you one last time, Morgan. I prayed so hard."

He sank to his knees beside her, gathering her fiercely to him, his voice breaking. "Why? Why did you do it?"

"I couldn't let you lose everything."

"Goddammit, Selina! *You are* everything. Nothing else matters."

"I'm sorry."

He kissed the top of her head, then her forehead, her cheeks, her lips. "We'll find that boy. I swear to God, we will."

"By dawn?" she said sadly. "I think not, my love."

He pulled free his derringer. "Then I'll kill anyone who comes for you. Or I'll die with you."

She pressed her fingers to his lips. "No. Celia needs her father. We can't both die tomorrow."

"I can't lose you, Selina." His tears dampened her cheek, his heart threatening to collapse from the pain. "I can't." He cradled her against him. "I love you, Selina. More than my life."

"Then grant me one last wish, beloved," she murmured, tracking her hand along his cheek and down his arm to capture his hand in hers. "Let me lie here with you—touch you, hold you, be part of you."

He forced back the agony that threatened to consume him. He had to be strong for her, for them both.

But he couldn't suppress a tortured groan, as she started to unbutton the front of the shapeless prison dress she wore. "Selina, please, we can't . . ." He'd never known such pain.

"I want you, Morgan. I love you." She slid the dress from her shoulders. "Touch me. One last time. Touch all of me."

He scooped her into his arms, burying his face against her neck, his hands roving the beloved curves of her body, skating past her breasts, her belly . . . "For the love of God, Selina . . ." He stopped. His heart constricted. "My God." He stood up. I have to go for a little while."

"No! Morgan . . ."

"It's all right. I'll be back." He got to his feet.

"Please, you can't leave me!" She clung to him, trying desperately not to cry.

"I can't stay here and let this happen. Every minute, every second we have left I have to use to try to save your life."

"It's too late, Morgan. Please, don't deny me these last hours together."

The look in her eyes was almost his undoing, but he held to one last desperate hope. He longed to share it with her, but didn't dare lest it come to naught.

"I'll be back. I promise." He banged on the door, shouting for the guard. The hinges creaked, and then Morgan was gone.

Selina had held back her tears for Morgan's sake. But now she sagged against the cold stone wall at her back and sobbed brokenly. Only precious hours remained of her life. Why had he abandoned her? She knew Morgan would try to her last breath to save her, but it would be futile. Marelda had woven her vicious web too well. The woman had used Selina's months of freedom to manufacture evidence that would have convicted a saint.

Selina's sobs lessened as her thoughts drifted to Celia, Wolf Trail, and the strange twist of fate that had catapulted her into Morgan Kincaid's life. How unhappy he had been. If she had lessened the bitterness, eased the hurt, lightened his heart just a little, then all of her own pain was worth it.

The cell door creaked open again. She jumped up hopefully, her heart thudding. It was not Morgan who strode in, but a familiar-looking man in a dark suit and Roman collar. The priest from St. Mary's. "Father Thompson, isn't it?" she asked softly.

"Yes, my dear."

"I'm sure you mean well, Father, but . . . I really am not up to . . ."

"I don't mean to intrude, child." The priest paced the confines of the small room, seeming more ill at ease than Selina. She doubted he had often been obliged to bring comfort to women prisoners awaiting the hangman.

"I keep remembering how frightened you were that morning," the priest began. "I just wish I had known then . . ."

"There was nothing you could have done."

His gentle eyes held such pain that Selina found herself feeling sorry for him. "I . . . I'm all right, Father. Really."

"Oh, my child, my child." He wrung his hands together, seeming to want to say more. With a final, despairing look he turned and left.

Selina sank back onto the mattress, immersing herself in the memory of Morgan's touch. Why hadn't he stayed? Why?

The hours passed much too swiftly. At dawn the warden came to her cell, standing to one side as a guard unlocked the door. She straightened and walked forward unsteadily, but she took pride in the fact that she made it out to the prison yard without assistance. The walled enclosure seemed crammed beyond capacity by the crush of onlookers who had gathered to watch her die. Even the prison gates had been left open to allow for the additional throngs spilling out into the streets.

The wave of humanity parted as three guards formed a wedge in front of her, leading her toward the weather-worn wooden gallows in the middle of the yard.

She almost collapsed when she reached the bottom of the steps. One at a time, Selina, she told herself. One at a time.

It was then she heard the reed-thin voice cackling above the din of the crowd. From a raised platform barely ten feet from the gallows—a structure apparently erected just for the occasion—Marelda Hardesty raised her arms in a triumphant gesture. "At last, witch!" she shrieked. "At last you'll get what you deserve for what you did to my Gideon."

Selina regarded her quietly, deciding at last that in her dementia Marelda had truly convinced herself Selina had killed Gideon. She felt a strange pity for her all at once.

Selina started up the steps, noting the texture of the wood in the railing, the roughness. She seemed to have a heightened awareness of everything. Instinctively, she sidestepped the trapdoor on the platform, but a guard firmly maneuvered her over it.

A collective gasp from the crowd made her look up. Marelda lay sprawled on her special platform, clutching at her chest, her hands twitching. With a desperate strength she forced her spider-thin body upright, her gaze locking for one frozen moment with Selina's.

Selina straightened, returning that venomous look with a quiet dignity.

Marelda wavered. "Hang her!" she croaked. "Hang her now. Hur-ry . . ." Her hands shook, her eyes going wide, as if stunned that her body would dare betray her with victory within her grasp. "No," she mewled, "no, I have to see . . . have . . ." She crumpled to her knees, a horrible rattling sound issuing from her throat, then she pitched forward and lay still.

A man bending over her muttered a crude expletive.

Selina considered the irony. Marelda had orchestrated every detail of this day, but one. She would have her revenge, but she had not lived to see it.

Selina stared at the prison gate, willing Morgan to come through it, longing to see him one last time. Tears coursed silently down her cheeks as a burly guard slipped a black silk hood over her head, then secured her hands behind her back. Selina breathed in and out, feeling her own hot, moist breath, the last breaths she would ever take.

"Good-bye, Morgan," she whispered. "I love you."

A drum sounded. The last thing she would ever hear?

But no, there was a shout. It was Morgan. But

he was too late. She couldn't say good-bye. And how badly she wanted to say good-bye.

A shot! Oh, God, he had tried something reckless. He was dead. No, no! Oh, someone please let her see him. One last time. Please! She struggled.

Hands grabbed at her, slicing the ropes that bound her wrists, ripping the hood away. But it all seemed to be happening from a great distance. She looked up to see Morgan's beloved face, then fainted into his arms.

She woke in the shadow of the gallows. "Couldn't they just have had done with it?" she sobbed. "They want to make sure I'm awake to die."

A man she didn't know hovered over her.

"Hush, sweetheart," Morgan was saying. "Hush. This is a doctor." Morgan was crying. God, how she hated to see Morgan cry.

A motion from the crowd caught her eye. People were shifting out of the way to let someone through. Father Thompson. A plump woman huffed alongside him. His housekeeper? What was her name? Mrs. Rafferty. Had they come for the hanging? Her attention was drawn back to the stern-faced man who hunkered beside Morgan.

"A doctor?" she said. "Does it matter if I'm sick before I'm hanged?"

Morgan cradled her in his arms. "Please, God. Please, God."

The doctor was nodding, looking at Morgan. "You were right, sir."

Selina's gaze shifted back to Morgan. "Right? Right about what?"

"You, little lady," the doctor said, "are going to have a baby."

Selina clutched her abdomen, gasping. "A baby! Oh, Morgan, they'll be killing our baby too!"

"No. No, love, no. They won't." He held her fiercely to him until she ceased her struggles. "Selina, my love, my life, they can't hang you now. They can't do anything to jeopardize the innocent party. That's the law." He kissed her, caressed her, murmured over and over how much he loved her. "We have another six months to find that boy."

Selina stood in the warden's office, scarcely able to absorb all that had happened. Six months. She stroked her stomach. At least she would leave a part of herself behind. For Morgan.

She sagged into a horsehair chair in the corner, the morning's events still difficult to believe. Marelda was dead. Selina was still alive. And now Morgan was standing in front of her, bellowing at the warden that he'd damned well better have Selina released into his custody within the hour or he'd have the governor of the state of California on his neck.

A knock on the door interrupted Morgan's tirade. Father Thompson strode in.

"I'm sorry, Father," Morgan said grimly, "but this is not the time for . . ."

Mrs. Rafferty peered in, her gaze shifting uneasily between Morgan and Selina. Selina frowned. The woman looked for all the world as though she expected Morgan to attack her. Then a smaller figure crept into the room.

A young boy.

Selina leaped to her feet. "Morgan! Morgan, my God! That's him. That's the boy who . . ." She covered her mouth, her gaze darting to the warden, whose ferret eyes suddenly gleamed with interest.

"This is Danny," Mrs. Rafferty said, an unmistakable pride coming into her voice, though she still looked very frightened. "My son."

Morgan stepped over to Selina. They exchanged looks, and he knew.

"Danny," Father Thompson said, "you don't have to be afraid anymore. Just tell the story in your own words."

The boy started haltingly. "I used to run errands for Nob Hill folks all the time. Mr. Gideon, he was always real nice. And then . . . that last time . . ." His words came in a rush, as though the faster he said them the less chance they would have to cause him any more hurt. "I'm so sorry, ma'am. I was so scared. He came at me. He wouldn't leave me alone." The boy was sobbing.

"He grabbed the knife, said he would cut me if I
didn't . . . if I didn't . . ."

"Please," Mrs. Rafferty begged, "haven't you
heard enough?"

Morgan nodded, giving the boy's shoulder a reassuring squeeze. "It's all right, son. Nothing is
going to happen to you. It was self-defense."

Even the warden offered no protest as they all
went out into the hallway.

"Mr. Hardesty was so rich," Mrs. Rafferty said
as Morgan and Selina walked along with them out
into the sunshine. "I was certain that woman
would find a way to have Danny hanged." She
looked sadly at Selina. "Please, understand. He's
my son."

They stood in the now empty prison yard. "How
did you come into this, Father?" Morgan asked.

Only then did Selina perceive the reason for the
priest's despair earlier in her cell. His words confirmed it. "Danny came to me in the confessional
about three months after Mr. Hardesty's death.
The poor child couldn't carry the burden anymore.
But I was bound by my vows not to say anything
to anyone." He looked at Selina. "You don't know
what I went through during your trial, child. If the
good Lord makes hell anything at all like
that . . ."

"It was Danny himself who came forward,"
Mrs. Rafferty said proudly. "He saw the papers. I
. . . I'd been trying to shield him. But yesterday

he found out and came to me." She looked at the ground. "God forgive me, but I tried to talk him out of it. So he went to Father Thompson."

Selina caught the boy's hand in her own. "You are braver than you can even yet understand, young man. I thank you for my life."

She stood with Morgan and watched the priest, Mrs. Rafferty, and Danny make their way through the prison gate. "He really will be all right, won't he?"

"With that witch dead there'll be no problem," Morgan assured her.

She slid her arm around his waist. "I can't believe it's over. That I'm free. That we can go home."

He trailed a hand down her cheek, his voice threaded with a note of defeat she'd never heard before, his words chilling her more than any hangman's noose. "I'm going back to Wolf Trail, Selina. But you won't be coming with me."

Chapter 22

Selina settled onto the silken coverlet of the four-poster bed, sighing wistfully. No doubt she would be spending yet another night alone. Morgan had reserved a room for her in a luxurious hotel overlooking the bay, but he did not share it.

"I have to give you time to think, now that you're free," he said.

Free? What freedom could there be in her life without Morgan to share it? He had become obsessed with the notion that she had not chosen to come to Wolf Trail, that she'd been driven there out of desperation.

He would do the honorable thing. He would support the baby financially, but he would not build another marriage forged by misguided emotions.

As was his habit every evening, he stopped by on the way to his own room. He stood there now, gazing out the window toward the bay. His tone of late smacked of a teacher attempting to instruct a slow-witted child. Selina dug her fingernails into the silken bedcovers as his latest lecture unfolded.

"Lenore was young, infatuated," he said, maintaining his rigid stance at the window. "But our marriage never should have happened. I didn't love her. And I should not have forced her to move to Montana."

Selina congratulated herself on how well she held her temper. "A marriage isn't a place for comparisons, Morgan," she returned evenly. "You and I were and are in love."

He went on as though she hadn't spoken. "I've booked passage on a train north tomorrow. I've arranged for you to stay here as long as you like. I've hired a nurse for you as well."

Her frustration gave way to despair. This could not, would not, be their last night together. Somehow she had to get through to him. "I ordered that supper be sent up. Join me. Please. Don't make me eat alone tonight."

"I think . . . I think it would be best if I just said good night."

She got up and crossed to the window, then gently turned his head to face her. "Your days of hiding yourself from me are over, remember? Do you think I can't see what this charade is doing to you? And surely you must see what it's doing to me."

"Selina, please, I'm trying to do what's best for you." His voice was ragged. "Don't make it any harder."

"I'll be damned if I'll make it easy!" she cried. "I *want* it to be hard for you to turn your back on me. I want it to be impossible!"

He stepped away from her, unable to bear the closeness. "When we met, you were running for your life."

"Blast it, Morgan! From that first night, from the first instant I saw you, there was something between us."

"I don't believe in fate."

"How can you not? Look at our separate lives and the thousands of separate pieces each of us had to put together before we could meet."

He regarded her quietly for a long minute, and she took heart that he was at least thinking about what she said. Again she moved toward him, but stopped short of touching him.

"So many separate pieces, Morgan," she murmured. "Selina Michaels was a pampered, adored child ill-prepared for the real world. Selina Hardesty was a terrified young girl forced to endure five years of hell. Ah, but Abby Kincaid, what a blessed life that lady has come to live."

She extended her hand, holding it toward him, palm upward, waiting. For what seemed an eternity he just stood there, looking at it. Then he reached out with his, lacing his fingers with hers. "Abby . . ."

She went into his arms, nuzzling his neck, kissing the straight line of his jaw. "Make love to Abby, Morgan. She loves you so much."

He cupped her face, his gaze fierce. "I don't want you coming back with me because you feel obliged, or grateful, or . . ." He swore. "You haven't recovered yet from the shock of all this. You can't be certain."

"Do you love me, Morgan Kincaid?" she whispered against his ear, lifting his hand away from her face and settling it over the aroused tip of her breast.

He groaned, shaking his head as though to clear it. "That doesn't matter. We're talking about you."

"Do you love me, Morgan Kincaid?" She kissed him, once, twice. "It's a simple question. Yes or no?"

"More than my life."

"I am very pleased to hear that. Because I'm afflicted with the same condition. You *are* my life. And I wouldn't change a minute of it, as long as I could be sure you would be there in the end to share it with me." She kissed him again, reveling in how fiercely he kissed her back. "Take me home, Morgan. Take me home."

"Count on it," he promised huskily, giving in to the wonder of loving this woman, accepting at last that she loved him back. With a whoop of pure joy he scooped her into his arms and carried her to the bed. His body, his heart, his soul, would never again be his alone, and he wouldn't have it any other way.

Later, much later, he paused during his worshipful exploration of her body just long enough to slip a small gold band onto the third finger of her left hand. "Wherever you are, Abby, I'm home."